THE MAIL ORDER BRIDE

Visit us at www.boldstrokesbooks.com

THE MAIL ORDER BRIDE

by

R Kent

2020

THE MAIL ORDER BRIDE

ISBN 13: 978-1-63555-678-0

This Trade Paperback Original Is Published By
Bold Strokes Books, Inc.
P.O. Box 249
Valley Falls, NY 12185

First Edition: March 2020

CREDITS
Editor: Cindy Cresap
Production Design: Susan Ramundo
Cover Design By Tammy Seidick

Dedication

Wendy

Brian

CHAPTER ONE

July 4, 1864, Molasses Pond, Arizona Territory

"Austin, my boy, you need a wife." The barkeep greeted me as if we had been in the middle of a conversation.

The cavernous room of the Watering Hole saloon was empty. Green shades blocked the intensity of the sun. Circular tables littered the front of the hall. Their scattered chairs had spilled or wandered away. Flies congregated on the sticky splotches along the bar top. And a hound sprawled in the middle of the floor at the base of a long dead, potbellied stove.

Summer's heat hung like a malevolent presence.

"Just a bottle of whiskey," I replied, walking to the far end of the brass-edged bar.

I spun a coin onto the bar, watching until it wobbled flat. That was my last coin. "And I'll take a glass of milk." I turned sideways to face the room, propping my elbow to affect practiced relaxation.

Folks in these parts knew me as Austin. They knew me as a young man, hiding in the wilds of the frontier from a vile past, struggling to survive where grown men had trouble doing so. I cultivated their notions with a cold demeanor, a hardened look, and a lump in the right place.

Stories claimed I was a savage suckled by wolves with the venom of rattlers running through my veins. I particularly liked the one about being a half-breed Apache. It was the hangman's scar that no one had a fanciful explanation for. My White pa used to say, "If it can't be explained, people will fear it." All good. Fear kept folks from being overly friendly.

Below the brim of my felted hat, nervous sweat slicked my forehead. I tucked a stray strand of hair behind my ear. My Sunday-go-to-meetin' shirt stuck to the middle of my back.

I couldn't relax around Whites. Even though I'm white.

Jack McKade, the barkeep, was also the owner of the Watering Hole. He shoved a bottle toward me, pocketing the coin. He didn't care for me much. Probably because I was a homesteader with no cattle to rustle and no family to harass. He couldn't control me. And that didn't sit well with the likes of McKade.

I didn't owe him anything. Mostly, I didn't have anything he wanted. My land, maybe. But only if I had a strike.

Wealth and domination over others were what a man like McKade lived for. Twisting folks up fed something dark inside of him. He wielded his power from behind the bar where pouring whiskey was the place to learn every man's secrets.

With a gruff bark, he ordered a woman to fetch my milk.

A crooked leg kept McKade behind the bar. He didn't limp or gimp. He wore a brace on that leg which made him more self-conscious of the weakness. He didn't tolerate any show of weakness. Weaknesses got exploited. McKade preferred to do the exploiting.

He was intimidating. McKade's bellow could scare the skin off a fleeing rabbit. His laugh was akin to a spook howling in the night. And when he smiled, he looked like a crazed coyote on the hunt.

Back East, my White pa had known a man with a leg brace. I don't believe it was an uncommon sight.

But this was Mr. Jack McKade of Molasses Pond who wore a brace on his left leg, and he didn't take it well. Some say he was born angry. He had small, piggish eyes, warning of a bad temper. Fortunately, he wasn't heeled. There was no fat gun belt encircling his generous gut. There was, however, a sawed-off, double-barreled scattergun handy beneath the bar. McKade was damned fast on the grab for his weapon. And not shy about pulling the triggers.

I'd heard tales of a Lightning Jack McKade who was a no good scourge on the face of the earth. Big city newspapers said he was a gunslinging manslayer. Man *or* woman. It hadn't mattered. He killed with equal callousness. *Lightning Jack.*

Lightning Jack was one of the deadliest men alive. There were wanted posters from here to the East Coast. Whites said the law would never catch up with Lightning Jack McKade. Apache warriors told of Lightning Jack riding, untouched, through a hail of arrows. Navajo believed he was a spirit walker. And common folk said "yessir" to the gunman.

I didn't put much stock in stories.

If this man was once Lightning Jack, maybe he was looking for a fresh start like the most of us. Pa had always said to take a man for who he was today. Today was what counted. He said, "Lucky enough to survive yesterday, a man was blessed with being allowed to scratch out a living today. He could be dead tomorrow."

I vividly remembered most everything about my White pa, but I could no longer picture his face.

"Here ya go, hon." Rose clanked the full glass onto the bar. Streaks of gray at her temples hinted that she was old enough to be my mother. Men called her "Cactus Rose." They said she was a bit prickly. But she had always spoke kindly to me. She was the closest resemblance I had to an actual friend in town.

"Thank you, ma'am." I wiped my slick palms on the sides of my hide-covered thighs, then yanked my hat lower over my eyes. I felt a flash of heat across my face. I hoped my cheeks weren't glowing. I didn't talk to women much. And I really liked them—in the way boys do.

"Cause for a celebration?" Rose asked.

"Put a claim on Homestead Act land." One hundred and sixty acres, to be specific. The process was all formal and important, befitting the lengthy time and considerable effort to have saved ten silver dollars. The registrar at the land office had filled out the federal application. He figured I couldn't read, much less write. I shocked him by printing my surname, Austin. Just Austin.

All I needed to do now was stay on the claim for five consecutive years in order to gain its title. The sprig of land was all mine—well, in five years' time. But nothing would shake me from my property. I meant to grow into a respected man, homesteading on the outskirts of Molasses Pond.

The thought of my dreams coming true softened my stance. I ran a dry tongue over my cracked top lip.

"Couldn't have picked a finer day," Rose chirped.

Gunshots assaulted the stale air.

Too quickly, I palmed the leather holster hanging from the heavy belt slung beneath my hip bones. I was as jittery as a long-tailed house cat sitting on a porch full of rocking chairs. Reminding myself to breathe, I kept my hand on the holster, keeping it away from my revolver.

A cannon thundered.

The wagon wheel chandelier shook. A candle stub dropped to the sawdust-strewn floor. The hound thunked its tail, not bothering to get up.

I straightened from leaning on an elbow. A skinning knife, tucked at the small of my back, pressed against my spine. I found its sharp presence comforting.

Rose sashayed to the saloon doors to watch the commotion. A red-feathered plume bobbed from her nest of blond hair. "It's the Fourth of July! Independence Day."

Her sudden burst of glee calmed my ragged nerves.

Though Rose was not the woman for me, my eyes lingered on her womanly attributes. A low-cut red silk dress plumped her stark white voluptuous bosom and squeezed her ample waist. Her skirts began as voluminous layers, but the front was tied up to her midsection.

I eased my hand from the holster and flexed my fingers. My pa's Smith and Wesson revolver waited obediently at the front of my left thigh. Its butt was forward for a cross-handed draw that I wasn't proficient at. Pa had bought the gun new before our family joined a wagon train heading west in 1855. I've kept it close since his demise.

Before putting my attention back on a delicious sip of milk, I flicked the restraining loop from the hammer of my gun. There was nothing innocent about gunshots in Molasses Pond. No matter the occasion. Not when McKade's hired gunslingers were the only ones carrying.

With a swallow of fresh milk, my eyes drooped. The soothing drink coated my parched throat.

Shots rang out like a string of firecrackers. Whooping and hollering sang under the high noon sun. A slight breeze kicked dirt and dust from the floor. An occasional rushing reveler set the saloon doors to gently swinging. The tang of gunpowder filtered into the dry barroom air.

I settled my side against the bar, concentrating on my beverage like it was the only thing in the world that mattered.

Independence Day, 1864. The eighty-eighth year of America's Independence from British tyranny. But the country was at war with itself on one front, and at war with the Indians on the frontier. Through sheer willfulness, Molasses Pond had survived in spite of the country's ills.

The town was overripe for an explosive occasion. But not because of pride or glory in our country. It was an excuse to drink and gamble. It was an excuse to take a day away from empty sluice boxes and dried up creek beds. An excuse to not face another day of disappointment, starvation, and desperation.

When I rode in, "Old Glory" was flying high from a crumbling, Spanish-Mexican fountain in the center of Main Street. The pastor had droned a sermon under the flag. While I signed for my claim of land, a banjo, with accompanying fiddle, had performed a rousing rendition of "The Star Spangled Banner." And men fought over raising a Confederate flag.

I had made it into the Watering Hole before guns blazed.

A whistle preceded the next volley of cracks and blasts. The intrusion resounded in the vast emptiness of the saloon. McKade was at the other end of the bar wiping a greasy glass with a greasier rag. Rose stepped away from the doorway, patted her hair, and smoothed her skirt. I was determined to enjoy the milk.

Holiday frolickers burst through the swinging saloon doors.

Confederate deserters bellied up to the bar. These were McKade's hired guns. Each was slick and lean. They wore store-bought shirts and kept their Confederate gray trousers tucked into stovepipe boots. Their weapons gleamed from polish. And their eyes were bright for a fight.

I kept my head down, focusing on the glass in front of me.

Litters of sorry looking prospectors tumbled in, jostling for chairs.

Out of habit, I sized up the odds—one gunslinger to every half-dozen down-on-their-luck types. Given six-shooters, the numbers were about right. McKade knew what he was doing. His hired men held the advantage.

Hard-luck diggers collected at the low tables, fussing with one another to pool their possibles for a round of drinks. Tattered shirts drooped from thin shoulders. Filthy pants had holes in the patches that were covering holes.

The miners mostly contemplated the gnarly nails hooding the misshapen toes of their bare feet. They stole looks in my direction.

My new shirt still had crisp creases from the shelves of Percival's Mercantile. Even in the July heat, I knotted a black silk kerchief around my neck. It hid a hideous scar. My breeches were of fine doeskin. And I had moccasins of elk.

Several diggers wedged in on either side of me to perch at the bar. Resentment wrinkled their weathered faces. The heat of them was intrusive. That was enough encouragement for me to move my gun-hand to the smooth worn leather of my holster again.

Destitute men had nothing to lose. Desperation made them viperous.

They didn't have much to gain either, except favor from McKade. That made them unpredictable.

McKade controlled their fortune. He wielded whiskey like a weapon. They could each only ever be as much as he allowed. And they would always be as little as he dictated. If there was any order in Molasses Pond, it could be found in a bottle of McKade's whiskey.

I'd never be a cussed miner clawing at rock on the speculation of a shiny crumble. I'd sooner sell my gun arms in service than squat in a trickling creek bed, rasping my fingertips bloody to pay for a lick of whiskey on Sundays.

I'm opposed to cashing in on precious metal. Unless it's lead.

Gold, silver, and copper encouraged evil. Greed prospered. Greed changed men. It made them ugly. Ugly made for dangerous. I wouldn't want to be ugly or dangerous. It was already rumored that I was evil.

The air in the overcrowded saloon grew thick and rank. The scar beneath my scarf began to itch. I stuck a finger in at the knot to scratch at my neck. The top pale edge of the marks must have peeked from the covering. Wide-eyed stares traveled the length of the bar.

I dropped my hand to caress the butt of my Smith and Wesson. It was the one thing every man understood.

"Hey, boss. Get a load of the beads on that bracelet." A gaunt man set back on his heels, stuffed his thumbs in a rope belt tied about his skinny waist, and whistled. "You get that from around here?" he asked then whistled again. "Turquoise."

At that word, the entire saloon hushed. Where there was turquoise, there was copper.

I drew my sleeve down to cover the brightly colored beads. It was too late.

The crowd flooded toward me. They scrabbled over one another. Crazed men shoved at me like corralled wild horses, frenzied against a fence. The rot of their festering breath trampled, hot and humid, over my cheeks. The stench of them pressed in on me harder than their rangy, sweating bodies.

My skin crawled. *Flight or fight.* There were only ever those two options.

A stout arm swung around my bunched shoulders.

I swallowed at the tightness in my throat. Shifting from one foot to the other, I willed myself to dwell on anything but the fear of being trapped.

A bony foot stomped mine. An elbow shoved into my ribs. A knee knocked at the protruding potato stuffed in the crotch of my breeches. And the riotous men clamored near to on top of me.

My mind was on fire, fishing for distractions. I focused on the vegetation sitting in my breeches. It bolstered my courage. But a drastic shift would have been difficult to explain. It was slightly more to the left than I liked. But didn't the majority of them hang to the left? It had to be perfect. I needed it correct. I needed to see me when I looked down.

I clenched my thighs against the jostling. My back teeth ground so hard the muscles in my jaw throbbed.

Flight or fight.

I tightly embraced the carved, antler grips of my Smith and Wesson like I was reuniting with a long lost lover. Deadly heat piqued inside me. My palms were sweat-slicked. My mouth was dry. My stomach rolled. Survival screamed too loudly in my head. *Flight or fight.*

The touch of the cool, curved, steel trigger made my finger twitch in anticipation.

When the brim of my hat got knocked to the bridge of my nose, I coaxed the revolver's hammer back.

Click, click, click, click.

The crackling of cocking stilled the swarm.

McKade perked at the ominous noise. "Now hold on there." He smacked his stumped shotgun onto the top of the bar.

Silence filled the room.

Under the threat of McKade's splattergun, men cleared away from me. Miners crept to their tables. Cards came out. Everyone kept their chins tucked, sneaking furtive glances at McKade.

Jack McKade lorded over the diggers. I speculated that he lorded over many of the town's businesses too. But I didn't know how far his reach extended. I did know that getting caught in his grasp would be fatal.

The moment of silence moved back into normal saloon cacophony.

"So how about it?" McKade swiped the barrel of his shotgun at a cat that jumped onto the bar. "No-good, greasy lout. Come back when you've caught a rat." Stowing his gun beneath the bar, he said, "A wife? The boys are thinking on putting in to get you one."

"No. I'm all set. The bottle of whiskey and the glass of milk will do." *No complications.* "No wife."

I can see McKade's game. He's looking for his next plaything.

If I cared about someone, he'd find a way to use them against me, until he owned me. And he's got his hired guns convinced there's something in it for them in setting up his twisted plot. If they had a vested interest, McKade could control them in controlling me. He would never leave a trail that implicated himself. If anything went bad, McKade would need someone to blame. Someone to hurt.

He always needed someone to hurt.

McKade leaned across the bar with a leer at my crotch. "Is that all? Maybe you want more than the milk," he stated. "I saw the way you looked at Rose."

Rose was a blond-haired beauty to be sure, but it was Lily, McKade's golden-haired daughter, who had caught my eye. I wasn't about to mention that though.

Lily McKade was too proper to be permitted into this establishment during business hours. I wouldn't have figured Jack McKade as a family man, but Lily was proof positive. And she was very fine. Very fine indeed.

The girl was about my age. Maybe seventeen? Her sunny yellow hair bounced in long coils from under a tiny cap decorated with netting, ribbon streamers, and flowers. Fresh flowers. She always wore fancy finery. I'd seen the likes in a big city.

Her silk dresses were full-skirted, relying on crinolines and hoops, and displaying a bulging bustle at the rump. The dresses were hemmed ankle-high to show off matching, tall, buttoned boots. Lily carried a parasol of lace that wouldn't hold water off her head, and doubtful gave much shade.

I sighed. On her dainty hands were pristine white gloves. They were all the rage for sophisticated ladies. I had seen gloved hands clinging to gentlemen in the big city too.

I wanted Lily's gloved hands hugging onto my arm. I wanted to be her gentleman.

McKade eyed me suspiciously. A squeak of his hinged leg brace brought on a childhood memory. *A monstrous man atop a huge beast of a horse and a blinding glint of sun off of steel.*

Two hired guns sidled next to me. It was best to ignore them. I stuffed the glass to my lips, much preferring the smell of clean milk to their hovering foul odor.

I wasn't fond of Jack McKade. There was something too familiar about the big man—not in a good way.

McKade slapped the bar with a filthy towel. When he spoke, his bushy black eyebrows took on a life of their own. "Austin, you're a good, upstanding boy." His ears were muffled with nests of dark, curly hair. A woolly mustache hid a pair of thin lips to a mouth that was more of a severe knife slash. "A young man should have his place looked after." His face reddened with the edge of anger. "He ought to have his meals warmed. Not to mention his *needs* met, if you know what I mean."

I didn't know *exactly* what he meant. But I wasn't about to ask either.

He leaned his bulging forearms on the sticky bar's surface and looked me in the eye.

A gunslinger named Seth draped about my shoulders uninvited. His cohort, Jeb, slapped me on the back. Others laughed. Their guffaws were grossly punctuated by sucking breaths of snorting. Reminiscent of pigs.

I glanced toward the tables at the calloused hands, raw fingers, and blackened nails of the prospectors. They had probably been good men once. They weren't much of anything now. Empty skin bags. I doubted their whiskey expenses left a nickel to patch a tent or put much in a cook pot. Not with McKade's inflated prices.

None of them could afford to live. The greater sadness was that they couldn't afford to leave.

Jack McKade moved off to fill glasses. I shrugged Seth from my shoulders. Men poured their attention back into their drinks.

My celebratory mood soured. I swirled what was left of the milk, watching its rich, creaminess lap smoothly around the inside of the grimy glass. *A wife? Absurd.* The saloon setters didn't know me at all.

Rose loitered at the back of the room. I felt her eyes linger on me. There was a flicker of melancholy in her stately bearing. In the next moment, she beamed a smile and collected abandoned drinks from the tables, tossing half of a neglected shot down her gullet. She chugged the contents of another deserted glass, then upended a bottle to poke her tongue at its last dribbling drops.

I gulped down the rest of my milk and shoved the empty glass across the bar. The bottle of whiskey sat waiting. I swooped it up then silently left.

Outside, a small dust devil kicked to spinning. I stood in its gritty, twisted wind on the board walkway, hoping the air movement would break the oppressive heat. My clothes clung to me. My scarf felt as tight as a noose.

I untied Charlie Horse from the hitching post then pulled at the kerchief hiding my scar.

Charlie Horse. He was a loudly marked Appaloosa stallion. The blue roan over his front was the color of an angry sky. I sat him bareback where a dark bay line separated the blue from startling white. Decorating his rump were large bay egg spots. His unique coat stuck out against the reds and browns of the surrounding landscape. Charlie Horse was the kind of horse revered by warriors. Stout and square built. But his small pig eyes cautioned he was cagey, fearless, and quick-tempered. Charlie Horse's parentage had seen a mix of modern ranch breeding that I didn't hold against him…most days.

He had come up lame the last mile into town. It was likely a hoof festering on gravel. He'd stay sound with shoes. If I could afford them. I couldn't. Not yet.

I'd have to walk him home. I tugged the brim of my felted hat low over my eyes to peek at the blazing sun. The day was getting on.

A shotgun blasted from within the Watering Hole.

A body flew from the swinging doors to lay lifeless on the dry road. Its belly bloated within moments in the blistering heat. Blood burbled from beneath, quenching the cracked patch of earth.

Charlie Horse sidestepped.

Lily strolled the boardwalk in front of Percival's Mercantile, at the other end of town. She twirled her frilled parasol, eyeing me from beneath her gay bonnet.

A wife? I had enough trouble keeping myself alive.

From inside the saloon, I heard glasses chink, an empty whiskey bottle rolling across the wooden floor, and cards slapping on tables. Conversations droned. Business went on as usual in the saloon.

I led Charlie Horse into the middle of Main Street and headed out of town.

Behind me, McKade bellowed to his audience, "Boys, Austin's perfect for a wife."

CHAPTER TWO

October 24, 1864, Arizona Territory

The colorful October evening descended into darkness. I jabbed at the fire illuminating an ancient stone corner beneath a rock overhang.

Early last spring, I was seeking shelter as a fierce storm rumbled in. The skies had blackened as dark as a petered out mine shaft. Cold, fat raindrops pelted my skin. So, I took refuge in a thicket of mesquite and shivered while the air sizzled. Thunder crashed about an angry sky. Water sluiced in a flash flood down the arroyo beside where I squatted.

Charlie Horse had run off. Again. Hungry and alone, I slumped my shoulders toward my chest, wrapping my arms around my skinny legs. My teeth chattered. I was thankful for my wide-brimmed hat. It added to the scrub's meager attempt at breaking the watery onslaught.

Sucking on my discomfort, much like a sorry, sopping, house cat, I watched the rolling storm from under my hat. That's when I saw it. The next flash of lightning sent a jagged spear pointing to the flat top of the overhang, illuminating the corner weather break. The solid rock formation had long ago split, as if the two sides had had a lover's spat.

I ran toward that near-hidden alcove, dodging hunkering shadows and jumping over wild runoff. The spacious shelter proved dry and vacant, though scattered bones and broken branches attested to a recent occupant. I've bedded down in the huge hideaway ever since. Even after I built a sizable hogan nearer to a dug well. I liked the company under the overhang.

Charlie Horse and I watched the last reds and oranges of the day's setting sun shake its fist in defiance at evening's reign. Fall blazed bright with beautiful colors. And in the darkest of the night, light from the firepit danced a picture show on the looming stone walls. Beneath the overhang, I didn't feel so alone.

The hogan was a dark hovel. I'd be glad of its closed warmth come snow, but—

I whirled around. My gun leveled at the intruder's midsection. Hammer cocked. Trigger finger snuggled against steel.

"TwoFeathers." I grabbed the hammer with my thumb and gently squeezed the trigger, easing the firing mechanism back to resting. "One of these days you're going to get shot," I squeaked without my practiced pitch.

"One day I won't tell Os-ten I have come. I will take the gun." His timbre was enviously low. He shrugged. "I like to look at this." TwoFeathers touched the corner of his eye then twirled his finger in the air.

I spun my gun, fancy-like, then flipped it into the air. When I caught the revolver with my other hand, I twirled it with equal dexterity, before seating it back into the holster. "All you need to do is ask, brother."

TwoFeathers jerked his fingers up as a gun. "This more fun." He laughed and rolled his head forward to pop a fat deer from across his massive shoulders. "You bring the killing thunder faster than the lightning in the sky." The carcass slammed with a thud that kicked dust into the air. "But this one?" TwoFeathers pointed. "Already dead." He moved to the fire and rubbed his hands over the warmth.

TwoFeathers had been a young shaman before his tribe, too, was rounded up by the White soldiers. He escaped their forced march. Like many young braves, he fled to the Apaches to fight. He was now a fierce warrior. He was still the best healer I'd ever crossed paths with.

A single-shot, muzzle-loading .53-caliber Hawken rifle hung slanted over his back. The massive, long-range plains rifle could drop a full-grown bull buffalo from a considerable distance. TwoFeathers also carried the biggest Bowie knife I'd ever seen.

He laid the powerful rifle, its powder horn, and several rabbit skin pouches on the ground. Then he shed a rolled and tied wool greatcoat from his back. The insignia told of its previous owner having been a Union officer. He shook out of a thigh-length deerskin smock that had probably been worn since the second he liberated it from the animal. *Ick.* And lastly, he kicked off his moccasins.

TwoFeathers always painted half of his face. This time in red. Which made him appear to have blood gushing down one side of his head. I asked him about it once. Why one side was solidly painted and the line so sharply defined along his nose, splitting his lips in two and dribbling through the center of his chin?

"Walks with two spirits," he answered.

The skirt of a lady's dress encircled his stringy waist where a traditional breechcloth would have hung. My White ma had had a dress of similar flower print, but it was blue, where TwoFeathers's was the palest of yellow. Sometimes I'd think of Ma when I saw him. Not that his man's muscular physique could be mistaken for a woman. It was more from the way he gracefully moved and how he fiercely beautified his world. Ma had been like that. Chock full of grace and fierce beauty.

The shortened hem of his floral-printed skirt was lightly weighted by adorning quills. He had foregone leggings to adopt the White's pants. His were made of a very supple deerskin. A slit over each bronze ankle was decorated with intricate, colorful beadwork. His low moccasins were also elaborately ornamented.

"Now we trade." TwoFeathers plucked a copper band from his wrist. The hammered band was etched with a border pattern of spirals, symbolizing the never-ending cycle of growth, change, then eternal life. A polished turquoise stone peered from the center like one giant blue eye.

TwoFeathers pointed at the stone. "Os-ten," he said in low guttural tones that swallowed the "au" sound backward. Then he touched the corner of his eye.

I didn't know exactly what he meant, but I knew what he wanted.

I filled two sugar sacks with different colored rubble that fell inside the crevice at the back corner of the formation. On the exchange, he secreted a small round ball the size of a large pebble into my palm. It was a .53-caliber copper ball that went to his massive Hawken.

Trading done, we both set upon rendering the deer carcass. TwoFeathers was faster, taking long swipes that deftly shed the meat of its hide. As he bent over the work, black hair bound in crisscrossing rabbit skin ties never strayed from the middle of his back.

TwoFeathers had deep, powerful eyes, like windows to an old soul. I heard stories that a man could see his own death if he stared too long into the eyes of a shaman. It's not a tale I was willing to verify. I had already known that looking in TwoFeathers's eyes was akin to peering down a dark well as a drop of sweat plunged to smack endless ripples into motion. The thought of it sent the crawlies up my arms.

My eyes were blue. My White ma used to say they were the color of the sky after a long-awaited summer storm had purged the oppressive air. My adoptive Navajo mother saw blue eyes as sickly. She had covered them for several days with strips of soft, thin hide slopped with a thick, porridge-like goo. She sang and chanted and wafted smoke around me, hoping to drive away the malevolent spirit that paled my eyes. To no avail. The evil was there to stay.

Most had thought I was "touched." Not just for my eyes. Regardless, my adoptive mother loved me. She took me in at nine years of age and raised me to be Navajo. This "daughter of Whites" was one of The People, one of The Dineh.

TwoFeathers threw gristle onto the fire. It sizzled, breaking me from my thoughts. I chunked into the haunches, splitting sections away from the skeleton. With my knifepoint, I thrust through the stifle and hock joints. The massive hindquarters were skewered on hooks and hung from a rack over the fire.

My fascination with TwoFeathers appeared akin to a moon-eyed girl with a crush. But I wasn't in love with him. I did love him. I considered him a brother. But I wasn't *in love* with him. I wanted to be him. Parts of him. The parts that were strong and rugged and all man—virile, potent. And the part that embraced his different nature and was revered for it. *Everybody wanted to be somebody else at some point in life.*

The Bible-thumping pastor in town would say envy was a sin. I didn't trust the pastor. There was something off about him, as if he preached to convince himself, not others. He was milquetoast too. I couldn't trust a man without a spine.

I placed thin strips of meat on the hot stones surrounding the blaze. We gnawed on slices before they were fully cooked. The juices drooled down our chins. Feast or famine. I was planning to stay on the feast side.

The fire popped. Mesquite smoke trailed in thin wisps toward the rock slab overhead, flavoring the hanging chunks of haunch. "Come winter, food's going to be scarce."

"Mm," TwoFeathers said, nodding. He looked off into the darkened night, outside the fire's ring. "Miners hunt much. Leave meat for coyotes to feast." His shoulders slumped. It was the first glimmer of defeat I'd seen in any Apache.

After the stillness grew stale, TwoFeathers stiffened. "Could eat horsemeat," he said with a toothy grin.

"A warrior needs horses," I replied.

"You could make a good Apache. You could fight."

"I'm not a warrior." I've killed before. Gun fighting doesn't sit well with me. The dead man is always someone's father or brother. I just haven't learned not to feel bad about that.

"You should have sheep." Bright white teeth gleamed from his two-colored face.

I threw a hunk of fat. It smacked onto his unpainted cheek.

He peeled the goo from his skin and sniffed at it. When he threw the mess into the fire, it sizzled and crackled. TwoFeathers jumped to his feet, scenting the air like a hungry wolf.

He waved in front of his nose. "Horse?" His face wrinkled at the foul odor, like a prissy girl smelling a bad fart.

Charlie Horse nickered. His hoof had been festering on another abscess.

TwoFeathers hefted the lame hoof. With his big Bowie knife, he carved the gravel track open. As he pushed on the sole of the hoof, a bubble of acrid pus erupted.

Per routine, I pulled the cork from a bottle and handed it to him.

TwoFeathers swigged a gulp of whiskey, wrinkling his face into amusing contortions, then splashed the liquid into the open, oozing track.

The horse blanched at the sting but didn't pull his hoof away.

From inside his skirt, TwoFeathers took out a pouch containing a moss poultice wrapped in wet rawhide. The rawhide would dry, harden, and tighten, holding the drawing poultice in place and protecting the tender toe.

When he was done, TwoFeathers ran his hands over Charlie Horse's head, staring into him as if he could see his soul. Charlie Horse was so entranced that TwoFeathers could have stolen off with the bay egg spots on his rump.

"Warrior's horse. Spirit guide."

I dug back into the work of rendering the deer. Their conversation was their conversation. That horse and I had a different understanding, mostly built on too many differences of opinion.

My hands were slick with lard as I stacked hunks of meat, and some of the bones, in piles on the outstretched hide. There was still much to do in preserving every tiny bite for the harder season. The raw cuts required heavy salting, and there were more chunks to roast, smoke, or salt. Then everything needed to be tightly bundled for cold storage.

These past weeks, I had dug and mounded a considerable cellar hole. The earthen roof disguised its whereabouts. A wooden door in the side of the hillock made it easily accessible. The few vegetables I was able to grow were already stockpiled inside. The added meat would be a welcome addition. Winter was coming. I was nowhere near ready.

I had built my hogan among bursts of erupted stone making it difficult for visitors to quickly advance on. The octagonal shelter was sealed with clay and tightly packed in the seams. The cedar logs kept out inclement weather, bugs, and rodents. Instead of a center firepit, I built a stone fireplace and chimney in one wall, like the Whites. A strong, domed roof of brambles and clay was weatherproof. The heavy earthen material guaranteed that the temperature stayed cool in the summer and warm in the winter.

The dwelling had no windows. The fireplace lit the entire cavity. I tried to convince myself it was homier than the overhang. I tried to live inside. I couldn't. The gnawing sense of being trapped, alone, in the blackness, drove me back beneath the open shelter of the outcrop.

A drastic drop in temperature woke me too early in the morning. Predawn appeared like a purple bruise covering an injured sky. I wrapped my arms around myself.

TwoFeathers had quietly vanished, which was his way. My world felt somehow empty for his silent leaving. But there was no time to dwell. The venison had to be stored. And there were chores. And I should be setting my sights to checking traps. And gathering firewood for the colder months.

My tanned hide shirt was greased with the muck of last night's meat carving. I shucked the soiled smock, trying not to look at the wraps binding my chest. The grimy tunic would dry if laid in the sun. When it dried, I'd scrape the hide before wearing it again.

A bucket of cold water was not what I wanted to confront in the dawn hours of a frosty morning. But I splashed the icy water onto my face and underarms, careful not to soak the doeskin bindings. If they got wet, they'd tighten too much. I'd have to take them off. I couldn't. I couldn't bear to look on the budding womanhood of the body that didn't match the boy I knew I was inside.

In the frigid air, I danced from one foot to the other, not looking down. I only owned one other shirt. My Sunday best. I was sore about using it. Tucked in, the flimsy cotton showed the lines of the wraps. I had to wear it billowy, which could catch and rip during chores. To protect the cotton shirt, I stuffed my arms into a warm coat, flattening the shearling wool collar.

I stroked the ravaged skin of my neck. The rope burn scar alternated between shiny, smooth patches and lumpy, jagged areas. My eyes glazed over with assaulting memories.

Shod hooves rang against stone. Hearty laughter. Blinding sun. Gunfire. Too much gunfire. Navajo dropped in fleeing poses. Children wailed. Gunfire. Lifeless faces twisted in anguish and horror. Flames. The choking, burning tug that went on and on. Then black. Nothing but black.

I shook myself. It was the same each time. Horrifying snippets in the same sequence, with the same missing gaps.

I pulled the kerchief twice around my neck before cinching the knot then stepped into the early morning sun.

A sorrel colt stood in the split rail paddock. He glistened in the bright rays. October's cold nights had teased his coat to grow for the coming winter. Even shaggy, he shined. I worked my fingers through the horse's flaxen mane, speaking words in the language of my adoptive family. Practicing the low tones that sang to the animal's twitching ears.

He was a big colt with long legs, having seen five summers before I roped him last March. Charlie Horse and I had found the sorrel mired in the melting snows. Thin and exhausted, he was willing to follow behind Charlie Horse. And though Charlie Horse found reasons to run off this past summer, the sorrel had always stayed.

I gentled the sorrel. Now that he was well-handled, I could ride him just about anywhere, doing just about anything. I wanted to keep him. Especially since Charlie Horse lamed up if the wind blew wrong. Or ran off whenever a mare whinnied. But I couldn't keep him. Feed was short and I was desperate for trade goods. The sale of a horse meant my survival.

Did I really need to trade the sorrel? Was I only trying to convince myself? I really liked the young horse. Maybe I could survive the winter without store-bought goods. I had a short stack of tanned pelts to trade. It might be enough for bullets. I could do without beans and salt. I didn't need much.

I rolled a patched blanket to fashion a harness collar low around the sorrel's neck, settling it against his chest. Then, I ran ropes down either side. At the ends, I kept the ropes spread using a sturdy branch. With the harness contraption, the sorrel hauled the bundle of meat to the cellar hole as I led him.

A small cache of carrots, potatoes, radishes, and onions were piled toward the back of the dug out room. Along one earthen wall were salted pelts. Hanging above the pelts were cured and smoked meats from my traps. It looked like a bounty. Worth more than any sorry riverbed plot panning for gold. But I still worried it wasn't enough to see me through the coming winter months. *If I was careful... If I ate sparingly...*

I stacked the salted meat on the cold floor and shuffled out.

The sorrel had waited patiently. I took off his trappings then offered him water from the well. His soft muzzle gingerly touched the surface of the water, stilling for a moment, then splashing before drinking. He was mesteño. Whites called them mustangs. The little wild horses were suspicious by nature. It kept them alive.

I rubbed his coat as he drank deeply.

My browning garden was also thirsty. I tipped several buckets into the channels, soaking my short plants. Corral fences needed to be mended. A new breaking pen had to be built. More scrub should be piled for winter's feed. A captured mare had foaled out of season. I'd have to pamper the pair in my existing round pen.

The mare and foal gave me thoughts toward ranching horses by breeding them. I could raise the best horses in this part of the country, not just rope 'em and break 'em. But that was for another time. Now, the hard-packed, rocky ground had difficulty feeding mesquite thickets and cactus. It wouldn't feed many horses. Not this year.

I had a spit of grass along the Gila River. It wasn't much. My land would need to be cultivated to produce proper feed if I wanted to breed horses. I tugged at the silk kerchief knotted at my neck. Rounding up stray cattle would be more lucrative. And I still wanted a milk cow. I loved milk.

To be honest, cows were for cowboys. My heart was with the horses. It always had been.

If I gentled horses under saddle, I could sell them to the blacksmith, who also owned and ran Molasses Pond Livery. Broke horses were hard to come by in the Arizona Territory.

A jingling of harness stopped my runaway thoughts. A horse and buggy picked its way through the rocky expanse. I tied my holster down to my thigh and plucked the hammer loop off. Then waited.

"Ma'am," I said, pleasantly surprised when Rose drew in the lines and slowed the fringe-topped buggy to a stop alongside me.

"Good morning to you, Austin."

I liked how Rose said my name. As if it held importance. My face instantly grew hot.

"You have a package arriving on the stagecoach," she said with a sunny smile, bobbing her head. The plume in her stylish hat nodded. She looked a lot like Lily just then, with her fancy dress and the netting corralling a feathered bonnet. Gloves accented her delicate hands. A scraggly bundle of wildflowers wilted next to her on the cushioned bench seat. "Heaven's sake, Austin, don't just stand there. Come on."

It hadn't mattered that I didn't order any package. And it hadn't escaped me that no one would send me a package. I tied the sorrel to the side of the buggy, then hippie-hopped aboard like a starving rabbit to lush, green grass.

What boy wouldn't take a long ride into town with a pretty woman?

CHAPTER THREE

I slowed the buggy horse to a quiet walk on the outskirts of town. Molasses Pond was still asleep. The road was empty. The boardwalks were barren. A couple of tent flaps lifted. A bell jingled as the door of Percival's Mercantile opened to greet the early morning chill.

Wood smoke hovered low as cook fires coughed to life. My mouth watered at the aroma of fried bacon. The scent of strong coffee drafted on the breeze. A rooster crowed. Chickens cackled as they were harried for their eggs. Steel rang in the distance, announcing the blacksmith was already into a long day of work.

"In front of Percival's Mercantile, if you please." Rose flapped her gloved hand toward the store, then adjusted the shawl that slipped off her shoulder. As we came to a halt, she bundled the bunch of flowers into the crook of her arm like they were a newborn babe.

In a gentlemanly manner, I offered to take Rose's hand, helping her from the fringed buggy.

"The stagecoach stops here," Rose said. "Don't forget to pick up your package." She waved at the mercantile's boy, giving him a coin to take the buggy back to Molasses Pond Livery.

I gathered the sorrel. It would be a long ride home, but a smile on my face from the buggy ride with Rose would last the entire way and then some. I flipped a rein over the off side of the sorrel's neck. There was no package.

Rose pursed her lips and eyed me.

"I need to get a few things in the mercantile," Rose said. "Will you be here when I come out?" She flung the door wide and waltzed in, not waiting on my reply.

I tethered the sorrel to the hitching post then perched on the boardwalk outside Percival's Mercantile. *What was another few minutes?* I waited for Rose. I'd also wait for the stagecoach, figuring I was here, I might as well see what the fuss was about. I hoped the waiting wouldn't be overlong.

It wasn't the waiting that bothered me, though I was not generous with my patience.

The town was waking.

I fidgeted at my neckerchief, then smoothed the front of my coat, checking the pockets. I had too few, with nothing in them. For something else to do, I stabbed my toe at the mud-spattered planks.

The weather was cold. I was too hot. The sky had grown cloudy, and I preferred the sun.

Snow was accumulating in the higher elevations. Its patches of white could be seen from here. That meant an early winter. Streams and rivers were swelling to eventually freeze. And game was descending into the lower basins too soon.

Children dashed from around a corner, chasing a rolling barrel hoop. They stopped to stare. Men on horseback rode through town watchful of me. People gathered in clusters to whisper. Molasses Pond was slowly coming alive with the new day.

I smoothed the kerchief against my neck again. Curious eyes followed the movement of my hand. I'm sure the prospect of catching a peek at my hidden scar had townsfolk twittering gibberish as usual.

The stiff heels of Rose's ankle boots tap-tap-tapped as she pattered from Percival's Mercantile. I was relieved to have the distraction.

Rose uncorked a small silver flask, tipped it to her lips, then took a long swallow. "Medicinal," she mouthed as our eyes met.

She puckered as if she sucked a sour lemon. "I got you a little something," Rose said, "for the homestead and all." She presented a wicker basket covered with a red-and-white checkered cloth.

I reached for the cloth. "Not now." Rose slapped my knuckles with her gloved hand. "What are you staring at?" she barked at the children. Their hoop fell over into the mud. "Haven't you ever seen an honest, hardworking young man before?"

I thought she said "man" kind of funny, but maybe I was just sensitive to it. I stood a little stiffer and widened my stance. "I'm used to the stares," I said.

When she turned back to me, her painted face was all soft and soppy. "Staring is rude." She patted my cheek. "Besides, there's nothing wrong with who you are."

And I didn't know what exactly she was referring to. Hiding the hideous scar? Dressing in fringed buckskins like a savage *breed*? Or suffering the body of a female while my mind, heart, and soul has always been a boy's? *Could she have known?*

Slight for a young man and ever cautious about that, I hooked my thumbs in my fat gun belt then scraped at the leather of the holster with the bitty finger on my left hand. Hovering little boys' eyes grew wide. The children scampered away.

Packing a hogleg on the frontier was a necessity. The law was afraid to venture this far into the new territory. Predators, both two- and four-legged, preyed on the weak and defenseless. For me, toting a sidearm provided considerable peace of mind.

On the edge of wilderness, a gun was the great equalizer. The fastest gun... Well, the fastest gun usually got anything they wanted.

I patted my "Slim Jim" style holster. I was proud of it. It had cost me half of last winter's trapping.

The gentle morning breeze was being chased out of town by a brutal wind. The dark sky turned even more threatening. I tugged at the fleece-lined collar of my waist-length coat to adjust its bulk to my earlobes.

Folks milled like penned cattle. Their raspy whispers scratched at my ears. I could feel their eyes on me. The muscles across my back and shoulders tightened. The small hairs on my neck bristled.

The attention of the townsfolk was more than mere curiosity about my scar. But I was probably being oversensitive.

"This is quite enough." Rose placed the basket on the boardwalk. "Austin, stay." She stepped down into the muck. Her ankle twisted, nearly knocking her off her feet. She recovered clumsily. Rose lifted her foot and tortured the high-heeled short boot on more securely. She stomped directly across the muddy roadway, regained the boardwalk on the other side, and headed off to the Watering Hole.

With nothing but the waiting, I propped my heel against the hand-cut clapboards of the store's rough-hewn facade, leaned back, and rolled a cigarette.

I didn't smoke. I barely tolerated it. The taste was rank. The stench foul. Its acrid smell biting at my throat also stung my lungs. Hateful. But I struck a sulfur-tipped match after shoving the bag of works back into a breast pocket, then puffed the rolled paper to glowing.

The act was part of *who* the fine upstanding townsfolk expected me to be. I pressed the cigarette to my dry lips and sucked the sour smoke until it filled my mouth. After holding the fumes in momentarily, I blew them out in a slow, steady stream. The tendrils of my exhale could be seen from a distance.

I'd give them all their show.

The Concord stagecoach clambered into sight. Its chinking harness brass, clanking tug chains, and creaking greased wheels were punctuated by harsh grunts from the driver as he chastised his team of six sweat-lathered horses. Loping hooves slopped and slapped the wet, cold earth. The animals were charging down Main Street like their tails were on fire.

The driver yelled whoa and scrambled to take up his lines. Sloppy work for a six-in-hand teamster. I made a mental guess as to where the stage would actually stop, given the out-of-control nature of the rig. The coach sped past my expectations before jolting to a standstill. I'd bet the passengers had had one helluva rough ride for their money.

Dust-smudged faces emerged, attesting to the wear and tear of their long journey.

I didn't much care about people. Especially strangers. But I'd exercise just enough graciousness to make sure the weary stage riders were clear of my path.

The glowing end of my cigarette crept toward my fingers. I flicked it into the mud.

Two women and four men wore grit from top to bottom. Grimaces contorted their worn faces. They were visibly unimpressed with their travel accommodations. Luggage was haphazardly tossed down. A satchel of papers burst open. Mail and posters took flight on the wind. The clerk from Percival's Mercantile scurried after them. I stomped onto a skittering stack. WANTED was printed in bold black letters. I thought it was my own face that stared back at me.

"I got them, Mr. Austin," the clerk said. I automatically lifted my toe in response. "Mr. McKade can post these in the Watering Hole." The clerk scurried toward the saloon.

Passengers snagged their bags and wobbled off along the board walkway.

Last year at this time, the only hired way to journey this far was by freight with mules. That took a lot longer, with the trip being absolutely miserable given the nature of the beasts and the kind of men attracted to driving them. But now there was stagecoach delivery. Even a lawless tent town like Molasses Pond showed signs of getting civilized.

That cold wind burst especially sharp. My insides shuddered.

Barflies congregated into the street from the Watering Hole. A couple of hounds scuttled across Main Street. Percival's Mercantile emptied of patrons. Men on horseback were busily riding nowhere. And too many mud-caked miners slouched around the crumbling fountain in the center of town.

On the boardwalk, outside of the Watering Hole, Rose appeared to be spitting stern words at McKade, as only she could do. McKade had shot others for mouthing off. He never paid Rose any heed though.

I attributed the town's newfound life, and my growing unease, to the advent of the stage's arrival. It must have been big doings for a little town.

The ominous weather turned to drizzle. I picked up the basket from Rose then stepped forward. "The name's Austin. Got a package for me?"

The driver craned his head this way then that. "Nothing left up here. Sorry, son."

The lead horses jolted, loosening the man's grip on his lines. The stagecoach was off at a brisk jog with the driver letting the six-up cover the distance to Molasses Pond Livery unchecked.

I set the basket on the edge of the boardwalk then stepped into the sloppy street to collect the sorrel from the hitch rail.

A small hand tapped my shoulder. "Did you say your name was Austin? I'm Sahara. I'm, um…your 'package.' Your bride."

"Huh?" I think I whipped around too fast because my brain didn't keep up. "Excuse me?"

"I'm your bride. Sahara."

What did she say? "Sahara—"

"No. Sa-HAR-a. Not Sahara like the desert. Although that is my namesake, it is a different pronunciation." She looked at me with distaste, as if I'd purposefully disappointed her somehow.

I jammed a finger in my neckerchief and tugged back and forth like I was attempting to wrest a bone from a growling dog's jaws. *I didn't order any bride.*

"Must be some mistake," I declared. *I don't need a bride. I don't want a bride.*

Her strawberry blond eyebrows lunged toward each other like they were squaring off. A flush crept over her cheeks that almost blended her freckles into an overall darker complexion. She adjusted her bonnet, then tugged at the bow under her jutting chin.

"Um...I'm sure you're a fine woman and all..." I scoured my sweaty palms along the outsides of my thighs. "You see, my circumstances are a little...delicate. Er, difficult. I don't need a package—a person—a bride."

"What are you saying?" She looked at me with horror-filled eyes. *She had the prettiest green eyes. And a heart-shaped mouth.*

"I'm saying there's been some mistake. Maybe you can get a room at the Water—" It hit me. *This was McKade's doing.*

"I'm a mail ordered bride," she announced pridefully, as if that explained everything.

There was a moment where the air just hung, waiting.

"I don't need a bride."

She splashed down into the mud from the boardwalk. "You ordered me."

"I didn't." Panic ripped through me. I felt a rush of blood pounding in my chest. I cleared my throat as bile burned in the back. *I didn't. It was McKade. She was a pawn in his game.*

Sahara dropped her carpetbag into the muck. "I have your receipt right here."

My mind raced. *Flight or fight.* I wanted to run but my feet remained bogged in the mud.

She bowed her head, digging into her tiny purse. The pooch of cloth matched her dress. It was looped at the top with ribbon that extended enough to have been hanging from her petite wrist.

Her sun-faded green store-bought dress was dusty and yellowed with sweat under the armpits. The acrid wetness had, at one point, run along the bodice to her slender waist. She wore white gloves on her hands to attest that she was a proper, civilized lady. But the white had been soiled with use.

"Here." Sahara waved a folded paper in my face. It flapped open and looked official, like a land deed, except not typewritten.

The page was crowded with thin, squiggly letters threaded together in a running stitch. It didn't resemble the writing that I knew how to read. There was a date in block letters that I could figure out. And a fancy wax seal, out of which two little red ribbons hung as tails. It sure did look official, but a deed would have been worth more. "I...I can't read." I stammered. "I mean I can." I stabbed at the loop-the-loop writing with my pointer finger. "But not that. I can't read that."

I snapped my finger back, hearing Ma chastise me as a little girl. "Pointing is impolite." I brushed at the front of my coat then stuffed my knuckles to my hips, cocked my head, and leaned in, interested like. I *was* interested in what that paper read.

Sahara slumped, making herself appear shorter than she already was. She sighed loudly and rolled her eyes skyward in a colorful display, then made a big to-do over smoothing out that paper. She held it to her nose and read aloud. "One mail order bride, Sahara Miller, paid in full. Delivery to Austin, late of Molasses Pond, Arizona Territory."

I interrupted. "There must be some mistake." I knew there wasn't. This was McKade's doing. He would control me through a woman. He would use Seth and Jeb, with their unscrupulous interests, to threaten me.

I didn't want her but, doubtless, she wouldn't be safe in town. Whether I wanted her or not, taking her was the right thing to do. *Just until she can go back to wherever she came from. But maybe Rose...*

Chattering townsfolk began encroaching. The sorrel danced lightly from side to side.

"How old are you?" I asked quietly. I looked to the boardwalk of the Watering Hole for Rose.

People were closing in, loosely forming a horseshoe shape in front of us.

The sorrel thrust his tail out and snorted into the damp wind.

"Plenty old enough. My mama was married and widowed at fifteen." Sahara erected her tiny frame to stand fully upright. "I turned sixteen last June. I'm near to sixteen and a half years now."

A horde banded together and closed in. Barflies. Merchants. A few women. Miners. Cowboys. Kids. Seth was grinning. Jeb bounced on his feet like he needed to visit a privy.

The sorrel wanted nothing to do with any of them. I couldn't blame him for his sentiments. Their invasive approach was threatening. *How could I leave a girl to this mob? How could I leave her to the likes of Seth and Jeb? It wasn't right.*

I maintained a manly stance as the convoluted concerns of two fiery redheads got difficult. I dipped my forehead and tucked my chin. Only momentarily.

Attempting to hide my frustration, I lifted my head and stretched my shoulders as if the event were tiresome. I was too aware of not showing weakness. Predators preyed on the weak.

It would be easiest for me to jump onto the sorrel's back and hightail it out of town. But I couldn't leave Sahara.

As a warning to those encroaching, I slid my left hand to caress the hard shaft of leather in front of my leg. I switched the horse's reins and overtly flexed the fingers on my gun hand.

There was a collected intake of breath. Those with any sense set back on their heels.

"My bag." The girl showed absolutely no concern of being crowded. But she was concerned that the sorrel would run over the top of her bag.

I scooped the carpetbag from the mud.

A cheer went up. Rice and the like was thrown. The sorrel bolted sideways within the short length of the rein, swinging his rump into the projectiles.

I thrust the carpetbag and basket at Sahara Miller.

Having had enough, the horse ran backward, squatting low over his hocks. I went with him for a few strides, so as not to let the animal jam on his bridle. My face was pelted to stinging by one overzealous well-wisher. *Seth.*

I batted pebbles away from my eyes and cheeks, but they continued nipping at my clothing.

I shoved my hand to the butt of my revolver, too fast, too easily, and too naturally. The gun's comforting familiarity filled my palm. It sang to me. Wanting to be pulled. Needing to spit fire at the threat.

My surroundings came into keen focus. I concentrated on Seth's stance. I saw how his arm was loose and relaxed with the throw of a few last pebbles. His holster was tied down for serious business. Just above his knee. The butt of his revolver was perched. Ready.

I honed in on him. I heard the excited rhythm of his fast breathing. And I waited for the telltale lump I knew he'd swallow before committing himself to draw.

My hammer loop was clear. But my weapon would be a split second behind his if he drew on me.

I was itching to grab the handle. Itching to cock my gun on the draw. To hear the *click, click, click, click* of assurance that the next moments would come together in split seconds of deadly clarity, speed, and accuracy.

My senses heightened. My adrenaline surged. My muscles grew tense with anticipation, and restraint.

"Enough. That's enough." Rose shouted.

Flight or fight. There were only ever those two options.

Rose stomped and stumbled her way to the middle of the churning mess. She crossed her arms over an ample bosom and glared at Seth and Jeb. "The two of you. Enough." She pointed at Seth. "You." Rose shook her finger as if scolding a naughty child.

Both held their hands up in mock surrender. Feral smiles slithered across their stubbly faces.

Rose shoved her bouquet of wilted flowers at me. She whispered so that only I could hear her, "If you have any thought to the poor girl's safety, you must get her out of town now."

McKade raised his hand. A chorus erupted. *For he's a jolly good fellow.* The obliterated song was no doubt heard in the next valley. *For he's a jolly good fellow.*

"Jack McKade," Rose shouted above the raucous noise toward where McKade still stood on the boardwalk outside of the Watering Hole, "let these folks go home." She adjusted her small cap and patted her damp locks. "It's starting to rain for godsakes."

McKade lowered his hand. The crowd hushed and began to disperse.

A gulp of cold air hit my lungs, making me realize I had been holding my breath. The sorrel got all four of his feet to touch the ground at one time. Sahara continued to stand rooted, clutching a motley carpetbag and the mud-splattered wicker basket to her chest.

Gunshots snapped the chill air.

The sorrel spooked anew. He barreled sideways and back. My sight filled with bulging, white-ringed eyes; flaring, snorting nostrils; and scrambling, sweat-lathered red. I swung onto the flailing sorrel before he hauled loose from me.

The sorrel steadied under my solid seat. Just long enough.

I grabbed hold of Sahara and hoisted her behind me, wicker basket, carpetbag, and all. I wouldn't have been much of a man if I'd abandoned her to a mob.

I gave the sorrel his head. He burst into flight.

A gruff voice from the crowd jeered, "Half-breed."

Mad whooping, like a band of whiskey-liquored Indians, followed in my wake.

CHAPTER FOUR

Past the outskirts of town, I cupped my foot under Sahara's dainty shoe and slid her from the frightened sorrel. One of her arms was looped through the wicker basket, the other through the handle of her carpetbag. With white knuckles, Sahara clutched at me, making her dismount difficult.

"We'll walk a bit." I needed time to think. I needed my world to slow down.

"Where are we going? Why did you have to be so rough? Couldn't we have rented a buggy? How long do we have to walk—"

I spun into Sahara's face.

Her eyes jarred open as wide as a night owl's. For a second, she looked like a bewildered fawn. Sahara shrunk back in a twinge of alarm.

I hadn't meant to scare her. I just wanted the chattering chit to shut up. *This can't be happening. She has to go. I can't have a wife. I don't even want a wife.*

Her brows scrunched. Her pasty white face flattened and tensed, as if she expected me to hit her.

Stupid girl. What did she think? I relaxed my posture and stepped away. Sahara was too small for the frontier. Too weak. Too vulnerable. She'd never survive.

Sahara stiffened her back, tightening her lips.

After staring her down, I walked off. I was married.

This arrangement wasn't going to work. No. No, this wasn't right. Totally wrong. It was totally wrong. And how was I supposed to live as me? How would I keep my secrets? "Grr." I had too many secrets to have a wife.

I stomped along the trail. Wheel ruts had worn into the ground from over-burdened Conestoga wagons and heavy mule trains passing through the land in their haste for gold. I kicked at anything in my way. Rocks skittered at my punts. With the toe of my moccasin, I sent a soggy meadow muffin to heap elsewhere. Even mud readily leaped from a solid wallop. My mood turned as cold and foul as the fall drizzle needling its way to prickle my skin.

Around folks, I was socially awkward, easily derailed, full of self-doubt, and always on guard. I never relaxed around Whites. I wanted to be alone. To be an upstanding man, I'd have to live alone.

And none of it was Sahara's fault.

It was McKade's doing. If not directly him, he'd have put his hired boys up to it. Why? Why me? Why not the butcher, or the baker, or the candlestick maker? What was I to him?

I flung myself back onto the sorrel. "Let's go home." I gestured for Sahara to step on the top of my foot then offered her my hand.

She shoved the basket and carpetbag at me, before climbing behind.

The horse jigged. The pace was quick and jerky. I felt her thin arm slap across my midsection in reaction. The girl couldn't ride. Her body was too rigid. Her butt smacked the sorrel's loin each time he rose up. I swallowed a word of disgust before it escaped my lips.

"Don't be foolish," I snapped, "wrap both your arms around me and hold on tight."

Bony arms barred across my stomach with the pressure of a blacksmith's vice. Claws dug at my waist. The girl shivered against my back, quaking enough to disturb the horse anew.

"Do you have a shawl or cloak in your bag?" I felt a nod in reply and set to work at the clasp.

What I pulled out was a rag. It was clean but much too delicate. The thin shawl wouldn't hold against this biting fall weather. There was pitifully little else in Sahara's bag.

At nine years of age, I had been lost and wandering without much in the way of clothes. Like Sahara, I had once owned pitifully little. I wore undergarments and a torn boy's shirt. My exposed legs had burned to blisters under the severe summer sun. My feet had swelled and cracked as I limped along, dragging overlarge saddlebags like a tiny version of an overburdened pack mule.

Our wagon train had pulled out of Henniker, New Hampshire, in 1855. The people leaving waved to the people staying. Those who stayed shook their heads, muttering about "foolish pioneers."

My folks had been pioneers. I'm pretty sure now that they had also been foolish.

"Wrap yourself up. It's a long ride to the hogan." I balled the flimsy shawl and passed it off to Sahara.

Sometime in 1856, on the Cimarron Route of the Santa Fe Trail, Indians had descended from the rocky cliffs toward the stalled Conestoga wagons. The band emerged as if birthed from the boulders themselves. They looked savage, yes. Wild. I fancied they were free.

I ran toward them for a closer look, scurrying through low scrub, tumbling weeds, and ragged rocky ground. From behind a red boulder, plagued with a thicket of brown mesquite, I stared up at the Indians on their painted ponies. They passed so near that I could have petted the hairy legs of those splendid little ponies.

Our wagon train had crossed the paths of several bands over the year's travel. Most of the Indians were harmless. Some were beggars. A few were thieves. Fewer were hostile. Those that were hostile had been liquored on Whites' whiskey.

None of them were anything like the chilling stories told around the campfires at night. Stories depicting horrible red savages with war-painted faces, charging down into White settlements on their seasoned warhorses. These Indians were not "whooping and crazed, set to hacking innocent folks to death, taking prisoners to torture, and lifting scalps." They were just people.

Savagery was what the Whites made up.

Sahara shivered too loudly behind me, distracting my mind from its memories. I halted the sorrel, tied the baggage handles in his mane hair at the withers, and wiggled from my warm jacket. Her lips were tinged blue as I fastened my coat around her damp shoulders.

The anxious sorrel jolted in anticipation when I turned back to looking through his ears. Without my asking, he spurted into a jarring jog. Sahara wrapped her scrawny arms back around me in a death grip. My Sunday-go-to-meetin' shirt was too thin. The bindings were too thick. Would she notice?

With my legs, I squeezed the nervous sorrel forward faster.

Sahara rooted her head into my back like a piglet looking for grubs. Her shivering had calmed. The sorrel loped more easily.

In the hills, in 1856, I remembered, the wagons had sat lodged on an untamed pass. The pulling stock were exhausted. Men lolled in sweat-soaked shirts. Older children ran water to the thirsty. Women prepared cook fires for hot coffee to sooth the pains of encroaching futility.

That's when the Indians emerged from the unforgiving landscape in a magical, mystical way.

A big beast of a horse and its grizzly bear rider topped the ridge in their wake. The pair stood, silhouetted by the fierce sun, watching, waiting. Neither horse nor rider were Indian—both too big. The monstrous animal pawed the ground and tossed his head in the air, protesting the restraint of his brutal rider.

No one had heard the Indians until they descended from the rocky ridge. No one had seen them until they had wanted to be seen.

Indians could reach out and touch a person before anyone was even aware of their presence. Several such occurrences had happened along the journey. Spooky, but harmless.

Counting coup. I hadn't known what a coup was. As a child, I hadn't felt like a coup. I remembered thinking that the Indians shouldn't have to get so close to count. I could count from far away. That's what I was doing, counting, from the brush as warriors rode toward the broken-down wagon train.

Sahara squirmed against my back. The girl was skinnier than her clothes made her appear. Her fussy, sharp arms raked my lower rib cage. "Are we almost there?" she asked in a timid voice. It wasn't the same brashness that had met me at the stagecoach.

"Soon." I slowed the sorrel to a jog, then to a walk, and halted. His actions had smoothed. His gait transitioned downward easily. Yet Sahara jammed between my shoulder blades, bracing against the horse.

"We'll walk for a bit." I said.

When Sahara loosed her death grip from my midsection, she slid down the rain-slicked, angular rump of the sorrel. Her gloved hands grasped at tail hairs and air.

Sahara heaped onto the wet soil with a resounding thwack. Lathered sweat from the anxious animal had already soiled her dress. But red earth now upstaged the white lather, leaving the green dress suffering.

When she gained her feet, Sahara slapped at the grime, spinning in place like she was chasing off a clinging kitten.

I hopped down then led the sorrel. Carpetbag and basket in one arm, I towed him in my gun hand. The rustle of material and the pattering splash of store-bought women's shoes told me that Sahara quietly followed.

I wanted to forget she was behind me. My mind wandered through haunting memories again.

Bronze men with shiny black hair rode astride smaller ponies of mixed parentage. Spanish. The ponies, not the men. Left behind from the days of the conquistadors.

The ponies were all unshod, yet their feet were perfect. Each animal was a stallion with a heavily crested neck. The sight of so many uncut males ridden together was uncommon in civilized circumstances. Amazing.

The riders had the utmost control over the ponies, using very little in terms of physical restraints—ropes, bits, or bridles. A single leather line was tied around the lower jaw and held in one hand. I was envious. If they weren't riding bareback, the men sat only on a woven blanket. I wanted one of those cayuse ponies on a string, ridden with just a whisper.

The man on the monstrous horse atop the ridge sat in a saddle. That horse wasn't any cayuse. And that man was no Indian. Six other big men on big, saddled horses flanked him. The sun was at their backs, obliterating details.

The nimble compact Indian ponies floated over the boulder-strewn, steep land as if walking to church on Sunday. The cayuses were made for this land—small horses with colors and broken coat patterns capable of blending into the harsh background.

I had stared, marveling at their mystique. Enthralled.

A body hit the dirt in front of me. I jerked back against the boulder, silently clawing at the ragged rock with my filthy nails.

A golden body spraying crimson blood had thumped onto the ground. The report from a rifle cracked secondary.

"A man never heard the bullet that killed him," my White pa had said many times over.

The fallen Indian's body gurgled and hissed, twitching convulsively.

Horses screamed. Warriors wheeled their mounts in circles.

Through squinted eyes, I scanned for the smoking gun. There. On the ridge. His rifle's butt rested on a thick thigh. Steel blinked in the sun. A tendril of smoke wafted from the barrel.

With curdling whoops and thundering hooves, the Indians swooped toward the wagon train like a swarm of angry bees.

Clouds of dust obliterated my sight. But I heard sharp snaps of gunfire, shouts from men, cries of children, and the wailing of women. I slapped my hands over my ears, pressing in hard enough that my head should have exploded. Tears rolled from my clenched eyes.

The dust cleared on a hot blast of wind. Grit stuck to my wet cheeks. And the scene came into focus with horrid bursts of red.

Through the slaughter, I scanned for my pa.

He stood on our Conestoga's bench seat. Ma huddled below in the boot, clutching my two little sisters. Her face was smudged. The clean streaks down her cheeks attested to her crying. Her auburn hair tousled on quick whips of wind. Her pale blue dress strained tightly over bunched shoulders. I knew the material was pockmarked with tiny flowers, too numerous to count. And I had wished I could bury my face in its voluminous folds right then, where moments previous, I was fiercely displaying the independence that I had often been chided for.

Pa looked out at the horizon, searching. He might have been looking for me. His face was tense. He squinted. I remembered he had had blue-gray eyes that could be as hard as steel when he was angry. I had never known him to be scared. I could almost see his white-knuckled grip on the rifle. I knew how strong his hands were. He'd taught me to always grab hold with a powerful grip and keep holding on with all my might. *Never quit.*

Pa's gun barrel drooped.

I'd never seen him give up. He'd made me promise time and time again to never, ever give up on anything, especially a dream.

That barrel pointed at my ma and baby sisters. Their forms dropped. They appeared to be sleeping soundly long before I heard the rhythmic report of his rifle.

Horror struck me in the chest, like that bullet that hit the Indian lying on the ground in front of me. *Pa.* I wanted to run to him. My body would not budge. I bit down on my lip, tasting a metallic tang as my teeth had cut into flesh.

Pa killed my family. He shot his own family.

I stroked at my pained chest expecting gooey, gurgling blood, gushing from a gaping hole. Nothing. Though the pain in my heart crumpled me farther into the dirt.

Through tear-blurred eyes, I watched as Pa dug his Smith and Wesson from the gun belt at his waist. He turned it on himself.

The Indians stopped their whooping and hollering and quieted their frenetic mounts. The air grew still with deathly silence.

I pulled brush on top of my shaking body and held my knees to my chest. Hiccupping, I no longer cried. I had vowed to never cry again.

My gaze locked on the fallen Indian. His large, round eyes were already glazed with the hazy film of death. He lay there quietly, as if pausing to rest. No twist to his form. No mangled bones. He looked whole and at peace, except for the darkening slurry of thickened blood enveloping his torso.

I had been nine years old. Now? "Seventeen," I said aloud.

"Seventeen what?" The pitter-patter of those fancy shoes scampered up next to me. Delicate footsteps fell in line but not entirely with my steps. My stride was much longer. Stronger.

"I am seventeen summers." What did it matter? Why tell anything to this girl? She would be gone soon. I flung myself onto my favored colt. He had the majestic head of the cayuses. And though he was too large, he showed a bit of Spanish legacy through his sloping goose-rump.

Sahara's huff followed my ascent.

"My hogan is ahead. Not far."

I took Sahara's offered hand and swung her up behind me. Before she even settled, I squeezed the sorrel into a lope.

A trail of smoke drifted skyward from the distant butte's top. I slowed the sorrel to a walk.

"What's that?" Sahara asked.

"Indian sign."

"Are there really Indians close by?" She sucked a huge intake of breath before continuing. "Ya know, savages?"

"Closer than you can imagine."

I felt her shudder.

"What are they like?"

"People. They are The People."

Sahara clucked her tongue from the roof of her mouth, then followed with an exasperated sigh.

I continued. "What is anyone like? Each is different from the other, but we're all of the Great Spirit who made The People."

"You sound like an Indian. That's savage talk."

"How would you know what an Indian sounds like?"

"I read all about them. How they war and hate. They even fight among their tribes. And they kill anyone trespassing on their hunting lands or sacred grounds. I've heard how they covet whiskey and get all liquored up."

"Sounds like the Whites too," I said.

"I read about the gold here," Sahara continued as if she didn't hear me. "And there's land for the taking. And the Civil War doesn't reach this far. Best of all…no big city living on top of one another, with everyone in each other's business."

The hogan came within sight. The sorrel picked his way through the rocky landscape. He halted at the built shelter, blowing encrusted mud from his nostrils.

The sullen sky poured rain in earnest.

I pushed open the doorway. Gray light touched what it could reach. Beyond, was darkness. I struck sparks into a mound of dried horse chips and twigs stacked in the fireplace. When I gently blew on them, flames grew to lick at my nose. I stuck a stick to burning from a stacked woodpile, then went outside to retrieve the carpetbag and basket.

Sahara had barely entered, remaining against the wall.

I dropped her baggage on the straw pallet.

"I'm not a whore," Sahara announced while eyeing where I tossed her bag. "Men just want whores." She crossed her arms over her chest. "You men are all alike." Her soiled, white-gloved fingers clawed at her upper arms.

If she was looking for a reaction, she'd be disappointed. What did I care? I'd have her gone as soon as I could arrange passage back to wherever she came from.

"Men kill over whores." She shifted her gloved hands to her hips. "They kill over whores, and money, and power."

I pulled my hat from my head and fussed with it in my hands.

"Once they get the fever, it's like having to put down a rabid dog. Just can't stop 'em unless you kill 'em."

That was enough sermon for me. I shoved my felt hat on and left, closing the door behind me. Whatever Sahara was going on about didn't interest me. I walked the sorrel to the overhang.

With a fist of scrub brush, I rubbed the angular sorrel colt then tossed feed to each of the horses.

I was wet, and cold, and sore around my ribs. I wanted nothing more to do with the White girl and her White ways. I wanted nothing to do with the Whites at all.

Beneath the overhang, I poked at coals inside a stone ring. With kindling and coaxing, a fire leaped to life. I sat feeding it slowly. When I threw green mesquite onto the engorged flames, smoke billowed into the air. A low draft chased it out. The rain fought the signal's passage into the ever-darkening sky.

I set strips of meat to warming. The doeskin shirt had dried enough to scrape at it with a knife. I was anxious to shuck my wet, store-bought shirt in favor of the fringed hide covering.

When he came in, I didn't turn around. "I saw your sign," I said to TwoFeathers.

CHAPTER FIVE

November 6, 1864, Arizona Territory

It had been over a week. Bordering on two weeks. We hadn't been getting on. I wanted to make peace. But what I wanted more was for Sahara Miller to get gone. There *was* a way to make that happen.

"I'm going into town," I said to Sahara through the hogan's closed door.

Before dawn, I had tied a bead necklace in Charlie Horse's mane as a peace offering. It would look pretty on the girl. A trinket Sahara could take back to wherever she came from, adding credence to the tales of her frontier adventure.

TwoFeathers had left the string of rolled copper and polished turquoise beads in exchange for five-pound flour sacks of raw materials. I had laid the beautifully strung necklace by the fire last night, to watch the reflection of the flames dance over the tiny copper balls. The turquoise also shimmered in the firelight, not wanting to be upstaged. I had thought of Sahara and her fire-red hair. I thought the necklace truly belonged on her.

I checked that the necklace still hung in the short strands of mane over Charlie Horse's wither. "I'm leaving Charlie Horse here. I'm heading out."

When I turned to leap onto the sorrel, she tapped me on the shoulder. "Could you boost me?" She wore my coat and was shoving her fingers into gloves. Her bulging pouch purse swung from a ribbon on her wrist. I boosted her onto Charlie Horse.

The ride to town was long. The feisty sorrel jigged. I held on to him with one hand and ponied a bay colt with the other. We were all held to a sauntering walk by Sahara's inability to ride. And the trip was made longer by the fact that she twittered nervously with complaints about the horse, the cold weather, the food, even how my coat smelled of animals and wood smoke. *My coat.*

At least the incessant chatter kept Sahara on top of the horse. She hardly seemed to notice that she was riding. And after a while, Charlie hardly noticed either. He was a good egg. Mostly. Sometimes. Well…he was a darn good riding horse.

"…and I'm going to need a winter coat. Was that a store I saw in town? In Molasses Pond? What a strange name. I haven't seen a pond since back East. As for molasses, I highly doubt there's any around for miles. Mm…but sweet bread would be good. Have you ever had molasses bread?"

I hadn't answered any of the questions. There was no reason to. Sahara jabbered on. Ignoring her left me time to think.

That's what I'd been avoiding these last days—thinking. I was riding my sorrel. I was thinking about him. Though I'd never part with Charlie Horse, the sorrel had grown on me. I had worked extra hard to finish a bay for something to sell or trade, not wanting to part with my sorrel. All of it was coming down to survival. I could get along on my own with very little. I needed to buy a stage pass to get Sahara Miller gone.

My traps weren't panning out. Truth be told, I hadn't put the time into tending them properly. There were days I couldn't face checking them at all because of the disappointment. Hunting game had become just as difficult. More often, I felt, why bother, as immediate needs in providing for Sahara took precedence. I needed money. So I needed to gentle the unbroke bay. That's where all of my time went.

I had ridden the bay to the base of the foothills, looking for signs of game. A bull elk surprised us. I got excited and pulled my revolver, taking the shot, not thinking about what I was sitting on.

The bay about busted himself.

He turned inside out. Twisting and bucking. I grabbed a hunk of mane and tried to get his head around with one rein. The revolver in my hand pressed into his neck as he tossed to a frenzy.

I had missed the elk with that shot. To rub salt into my wound, the big bull stood his ground. He lazily turned his head to watch our antics.

I grabbed mane with both hands. I grabbed all the mane I could. As strands pulled out, I grabbed more. Desperate to hang on, I dug my heels into the bay's sides. I was sure that the death grip of those heels egged him to keep pitching. But what choice did I have? He was all in.

It was getting dark before the bay found his lost mind.

Needless to say, I spent the ride home that day gun training him.

I was low on bullets. I was low on winter stores. With no stake to buy either, except for two bales of tanned pelts from last year, I'd planned to sell the bay.

The bay was as typical as any red horse with black points. He sported a heavy head and Roman nose, declaring mesteño blood. His only difference from every other solid bay was the white crescent shape in the middle of his forehead.

The bay walked lazily beside my sorrel, laden with tied packs. He was a good horse. Sturdy. Not too tall. Not too smart. He had a gentle nature about him after that bucking fit got out of his system. He'd make a quiet lady's horse, but I could see him pulling a buggy too. The bay was tractable. He wouldn't get anybody into any trouble now.

The cold, blustery morning kept the street deserted of folks. That was more about being morning and less about being cold and blustery. Not many around town got going before noon. I could still smell coffee on the winds.

We rode to the mercantile. Sahara slid off Charlie Horse in haste. The necklace was gone from his mane.

She had shed my coat and dashed indoors. Which left me a moment to jam a small potato I'd secreted into one of the bay's packs down the front of my hide britches. With a sigh of relief, I straightened my shoulders and stood taller.

"Well, if it isn't Austin."

I jumped.

"You seem as skittish as a spring colt cut from his mama's teat. I do declare."

I turned slowly, hoping everything was adjusted properly. "Miss McKade." I tipped my hat to her with a nod, silently pleading with my face not to turn bright red.

"Call me Lily. Please." She tucked the ends of her shawl behind her elbows and smoothed the front of her bodice, fussing at the crisscross of lacing.

My face flushed.

I felt the heat rise from beneath my kerchief to flood over my cheeks. I busied myself with untying the bales of pelts from the bay. Then I tossed the packs and the rope onto the boardwalk.

"My, that is a lovely color on you."

"Ma'am." I tipped my hat and turned to walk down the road.

She stepped from the boardwalk. Her white gloved hand gently laid over my forearm. "I'll walk with you to Molasses Pond Livery. If that's where you're going. I was headed that way on my stroll." Lily tossed her head back and laughed.

I didn't know what was so funny, but I smiled.

Sahara stood in the storefront window, shooting flint-tipped, flaming arrows at me with her eyes.

What? I shrugged. I didn't understand women.

With Lily on my arm and the colts in my other hand, I waltzed off to the livery.

Her shawl slipped. Lily's shawl slipped from her shoulders to across her back and around her upper arms. The movement had caught my attention. Then I noticed that her intake of breath heaved her chest to plumping. It was distracting. I cast glances from the corner of my eye. I did like bosoms. I mean, I guess I shouldn't. But I did.

"How is the mail ordered bride?" Lily asked. "I heard she was the daughter of a whore. And no pappy stuck around." She fanned herself with a gloved hand. "Those ordered brides don't come from the best families." Lily looked downward and fussed with her skirts. She had the decency to at least act demure.

"And what's with that hair?" she asked next. "Is that color real? Do tell." She gave a tiny tug to my arm and whispered, "You would know by now."

I stared at Lily. I blankly stared because my shock wouldn't allow any expressive facial contortions.

"Oh, Austin, I do believe you're a man prude. How noble." Lily threw her head back, opened her mouth wide, and laughed with no hint of shame.

I draped the reins of the sorrel over the hitching post in front of Molasses Pond Livery, keeping hold of the bay.

"Well, here we are." Lily feigned a pout. "Oh, business is so tedious. I'll leave that to you men." In a proper ladylike manner, she dropped a slight curtsy and said, "Good day to you, Austin."

The barn was large, covered by a spacious gambrel. Wings stretched from either side. Inside, stalled horses munched on stored hay, and saddle horses stood patiently in tie stalls. A buggy, a wagon, hanging harnesses, and saddlery were put up neat and proper. Their scents tickled memories from my early childhood. But I couldn't think on them now.

"Was that Lily? Why didn't she stop in?" The man's gaze stared after her. "She tries to be a good girl. There's not a lot for a young lady to do in Molasses Pond. She tries," he muttered more to himself than to me and continued to watch her stroll in the opposite direction. "Sometimes."

He wiped his palm on the leather apron strapped around his generous midsection, then offered his hand toward me. "Justice."

He had a firm grip that went with his massive size. There was only one man in town as big as this blacksmith. But Justice seemed nothing like Jack McKade. I couldn't envision this man lording his bulk around.

His large, muscular physique was probably nurtured over years of hammering steel. His eyes were small but bright. Thick, expressive brows made him appear wise beyond blacksmithing and renting horses in Molasses Pond. His black hair, salted with gray, was cut short to the shape of his head. That, and his clean-shaven face, made him look kindly and trustworthy.

"How do I buy stagecoach passage back East?"

"Son, the stage doesn't run through here for another month or more. If you're wanting to get out…" His eyes drifted to the bay.

"He's broke to ride and to pack. Interested?" I fidgeted with the lead rope as Justice took my measure. "I need a cow. A milk cow."

"So, you're staying now?" He motioned me forward. "Let me have a look." Justice gently tugged at the upper lip of the bay. "Not too old. Over four. Not mature." He stood back to further contemplate the colt. "You take a look in the pens."

I handed the rope over.

At the side of the livery, the first pen held scrub cattle. Five rangy branded steers, two Longhorn cross heifers, and seven unmarked bulls. These would make for a fine beef stew, but a milk cow was different.

I jumped the rails into the next holding pen. All but two animals scurried away.

"How about that brown cow?" I asked as Justice rounded the corner.

Shed of his leather blacksmith's apron, he tucked his fingers into the waistband of his woolen trousers, causing the suspenders to strain. A smile twinkled in his eyes. "The young man knows his cattle." He clasped my shoulder in his meaty hand. "She has that calf at her side. Too young to be weaned. And she is bred back, pure. Are you selling the sorrel?"

No. I wasn't. I crawled from the pens. I didn't want to.

The two colts stood together at the hitch rail. I stroked the sorrel's forehead, then leaned my head to his. I didn't want to. My sorrel pressed into me and reached for my hide shirt, nuzzling it with his upper lip. "Winter's coming," I whispered. "You would have better feed. Probably oats." Was I trying to convince him or myself?

I hadn't wanted to let the sorrel go. I was sure we had a future together. *And that's the sound of a little White girl whining.*

I stood up like a man and plucked the leads from the rail.

Both colts. I led both into the barn, to a box stall. A twinge of regret tugged at my heart as I pulled the halter over the sorrel's delicate ears after sliding the neck rope from the sturdy bay.

That cow and heifer calf were worth more than just the bay, for a fact. I had no choice but to trade my sorrel too.

"I'm prepared to give you the difference in coin," Justice unstrung a purse of coins from a thong around his neck. The supple hide pouch jingled with weight.

"Son, stay out of the Watering Hole," he said, handing over several shiny coins. "That's no place for homesteaders. Getting prone to drunkenness will cost you everything and more. Might cost you your life." Justice leaned in with seriousness, thumping at my chest with his first knuckle. "Listen to me. Jack McKade wants to be king. He is filled with the blackest of evil. He is bent on taking everything from everyone. Don't get tangled in debt to him. Nothing short of death will stop him from taking away all that you love and live for."

"I'll keep it in mind." I pushed my hat off of my forehead. "King McKade. It does have a ring."

"King McKade," he chuckled. "It does have a ring at that."

Justice seemed familiar. Maybe not in looks, but in the way he moved, his intensity and his expressive eyebrows. He walked on the balls of his feet with his arms swinging loose, not befitting his massive muscling. I jounced the fistful of coins before stuffing them in my pocket. My eyes drifted to the sorrel. The bay was happily munching at hay, but my sorrel watched me intently.

"One more thing. Something you can use if you have a mind to bring me more horses in the spring." He jerked a tarpaulin from a clean, oiled saddle. The seat was smaller than usual. The craftsmanship was exquisite. Each hand stitch was perfect to the next. It had basket weave tooling over the doubled skirting. The seat and stirrup leathers were made with rough out for horse-breakin'. And a four-inch post horn was meaty enough to safely dally skittish youngsters. In a nutshell, it was a dream.

"I can't," I said, running my fingertips over the leather. I really couldn't. That calf had cost me dearly. I hadn't counted on her expense. The saddle was worth more than what I had left. And I didn't fancy owing anybody anything.

I tapped at the coins in my pocket.

"I can't," I replied. I drew the canvas back over the top of the buckaroo saddle.

"It's a gift. You're slight, like my boy was." He tossed the tarpaulin to the floor. "It was my son's. He was still too young when he took off adventuring after his uncle. He never came back."

The calf followed loose at her dam's heels as I led the cow down the middle of Main Street. The prized saddle was hefted over my shoulder. I think I strutted a little. I know I got to Percival's Merchantile before my feet wanted to stop parading.

Sahara stood on the boardwalk looking like a serious homesteader. She was engulfed in a boy's blanket-lined coat. Wellington pull-on boots peeked from beneath her skirts. "What is that?" she asked, swaying onto the balls of her feet and bouncing.

"It's a Jersey milk cow." I bowed, sweeping my arm in presentation of the bovine. "And her calf." I tied the cow to the hitching post and swung my new saddle onto Charlie Horse, who didn't look pleased—but with what now? *Me? The saddle? Or the cow?*

The cow was quiet enough to milk. I wouldn't find any better bred either. A purebred Jersey. She had belonged to a gold digger and his family. The wife traded for passage on a stage out of Molasses Pond. Jack McKade had set the miner off his claim by calling in a hefty whiskey debt. There was nothing left except for returning back East, empty-handed.

I hopped onto the board walkway then carried the waiting baled pelts inside the mercantile to stack them on the counter. Sahara disappeared.

The store was stuffed to the ceiling with trade goods. I had to squeeze sideways at the counter to allow the clerk by. As he climbed behind his center of business, I discreetly poked at my crotch to adjust the load. It had shifted, threatening to fall down one leg.

"She's been out back with my boys," the clerk said. "Your wife. She's good with children. They took right to her." The clerk riffled through the beaver skins. "Always a pleasure to buy your pelts, Mr. Austin. They bring a high price back East." He was a small, twitchy guy with round, wire-rimmed glasses and a bow tie.

"I'd like to get Sahara that coat and the boots." I only hoped there would still be enough money for salt and bullets.

The clerk giggled in his throat. "She's bought herself the coat and boots. In fact, all of these packages are hers. I sent a boy to fetch a buggy to deliver them out to your homestead."

Fortunately, he was scratching tallies on a sheet of paper and didn't see me grab the edge of the counter to steady myself.

I pulled at the silk neckerchief that felt as if it was intent on choking me. I patted at the coins in my pocket. There were too few.

"Anything I can get for you?"

I waved my hand over Sahara's packages. "Maybe you ought to get me the bill." If there was a bench, I would have sunk onto it.

"No. You don't understand. It's already paid for." He giggled again.

I wasn't finding the happy yet.

Outside, gray bloated clouds were moving overhead to darken the afternoon.

"Storm's coming," the clerk said, noticing my gaze.

Sahara must have traded the necklace I gave her. That hurt somehow. I rubbed at a tightness in my chest. The necklace was hers. She could do with it what she wanted to.

"The usual then? Salt, beans, and bullets?"

"That'll do." I waved him off. Deep in thought, I wandered out the door.

"Now that you brought the bride to town, she can stay with Rose." Seth settled against the wooden facade, blocking me from retreating back inside.

At his threatening tone, my hand automatically moved to the antler grips of my gun.

"Give him a reason, breed," Seth taunted me.

I heard a revolver's hammer ratchet behind me. Jeb was there, fully cocking his gun.

"We want the bride. She's ours. Bought and paid for." He inspected his fingernails. Against his nature, the nails were clean and manicured.

"I'd been wondering when we'd have this conversation," I said. "You're not having her. She's not yours to have."

"You had your little fun." His eyes slithered to my crotch. "She's not yours to keep." Yellowed teeth, with tobacco rooted between them, menaced from his carnivorous grin. "We want our turn. We want our property."

"She's mine. I've got a paper to prove it." I folded my arms across my chest, staying far away from any misgiving that I'd stray a hand to my gun. "My advice? Get your own."

"We can't," Jeb said from behind me. "The Agency done some checking. Besides, McKade said you'd make good on her. McKade has it all worked out." He prodded my ribs with the snout of his hogleg.

Sahara flew through the door, passing Seth as he continued to loiter against the wall. Her arms were crossed low in front, holding a hidden bundle. She looked to be in a family way.

I saw the bulk she cradled move.

One click. The gun that was pointed at my back disarmed. Its fat cylinder chafed a dry leather holster as it was dropped in.

Seth stood from shouldering the mercantile's wall. "Ma'am," he said, pulling at the brim of his hat with two fingers. Indecision raced across his face. His bluster faltered. Seth jerked his head in signaling to Jeb.

Booted feet behind me shuffled over the walk. The boards creaked and complained from Jeb's slovenly weight. With a splash of mud, I knew he had gone.

Seth hopped into the muck, skipping quickly toward the Watering Hole as if he were a high society city girl with juicy gossip to spread.

"I have something for you," Sahara said. Her face was split by the largest grin I had ever seen on a person. Pearly, straight teeth gleamed, exposing an adorable gap between the front two.

"I couldn't wait any longer," she said, dancing in place on her toes. Delight sparkled in her eyes. "Open it. Open my coat." Sahara jiggled and jumped.

It was difficult for me to get a firm grasp on the wiggling target. When I did, a squirmy, warm ball of fuzz popped out.

I held the pup in the air. Its pudgy body dangled. Legs paddled.

"She's going to be blue. I know she doesn't look it yet. Still too much white. But she'll be blue. With those black patches on either side of her head. And red legs. Isn't she beautiful?" Sahara clapped her hands together. Her face had softened with a wistful, dreamy look. "Quick, keep her warm. Stuff her in your coat."

"I...I can't," I said, trying to hand the wiggling puppy over. I couldn't afford a pup. Besides, a cattle dog could eat as much as a small person. Winter was coming.

"Yes, you can." Sahara stepped forward, ripped at the buttons on my heavy short coat, and shoved the young pup inside.

The animal's head poked out at the top. She licked my chin.

Sahara gave me a quick peck on the cheek.

My face flushed.

"Uh, Mrs. Sahara. Your change."

She turned to the clerk accepting several coins from his hand and squirreling them into her pouch purse.

The necklace. The money had to have come from the necklace. And there were so many reasons I wished she had not traded it away. Wasn't it good enough? Did it lack the refinement of White ways? I was sore at Sahara Miller.

"The buggy will be right around. Perhaps you'll be more comfortable riding in it with your supplies?"

"Why yes, thank you," Sahara said.

The clerk turned to me. "Austin, I have a total for you. Would you like the remainder on account or may we get you something else today?" He oozed too much cheer from his ear-to-ear smile.

"Just the bullets, beans, and salt. The rest on account."

Sahara was chauffeured home in a fringe-topped buggy. The puppy slept curled in a ball on her lap. The calf was securely hog-tied behind the seat. And string tied, wrapped packages mounded in the boot, on the seat, and around the calf.

Rain fell from the sky. It was shaping up to be the wettest fall Arizona had ever seen. I tucked my coat collar up and pulled my hat down as I rode Charlie Horse under my new saddle. He was content with the slow pace of leading the gentle cow as she followed her carted calf.

Not used to the saddle, but quite taken with it, I shifted my buttocks around, attempting to find a comfortable position. I'd been wondering on a lot of things on the ride home.

I'd been wondering on Sahara Miller, mail ordered bride.

CHAPTER SIX

"What did Seth mean by calling you 'breed'?" Sahara asked. "You aren't half—"

Without another word, I walked Charlie Horse and the cattle to the overhang. I didn't need to explain myself to the likes of Sahara Miller, mail ordered bride.

We settled into avoidance. She kept the pup and the hogan. I kept the livestock company beneath the overhang. So yup, nothing changed.

Hunting took me farther and farther away. Game got smaller and smaller. I set snares for rabbits and shot quail. They both tasted like chicken.

The sun was going down. The wind was picking up. It was time to be heading home, when there, descending through scraggly pinion and juniper, was a lone elk. He was thin and scurfy. Not more than three hundred and fifty pounds. With the looks of him, he was a pretentious spike, having overreached and gotten knocked around by a big bull elk.

Patches of dark brown hair were missing from his hide. His right foreleg gimped ever so slightly. I wished I'd seen the cows he'd sniffed after. Or the bull that ran him off. Either would have been a tasty prize. But I was plenty thrilled that the little scraggly buck came along.

Charlie Horse stood stock-still while I quietly teased my gun out of its holster. A .45-caliber bullet from a handgun was an iffy kill shot at this distance.

There was no way to get closer. If the spike spooked, I'd have trouble running him down over the rough country, even with his limp.

I didn't take aim. I fired from my hip. My gun was a part of me, as much as my arm and my hand were. I always hit what I pointed at.

The bullet deflected off his thick skull. The spike bobbed his head like a bug had taunted him. He quietly turned to leave.

Then, he dropped.

Dead.

A second later, a boom like thunder tore through the air. It was the sound of a Hawken.

"Os-ten." TwoFeathers emerged from a stand of prickly pear cactus more than a hundred yards to my right.

He was painted for war.

"This is Apache land. You must leave." TwoFeathers punched the air with his fist wrapped around the Hawken buffalo rifle. A feather fluttered at the end of the barrel. The stock garnered streaks of red paint.

I swung my leg over the saddle and stepped from Charlie Horse. "I have always been brother to the Apache."

TwoFeathers's face was half colored as usual. Bright yellow smeared over his bronze skin. Two thin black lines were added through the middle of his forehead, down his nose, and splitting his chin. Two matching lines slashed high across his bare cheek. There was a dot at the edge of each eye.

TwoFeathers eviscerated the young elk before I wandered Charlie Horse toward him.

"Os-ten must fight. Or Os-ten will be killed. You could come. Would make an Apache warrior. Better than getting killed. Come."

"I can't." There was a time I would have joined the Apaches. I would have fought at TwoFeathers's side against Whites. But I shook my head.

He stood. "You could come. Fight the White enemy." His voice held a mixture of resignation and anger.

There was something he wasn't saying. I knew him too well not to notice his rigid stance and flickering glances. There was something TwoFeathers knew that he wasn't telling me.

"White man is the same. Our enemy is the same."

Maybe he *was* telling me. I shrugged in frustration. "I cannot be an Apache warrior."

"Mm. Woman." He waved the air like shooing flies on a hot, lazy day.

I'm no woman. I fished a hand ax from my old pair of worn saddlebags. Leaving Charlie Horse with TwoFeathers, I stomped off to cut a pair of poles for a drag. My strikes were harder than they had to be. The ax stuck so I had trouble prying it loose each stroke. *Woman?* Chips flew. Several struck me in the face, nipping at my cheeks. Their bites fueled my anger. *Woman?* I slapped at the saplings with a steel edge. *I'm no woman.* My job was done yet I still wanted to whale into the wood.

I panted, letting the ax fall from my hand. *Or did he know about Sahara?*

When I returned with two saplings, TwoFeathers was gone.

I rode to the hogan. There, I dropped the shafts of the travois from Charlie Horse and dismounted. I stroked his neck and scratched his chest, thanking him for his work. Without the horse, we'd starve.

I shucked his bridle and loosened the saddle's cinch a notch before tying him with a neck rope. A slit burlap sack of scrub feed, hung in front of him, would keep him quiet. We were both bone tired.

There was still much work to be done. I hauled the eviscerated elk to thunk in a heap at the hogan's door, then kicked a moccasin covered foot at the wooden blockade.

When the door opened, I pushed through to dump the carcass in front of the fire. The flames were burning hot, and the stew I had smelled earlier this morning was bubbling with mouthwatering chunks of meat and potatoes. It would have to wait.

I shook from my coat like a dog shaking off water, then pounced on the carcass, liberating its hide. The meat needed to be cut and smoked or salted. Just like under the overhang, bigger chunks would dangle over the fire to smoke throughout the night. Strips could be cooked dry for jerky. And the remaining bulk would get salted and packed in tight bundles.

In rendering the carcass at the hogan, I was hoping for a second pair of helping hands.

Gelled blood oozed over the sod floor. The pup nosed in it. I cut a sinewy tendon from the rear leg and tempted her with that instead.

"Navajo," I said, surprised at hearing my brusque voice echo off the walls. I thought of TwoFeathers. I thought of The People...of all of the Nations. They were making their last stand. TwoFeathers stood as an Apache. A man had to stand for something.

Trouble was, I stayed out of everything. I was afraid. Who I was—what I was. My guns couldn't protect me.

Sahara looked at me with overly wide eyes. She wrung her hands until they glowed red.

"I am Navajo. Of The Dineh. Of The People. I was born White. But I was raised Navajo." I drove the tip of my knife deep into a haunch, working to sever the hip joint.

"The White soldiers came. They killed the sheep, the horses, the dogs, and burned our hogans." They killed old men, women, and many of us children. There were no warriors. No one fought against them. There weren't any weapons to fight with.

Sahara's small hand reached over, picking up already cut strips and cubes to set them on the smoking racks.

"I had a dog. A blue dog like this one." The pup had tired of wrestling with the string of sinew and curled up against my thigh. I reined in my vehemence, but it was seething under my skin.

"Now you. Tell me about you." I didn't look up. I didn't want to frighten her off.

For a few minutes, Sahara and I worked seamlessly, side by side.

After her silence stretched too long, I said, "Do you want to go home?" I stared into her eyes. She was very pretty with the firelight dancing over her face. Wisps of hair brushed her cheek. I restrained from my stray thought to tuck them behind her ear. "I'll trade for your stagecoach fare if you want to go."

"Home? I have no home." She was fiery when she raised her voice. "It was my mother's idea to send me away. It was her idea to ship me off as an ordered bride. That's fancy language for selling me." Sahara scrunched her face, pressing the heels of her hands into her closed eyes. "And I fell for it."

Was she saying no one wanted her? Was she saying she had nothing to offer? No hunting, no work, no skills? I glowered at the meat. This kill wouldn't be enough to feed an idle mouth through the sparse winter months.

Sahara sucked a breath through her nose and exhaled in a long sigh. Her body rounded around her work. "I thought it was a romantic idea," she said. "I had it all planned out. I would marry a cattle baron. Become a baroness and ride my fine, prized stable of horses across the range. All of which my husband would own." Sahara rubbed her forehead on her sleeve. "Now all I am is a silly girl living in a sod hut."

"Hogan," I corrected her. "And you don't know how to ride fine horses." I kept my fingers busy. What was she saying? Did she plan to do nothing to earn her way? I spread the thicker cubes and strips on the hide for salting. I didn't have the time or money to keep a pampered pet.

Sahara sniffled. She pressed the back of her wrist to her eye. "I'm not crying. Smoke got in my eye."

I dragged one of the salt sacks over, liberally tossing granules onto the meat. The girl could learn some skills. I rolled the cubes around and flipped the strips. "You can go from here," I said. "You can find the wealth you seek."

Of a sudden, it occurred to me that I no longer really wanted Sahara to leave. I needed her here. I needed her to help out, but I needed her here. Still, I wanted her to be happy. I didn't even know why I wished for her happiness. She had been thrust upon me.

I was tired. And I was angry. Maybe I was angry because I was tired. Maybe. Maybe I was angry at having to live in the wrong body struggling to be me. Angry for hiding and keeping secrets. Angry at who I am and who I'm not. Angry because I felt alone.

I was angry because I was scared.

"What is this?" Sahara held a copper .53-caliber ball pinched between her thumb and forefinger. "It's an odd thing to find inside an animal."

I sloshed tepid water over my hands and forearms from a wooden bucket. Sahara living here wasn't going to work. What about winter? What happened when I needed to live in the hogan? What about TwoFeathers visiting? No. Sahara had to go. I bundled a load of salted meat into my arms and left the hogan for the dug cellar hole, making sure to slam the door. Hard.

The night was pitch-black. Even the tiny pinpricks of stars hadn't come out to wink. Too much effort? Did they want to ride in on prize ponies too?

I felt my way into the dug cavern, to the floor at the back where the supply of deer was laid. That meat was older. I'd move that forward to stack the elk behind. It was work but it had to be done.

The door of the hogan opened with a creak. Sahara probably had to relieve herself. I couldn't do that for her.

My holster caught as I twisted in close confinement. The narrow space beckoned me to drop my gun. Instead, I untied the latigo that held it more solidly above my knee, then wiggled sideways. Lifting and shifting piles of meat was challenging. My arm kept hooking on the flouncing butt of my revolver.

Outside, the night air had a bitter chill to it. A shiver ran the length of my spine. I tied my gun back down.

Firelight came from the open door of the hogan. Shadows moved within the dwelling.

Shod horses were hitched at the side of the log structure, next to Charlie Horse. I heard their impatient pawing.

A loose front shoe clinked. One of the mounts blew through its nose then shook its head, rattling the heavy hardware of a bridle.

I slipped around their haunches. Their saddlebags hung limp. No overnight provisions. The riders had not planned to be eating and sleeping under the cold night's sky.

One of the animals nuzzled at my hide shirt. It was my sorrel, now owned by Justice. I stroked his face and touched my forehead to his.

The blacksmith had no reason to pay me a visit. Any business he had with me could have waited until daylight. So the sorrel had been hired out. And whoever did the hiring knew exactly where they were headed.

"Where's Austin, little lady?"

That gruff voice was familiar.

"I don't know. Perhaps you'll be kind enough to wait outdoors for his return," Sahara said.

"Nope. It's you we came to see. It's okay with us he's not here. I'm sure you'll let him know we visited."

"I don't think she'll tell him everything of our visit." The man had a nasal snicker.

"Seth. Jeb. Something you wanted?" I leaned inside the door's frame, pulling my makings from a pocket.

"Austin, we was just looking for you," Jeb said. The stench of his rotting breath wafted my way.

I shook crushed tobacco leaves onto a paper, rolled it, and licked at the edge.

"Yeah, that's right. We were looking for a claim out here. Heard there was yellow found over to the dry arroyo. Well, we figured you'd be good about offerin' supper to a couple of hungry neighbors passin' by," Seth said.

I shoved the finished smoke to my lips and purposefully searched the pocket in front of my six-gun for a match. The motion drew their eyes.

My hammer loop was out of the way. The handgun was popped slightly, loosened for a quick draw. These two understood this unspoken language.

I struck a sulfur-tipped match on the log wall. The tiny head flared. I sucked the rolled wad of tobacco to life. "Sahara, do you think you can find them a plate of supper?" I didn't mind polite guests.

Jeb looked around anxiously as if, of a sudden, he didn't know where he was.

Seth stared at Sahara, licking his lips as she walked past in her simple dress and bare feet.

"Then…they'll be on their way." I slammed the door against the chill of the early November night.

The puppy doddered over to sniff at Jeb's boot.

"Sahara. That's a mighty pretty name." Jeb ripped his hat from his head, holding it to his chest. At least he attempted to look like he had manners. Though it wasn't working for him. Neither was the knee-length canvas overcoat covering his gun completely. He kicked at my pup.

The pup squeaked and ran behind my heels, curling up against the wall.

Seth tore his winter coat off and lunged into the chair at the table. There was only one chair. A split-log bench offered seating on the other side.

Following suit, Jeb shed his coat, exposing the massive, holstered hogleg that hung too low over his thick knee. It had no tie down. He adjusted the swinging firearm when he climbed onto the bench, careful not to have his actions mistaken.

Sahara brought them steaming, heaped plates of the mixed meat stew that had been simmering since breakfast. My mouth watered. My stomach grumbled.

Seth caught her by the skirt. "Have some with us, little lady."

"No, thank you." Sahara yanked her dress from his hand and retreated to tending the strips of elk by the fireplace. She pressed her knuckle beneath her petite nose. And I agreed that the air inside had grown rancid.

"How 'bout you, Austin? Hungry? Looks mighty fine. Wish I had me a wife that cooked like this." Seth held his knife up, tipped with a generous hunk of meat. "Well?" He smiled, showing his yellowed teeth.

"Already ate," I lied, hoping they couldn't hear my stomach protesting.

"I see that she can satiate a man's other needs too," Seth said as his eyes strayed to my crotch. He bobbed his thin, peaked brows up and down.

I had forgone my trouser prop with all the riding today. A moment of self-consciousness made me feel less of a man—

"Now that's what we came to see you about," Seth said. He slapped another chunk between his feral teeth, chewing with an open mouth. "We were thinking you'd let us borrow your wife. Seein' how we're...partners and all." He talked with his mouth full.

Jeb perked his head out of his plate. "Yeah. The whore in town is getting old. And she ain't near as pretty as what you got." He pointed at Sahara with the tip of his hunting knife.

There was one thing I knew about Jeb. He could use a knife. Firelight glinted off his unusually polished blade.

Sahara balled her hands into fists. I caught her by the wrist.

"Are you going to let them speak about me like that?"

Seth interrupted, "We'll bed down right here tonight. Won't take up much of your time 't all, Austin. You go about your business while we conduct ours with this Sahara."

Seth obliterated the name, sounding it out like the desert. Sahara had wanted it enunciated with the accent on the second syllable. Highborn. Sahara wanted to be seen as highborn. And the grating of her name clawed at my innards.

"It's a shame you traveled this far for nothing. Renting those poor old nags and all. Sahara's my wife. You can't have another man's wife. Not in the territory."

"She's bought. Anything's paid for is a whore." Jeb roared. "And we done the paying."

Seth motioned to Jeb. Even with Jeb's anger, Seth held some sort of control over him.

"What my 'sociate is trying to explain to you is that we own shares in your property, so to say. We have rights to use part of that claim. Besides, you look more spent than I've seen you before. You won't be up to beddin' her tonight.

"Jeb and I figured when we went in that you had the place to keep her. We was figuring on cutting McKade out from the start. He didn't put no money in. We don't owe him nothin'. And we wouldn't have to share her around if she warn't in town. Which means you can use her most of the time. But we expect to be gettin' a little of what's ours anytime we want. No bother to you, of course." He swallowed a hunk of barely chewed meat. I watched the lump struggle down his throat.

"Then she don't have to move into town like Mr. McKade says. Not far's we'd be concerned." Seth stabbed his knife into the wooden tabletop, punctuating his intentions. "You keep her from McKade for us. And we'll stay peaceable with you."

Jeb leaned forward onto his elbows, bathing his blade with his thick tongue the way a cat washed its paws.

"Gentlemen." I stood from leaning on the wall. "Thanks for bringing your proposition to me. But I don't see it your way. And since you've had your fill of my supper, you'll be leaving."

"No. I guess you don't see it our way. You will. We're staying."

Jeb's weighty skinning knife flipped past my ear. But his throw was only the distraction.

Seth yanked his Colt Navy revolver.

My shot had already gotten off.

Distraction didn't work on me. Their game had been obvious from the way Jeb was particular about slathering that honed knife clean. It was akin to a gunslinger keeping his nails manicured, the calluses filed from his trigger finger, and his gun well oiled.

The echoing crack, the yip from the pup, and the smell of burnt powder brought to mind Pa's three rules on gun handling.

Never pull a gun unless you intend to pull the trigger. Otherwise it's a very thin threat.

Never wound. A wounded bear comes back enraged. Shoot to kill.

Never count on getting a second shot. You could still be killed if your first shot wasn't clean.

But I'm not a killer.

I'd do it my way and take responsibility for whatever comes. That's what being a man is about.

Jeb scratched gunmetal against dry, neglected leather. He was slow to pull the massive hogleg from its sheath.

I fired again from the waist. My gun spit a blazing metal shard from its barrel. Jeb's hand jerked upward. The Colt Dragoon spilled from his grasp as he cradled a bloody appendage to his chest.

Sahara jerked the hunting knife from the log wall. Screaming like a scalded cat, she threw it at Jeb with all her might. The bone handle knocked him in the forehead, just above his left eye. Sahara's aim was true, but she knew nothing of knife throwing.

"Get out," I growled.

The two fled into the dark. Galloping hooves attested to their further departure.

I holstered my Smith and Wesson.

Sahara's face was flushed. "Did you learn to use a gun from the Indians?" she barked with accusing anger.

"Navajo. No. The Dineh had few guns. No handguns. Only single-shot hunting rifles, if any."

She wrung her hands together. "What did they mean they bought me?" Harsh realization contorted her face. "You mean, you didn't send for me?" She pressed her fingers to her mouth.

"I didn't order a bride. I don't know who's money paid your passage. What I do know? McKade's hired guns think they have a claim to you."

"Stay the night," she said, collecting the filthy plates. She fed the tailings to the pup. Sahara turned from me, but I could see her stiff shoulders and the rigid set to her jaw soften. "Stay here. With me. Please."

"I think it's best if I don't." I liked her. The way she threw that knife? She was feisty and brash. She was beautiful. I wanted to stay. But me liking on her didn't change the truth of my situation. It was best for both of us that I didn't stay in the hogan with her.

"I don't believe you're a real man."

I emptied the two spent rounds from my gun and reloaded.

"If you are a man, take me."

"What?" I slammed the Smith and Wesson into its leather.

"Take me," Sahara repeated. "It's your right. You are my husband. You're the man. So take me." She had her hands on her hips. Her face had turned dark shades of red. "Those men would have taken me."

"Those men. Is that what you want? Men like that?"

I busied myself collecting the fallen hoglegs, the knife, heavy coats, and a hat. I tossed the armload onto the table then righted the chair and bench. "A man treats a woman properly. With kindness and respect."

"You don't even look at me."

There was a splatter of human blood on the floor. I looked at that. I remembered times gone by when I caused more than a speck of it. Sahara could never love me if she knew the truths about me. There were too many truths.

"Have you…" Sahara placed her hand on my arm. "Have you ever been with a woman?"

"I'll stay." I cut her query short. "But I'll stay here," I pointed to the front of the stone fireplace, "on the floor. To tend to the meat."

In the dark, I heard her toss and turn, and huff and puff. I almost felt sorry for the straw pallet as she punched it with her fists.

My eyes grew heavy sometime in the night.

His eyes were as hard as steel. They all huddled beneath his rifle. There was a man on the ridge—the White atop a massive beast. Steel glinted from his leg, below where the butt of his rifle perched. McKade. Jack McKade. Indians rained down, whooping from hell itself. My world was bathed in a bloody slaughter. My six-shooters spit fire and a golden-haired man slammed backward. Blood popped from twin holes in his chest.

I startled awake. Her soothing touch stroked my sweaty forehead. She was quietly humming a familiar tune. The one my White pa had played on his harmonica. "Foolish Pioneers."

In the dim light of the dying coals, I staggered to my feet in a sleepy haze then lurched to the door. I needed to get out. Needed fresh air and big spaces. Needed the swift legs of a fast horse.

I needed Charlie Horse.

I scrambled out the door. Stumbling in my haste.

Dawn was taking its first breath over the butte in the distance.

Charlie Horse?

Charlie Horse was gone.

CHAPTER SEVEN

Hoofprints told of Seth and Jeb stealing off with my horse. They wouldn't have gotten far. Charlie Horse was ornery about going someplace he didn't care to, with folks he didn't care much for. There was one place he would go every time he'd get loose. Charlie Horse liked to visit a small wild band that roamed the base of the butte, out past the arroyo. I'd bet I'd track him to there. If I was doubly lucky, I'd gather a stray, broke horse also.

Cattle drives lost a fair amount of stock on their push. At the end of a drive, leftover usin' horses from the remuda were sold or turned loose. Some of these gentled animals joined the wild mare bands or formed bachelor bands on the periphery of brood herds.

I needed a second broke horse if Sahara was going to stay. And it certainly looked like the girl was taking root.

Beneath the overhang, I stomped around attempting to get my brain in order. I milked the cow, turning her and the calf into a small fenced paddock after. I tossed scrub feed to the little wild mare in the breaking pen that had dropped a foal out of season. Back in the cavernous shelter, I rummaged through scant supplies, deciding what to take. The copper band bracelet with its center turquoise stone and a pouch full of coins fell from the wrappings of a heavy, bulky bundle.

A twin revolver to my Smith and Wesson nestled in a scrunch of cured rabbit skins. It had been a gift from a trapper I had worked for this past winter. At the urging from a wave of nostalgia, I flipped open the furs to run my fingertips along the barrel, pushing the cylinder to check its smooth, oiled action. I spun the revolver around my left trigger finger. The gun responded too easily in my off hand. But I nearly dropped it from a lack of practice.

"I'm going with you," Sahara said. She stood just inside the overhang, hands on her hips, with a look of determination. The morning sun set her red hair ablaze in surreal color.

Hastily, I folded fur flaps over the gun, tacking the bracelet to my wrist. "You'll slow me down." I plucked a deerskin satchel from the floor, upending it to shake loose any visitors.

"I won't slow you down." She stuffed a cloth wrapped bulk into my bag. Her fingertips lingered on my forearm. "Furthermore, we'll take the pup."

Sahara *would* slow me down. She was a house flower. I wasn't heading on a Sunday picnic. "I'll consider the pup, but you'll stay." I dropped the pouch of coins inside the bag with a slight of hand, then plucked her wrapped bulge from the satchel. "What's this?"

"Molasses bread. It's the first loaf I've ever made." She reached to flip open the cloth. The bread was a gnarly lump. "There's not much molasses to be found in Molasses Pond. And it doesn't come cheap," she said. Stray wisps of hair fell across her face. She pushed them behind an ear.

I looked at her. Really looked. Her forehead was tense with worry, but her eyes were soft with pride. Hair fell back over her cheek. She shoved at it. She was pretty—when she wasn't being irritating. Sahara brushed the front of her clothes.

"What's that?" I waved a finger up and down, pointing at her outfit.

"Store-bought clothes," she said with a huge grin, then chewed on her bottom lip as if she'd gnaw it off. "Men's store-bought clothes." Sahara took her hands from her hips and clapped them, bouncing on the balls of her feet. She twirled for me to digest the entire picture. "You like?"

The clothing was practical. Workable. Woolen trousers and a thick cotton, button-down shirt. Beneath, she wore a bright red long-handle undergarment. The clothes would have been a great expense. I was still struggling to accept that my gifted necklace had been bartered away. I'd have rather seen her wear it, just once, even if I'd had to incur the cost of her clothing expenses myself.

Sahara tucked the thick pants into her tall boots, "In case of brambles, burs, or snakes." Dangers the clerk had mentioned. With her heavy overcoat, the outfit looked bulky and straight. The slack garb toned down her full breasts, slim waist, and curvaceous hips. None of it could cover up the fact that she was all woman.

That was in her walk. The way her upper body flounced, jiggling her chest forward, shimmying her shoulders as no man would have. It was in the sway of her hips. The free swing of her arms. The little clap she did when she was happy or excited.

Sahara smoothed her hands along her sides, following her feminine form. She absentmindedly caressed her curves, straightening wrinkles and tucking bulk. No man cared to be that meticulous with clothing.

"You know, these clothes are quite comfortable." Sahara jammed her hands into her pockets then brought them out to hitch at her waistband, adding a few harrumphs. "Maybe I should have a gun," she said while clapping her hands together.

"No. No gun. Learn to use the clothes first."

She drew her fingers into guns and slapped them against her hips in the ready. Squinting her eyes, pursing her lips, and thrusting her jaw forward, Sahara spun on her booted heels to saunter off in an exaggerated manner. Her impression of a man?

Slowly, she turned, pelvis thrust forward, a snarl on her face. Sahara mocked a spit to the side.

When she drew, I was ready. I pulled a hair faster, leaving my hammer down.

She froze. Shock registered across her face.

Sahara opened her palms and slid them along her thighs. Her carriage shrunk. She turned away.

"Not bad," I said. "Pretty fast. Just needs a little work." It was only play after all. I hadn't meant to scare her.

"You're deadly fast. I've never seen anyone that fast."

Deadly fast? I had to be deadly fast. And deadly accurate. My gun had become a way of survival in the White's world. Sahara would never understand that. She was a White.

It was a White man who incited the Indians to massacre my White family's wagon train. My White pa killed my baby sisters and my ma. It was White soldiers who killed my adoptive Navajo people. White missionaries forced their religion onto me. A *proper* White family scrubbed my body clean and strapped me into White women's petticoats. And a White man called me out for a gunfight he had no business being in. That White made me a murderer.

I spun the cylinder on my revolver, then flopped it from side to side in a quick inspection.

"Did you know where you hit those men?" Sahara asked, turning back to me.

"I hit what I was aiming at, Sahara. I always hit what I aim at." I let a long sigh slip on an exhale. "I didn't kill them." My body caved a little, like when I got dead tired. "The one that yanked his revolver first? Seth. I sliced his ear for him. And the one with the knife that then pulled his gun? Jeb. I took the tip of his little finger off." I stared into her eyes. I thought there was a mix of fascination and horror. "I didn't kill them." I could have.

Silence. I watched the back of Sahara's head bob with its red hair shimmering in the sunlight. She said nothing for too long.

The gun in my hand was well oiled for smooth action. It was always ready to go to work. I shoved the killing instrument back into its holster, stuffing the leather loop over the hammer.

"Maybe you should have," Sahara whispered.

"What?"

"Killed them. Maybe you should have killed them." She faced me. "Have you ever killed anyone?"

"That's not a question you ask out here." I walked away, gathering bullets, jerky, a water skin, and a lariat. Stepping into the bright sunshine, I said, "Let's go. If you're coming, that is. And the pup stays here. She's too young and would only cause a wreck."

The trail wasn't easy to pick up. Seth and Jeb would have galloped for town, so I had a general direction in which to start. But Charlie Horse wasn't likely to have arrived in town with them. Each set of tracks running off the beaten path had to be investigated. Tracks scattered every which way. The difficulty was in singling out particular prints. At least there were prints.

Fresh tracks ran toward the butte. That's where Charlie Horse would go. I followed those.

In a dry gully, the hoofprints doubled. The hard pack was tortured, with its rocks strewn and the ground gouged. Stallions had fought. The herd then continued toward the butte. There was a smaller group following at a respectful distance.

I bent, prodding the imprints for a specific sign.

"Charlie Horse." I brought the tips of my fingers to my nose and sniffed lightly. "It's him." I waved my fingers under Sahara's nose.

Sahara grimaced, looking like she had smelled a bad fart from unsavory company.

"Charlie Horse is prone to gravel abscesses in his front hooves."

She didn't get it.

"He was sulking on one for weeks. It's finally blown out." I squatted to rub my fingers more aggressively through the crescent impression in the dirt. Sahara hunched down. "Smell." I held my gritty fingertips out to her.

"Oh. How awful." Sahara batted the fetid air in front of her face.

"Over there." I pointed to a band in the distance. The horses naturally blended into the landscape. Sorrels and bays were one with the brown and red rocky terrain. They moved slowly through jagged footing to pick at wisps of scrub.

My horse emerged from behind a large boulder. Big egg spots on a glaring white rump made him stick out from the others and the ruddy backdrop like a sore thumb. His coloring was unique and highly prized among The People. He was not a White's horse. So I had stolen him from the White soldiers.

Whites had stolen him from a Palouse River Indian tribe previous to my acquisition. I had a right to take him back. More right than the Whites had to owning him.

A short rope draped from his neck. He still wore my saddle.

I signaled Sahara to stay put.

Speaking in Navajo to Charlie Horse, I walked forward. He pawed the ground. The band of mares around him picked up their heads. I made the sign for "horse" and continued the silent language instead of speaking aloud.

Still, Charlie Horse proved difficult to approach. One wrong move and he would send the herd scrambling up the butte, following in their wake.

The clatter of foals' hooves sent gravel rolling as each clambered to their dams' sides. On the periphery of my vision, a tall, stout mare blew a snort. She was the alpha. The band milled closer together. Watching. Waiting.

Charlie Horse bowed his sculpted head, bobbing acquiescence several times. At this, I spun out a loop and let fly. He walked into it.

I signed "horse" in a respectful thank you. Then changed that to "my horse" by closing my right hand and bringing it toward my neck. I ran my thumb over my index finger and rotated my wrist, thumb now to the front. He came toward me. A barely noticeable limp shortened his gait.

I pressed my face to Charlie Horse's well-muscled neck, and ran my hand over his shoulder, finding new gouges and cuts. The short neck rope dangled. I took hold of it to drag the lariat to his throat. While I tightened the cinch, I said to Sahara, "You start walking Charlie Horse down. I'll be right behind you. I want to try for a stray saddle horse." I scuttled away before she said a word.

The band began herding closer to each other, preparing for flight. The lead mare poised to fight. Her ear twitched toward the rocky incline. Her eyes flickered with uncertainty. She was a rough bay with four white socks and a Roman nose. Nothing pretty to look at, but square and heavily muscled. She kept one ear and one eye pinned to me.

I zigzagged the rocky terrain quickly and quietly in a non-threatening manner. I watched the ground, not so much for where I walked, but for keeping my eyes from threatening the herd like a predator. I was a predator. Prey animals had eyes on the sides of their head. Predators had eyes in the front. The eyes of a predator could send prey into flight.

In close enough, I made a rope shot for a young gelding carrying a brand. At that same instance, a scream ripped the still air. The gelding whirled. The herd bolted.

Sahara. I ran, coiling my empty lariat as I went.

Charlie Horse blasted past me. The rope on his neck swung. I thought to grab hold as he whipped by. But I would have probably been dragged to death before he even noticed I was hanging on. Besides, Sahara might be injured. She was definitely in trouble.

I ran as fast as I could. Low brush scratched at my ankles. My flailing lariat snagged on a short boulder. I tripped, tumbling into a spiky cactus.

Still, I got up and ran to Sahara.

I jumped into the dry arroyo and followed its path to a dryer, open flood plain. There she was. Alone. Seemingly fine.

"What happened?" I gasped, gulping for air.

"Snake." Her face was puffy and red. Her eyes overflowed with tears.

"Did it strike you?" I pulled her to the barren ground, rolling her over to check where she was bitten. "Where—"

"No. No. It just scared me. The horse went into the air. He stomped at the snake."

"Did he pull you?" Charlie Horse was solidly rope broke. I'd never known an occasion that he'd fought a neck rope.

"No. He didn't pull exactly. I thought he might so I threw him the rope." Tears streamed in earnest. Sahara wailed and blubbered. "I don't know anything about horses. All I know is that they smell. They take a lot of work. And I'm safest when they're pulling a buggy, driven by someone other than me."

What was there to say? I stood, hauling her up with me. I needed a horse. I needed that horse. Charlie Horse. We had been through a lot together. He was my closest confidant.

"We could get you to town. We're near enough. I'll go back for Charlie Horse."

Her crying lessened to hiccupping sniffles. I waited. She neatened her clothes, tucking her pants back into the tall boots and her shirt into her pants. Sahara slapped at the dust and grime, then finger-combed her furious red hair.

We set off toward Molasses Pond. I started picking cactus spines from my buckskins, coat, and wrists. The needles that found flesh had already made my skin red and angry.

Within the hour, the sun hit its zenith. I handed the water skin to Sahara.

"What's that?" she asked.

"Water."

"No. That. That blinking." She pointed past a thicket of mesquite. "There's something shining."

I yanked her to the ground for a second time today. What would sunlight be glinting off of out here?

Sahara squirmed. "What are you—"

I slapped a hand over her mouth and shushed into her ear. "Stay here." Then, I circled wide in a low crawl for a closer look.

Charlie Horse. His neck rope was twisted in mesquite. I squatted behind strewn boulders. Waiting. Watching.

"For heaven's sake, Austin. What is it already?" Sahara stomped toward me as tall as a hundred-year-old saguaro cactus and as loud as a rutting bull elk.

Okie dokie then. If someone were laying in wait to ambush us, they'd have taken a shot already. "It's Charlie Horse."

Sahara craned her neck around the boulders. "Oh, the poor thing. He's caught in that awful brush."

Copper conchos adorned my saddle in each corner, under the latigo tie strings. They were engraved with the Spiral of Life.

I didn't see him. That didn't mean TwoFeathers wasn't out there. Actually, I was sure he was. I fished the jerked meat from my satchel and handed a few strips to Sahara before leaving the bundle sitting on the nearest rock.

Charlie Horse's rope had been tangled in the twisted fingers of a mesquite bush. I wrestled it loose then walked him off. He limped.

"I'm going to keep heading into town. I need Charlie Horse shod to protect his hooves." We resumed our pilgrimage. Sahara was quiet. I picked at more cactus spines.

Sahara emptied the water skin and chewed on the jerky strips. She looked worn out when we reached the outskirts of Molasses Pond. She hadn't complained once on the long walk. That told me she was done in. If the girl had any life left in her, she'd have been gibbering nonsense every second.

Main Street was certainly a welcome sight. I felt Sahara's mood lift as we marched into town.

Jeb staggered into the roadway in front of us with a bottle of whiskey in one hand. A clean white bandage wrapped his other hand. *That was probably where I had shortened his little finger with a bullet.* He grabbed after three boys rolling a hoop with their sticks. Too drunk to catch them. Undeterred, Jeb took a hearty swig from his bottle and eyed a woman crossing the street from Percy's Mercantile. Though she ventured wide, Jeb swayed his way to pinching her skirts.

At her squelch, the pastor, in a brown frock coat and white collar, hustled to escort the woman.

Wobbling drunk, Jeb pointed to the pastor. "He ain't one of us," Jeb shouted to the men lingering on the boardwalks and around the crumbling fountain. "You ain't one of us," he announced. "Pastor Goody-two-shoes. All high and mighty with the Lord." He poked the pastor in the chest. "He's a prissy dude, aintcha. A dude from back East."

He took hold of the pastor's coat lapels which steadied him, and bolstered his confidence. Jeb growled, "Let's see your God save you from this." He yanked a knife from his belt and held it to the pastor's throat. "Since you ain't one of us, you can go to hell."

He pressed the knife to the pastor's Adam's apple. "I'll kill all of you who ain't one of us."

"Austin, don't." Sahara clutched at my arm.

I shirked from her light grasp, tucking Charlie Horse's reins into her hand.

Jeb didn't see me coming. I reached across to clench on to his bandaged knife hand. He shrieked like a tiny church mouse nabbed by a rat terrier. Eyes wide with pain, he dropped the bottle of whiskey out of his other hand onto the packed roadway. It smashed.

I hadn't the strength to wrestle his arm from holding that knife up to the pastor's throat. I squeezed his injury, hoping he would let go of the knife.

Molasses Ponders lined the boardwalks, gawking like there was a parade stalled on Main Street. They poured from tents. Percival's Mercantile emptied. Hammers stopped pounding. Buggies halted. Horses stilled. It was as if the entire town held its collective breath.

Blood from a thin cut stained the pastor's pristine collar.

Seth hailed from the Watering Hole's boardwalk. I jerked my gun and shoved it over the pastor's shoulder to point at Seth.

Seth smiled at me. He held his hands up like it was all fun and games. "Jeb," he called as he stepped into the road.

Jeb attempted to shuffle around. I shook my head.

"Lookyhere, Austin, I can't help this sitchiation any unless you let my boy go."

"Isn't happening. I want the knife."

"Well now, that's not going to happen either. Ya see, Jeb is awful fond of that particular knife seeing how he's misplaced one of recent."

"The knife comes off the pastor's throat. I'll give it to your care."

"Now that sounds real good. Don't it, Jeb?"

Jeb twitched his eyes toward Seth. His left eye was blackened. Above, sat a swollen knot.

"Jeb's just feeling out of sorts. He'll be fine if I take him back inside." Seth approached with his hands still grasping for air. "I'll take the knife now, Jeb. You can have it back after."

Jeb flickered his eyes to Seth again. His bandaged hand relaxed inside my grip. He allowed the knife to fall into Seth's hand.

Hugging Jeb around the shoulders, Seth escorted him back to the Watering Hole. Jeb struggled against Seth's hold. He made a grab for the knife. Failing, he contented himself with hollering. "He ain't one of us. He's a savage breed. An injun. Unnatural. And he will go to hell at the end of my knife."

I spun the cylinder of my gun, checked its smooth action, then jammed it into its holster.

The pastor swabbed a line of blood from his neck with a clean handkerchief. "Son, those men aim to kill you one day."

It did appear that Seth and Jeb had a particular mad on for me.

Sahara rushed over as fast as Charlie Horse's lameness allowed. She thrust his reins back at me with a look I didn't understand. She took the pastor's arm and headed him toward the mercantile.

On a glance, I saw Jack McKade backhand Seth across that split ear. Jeb dumped onto the boardwalk in a drunken heap. McKade kicked him in the ribs. Sun glinted off the brace on his leg.

Charlie Horse and I doddered down Main Street under silent stares. Just when I was feeling all alone, Lily stepped into the road and took up my arm. "Our hero."

I couldn't help but smile. I felt my cheeks heat up. She was truly lovely. A luxurious wrap of blond curls nested atop her head, showing off her graceful neckline. Her porcelain shoulders were swaddled by the thick, soft, rabbit fur collar of her long, tailored coat. I felt the heat of her cuddling my side. "Austin."

When Rose said my name, it was with some importance. But Lily… When Lily uttered my name in a breathy whisper, it was like a special secret just between the two of us. I played the echo of her voice over and over in my mind.

At the livery, I tied Charlie Horse in the spacious aisle and took my satchel from his saddle horn. "Justice?"

There was no response.

"Hmm. It looks like we're all alone." Lily stroked her warm palm across my cheek. But her eyes strayed over my shoulder to where the shiny, silver-dollar-sized, copper conchos adorned my saddle.

When her rich blue eyes came back to mesmerize mine, my face glowed with heat. I wormed away from her close scrutiny. Would she notice I didn't have the fuzz of an adolescent beard? Lily was bound to find out. Sahara was bound to find out.

My gut wrenched akin to a gnawing hunger pang that I'd never be able to satiate. I plucked the loaf of molasses bread from my bag. The cloth fell open. I tore off a wad. Anything for distraction from Lily's fine form. When the bread hit my tongue, I closed my eyes. *Heaven.* I've never had anything like this.

"Oh, Austin. You make that ridiculous lump look too delicious." Lily plucked a nibble from the molasses bread. She popped it in her open mouth without a crumb touching her perfect lips.

When she smiled, I thought she smiled just for me.

Her arms came up over my shoulders. She was my exact height. I swallowed hard, forcing the molasses bread down my dry throat.

Lily lazily draped on me. And in that moment, I wanted to believe I was the only thing on her mind.

But, through the muscle movements of her arms, I knew the tips of her fingers caressed those copper conchos behind my back.

CHAPTER EIGHT

Her arms remained lightly on my shoulders. I could feel the flat of her belly pushing up against my own. Layers of clothing couldn't protect me from her scalding heat. I stared into her blue eyes. Her glance flickered past me to the copper conchos.

Through continued muscle movement in her arms, I knew she continued to swirl her fingertips over an engraved Spiral of Life. Admittedly, I was jealous of that copper disk shining under her touch.

"I know that saddle," Lily said. "It was my cousin's. Only it didn't have the copper ornamentation when I saw it last." Her eyes grew distant. "I loved my cousin Jamie." Her voice was soft. "Jamie had no fondness for the blacksmith's forge or this livery. My father gave him his first gun and taught him the quick draw. 'Pull that smoke wagon,' he'd call out to Jamie."

"Your cousin?" I asked.

"Cousin Jamie. He was gunned down in the streets of Durango by a horrible murderer." Lily leaned more heavily onto me. "I do like the copper decorations."

"That makes Justice your—"

"Uncle. Silly goose." Her breath tickled my lips. "I don't come here for the smell of horse manure or those nasty, bellowing cows." She snuggled close to whisper in my ear. "Where did you get the copper?" Lily pulled slightly away to peer into my eyes.

Were her eyes narrower than I remembered? The trapper last winter had spoken at length on the lack of virtue in yellow-haired girls that were narrow between the eyes. The trapper had spoken at length on everything. This last winter had been a long one.

"You look like him." Her cousin had had sunny yellow hair springing from beneath the brim of his jaunty bowler hat. He had been the nervous type. Too eager. His pearl-handled silver six-shooter sat high over his hip. He had had something to prove.

"I do declare, Austin, you are a million miles away." Lily's tongue darted out to lick at my bottom lip. She kissed me full on the mouth. Her lips were warm and wet. It was nice.

But all I could think about was Sahara. The way Sahara chewed her bottom lip when she worried. How her lips were moist and red and pouty. My mind pictured what it would be like to kiss her heart-shaped mouth. I wanted to taste her. I wanted to taste Sahara. A thrill ran through me at the thought, even as Lily's lips still trespassed on mine.

"Eh-hum." Justice interrupted.

Lily climbed off of me. She dropped her arms and spun to face Justice. "Uncle. I was—"

"I can see what you were doing."

"Uncle. I wasn't doing anything. Really." Lily winked at me then beamed to her uncle. "Don't be so stodgy, Uncle. You were young once too. Or was it so long ago?" she teased him. Lily walked over to her uncle, and wrapped about his bicep. She sidled up to him with a show of affection, much like a cat rubbing against a leg.

"Is there something I can do for you, Austin?" Justice asked. His face glowed with a taint of red high on his cheeks.

"Shoes," I stammered. "Um, yes. Charlie Horse, er, my horse needs to be shod." My voice squeaked too high.

"Will you be paying in copper?" Lily asked, perking her weight onto the tips of her toes.

"Lily, payment is none of your concern," Justice said.

"Oh, poo." She released her claws from her uncle's arm. "I'm just saying that Austin has the copper. A girl needs to size up her prospects."

"Lily. Austin is as good as married."

"Not truly, Uncle." Lily pulled away from Justice and tugged the fur-lined collar high around her neck. She looked at me and smiled. "They weren't doing you any favors," she said to me. "Seth and Jeb. They want the bride for whoring." Her lips held a devious, tight slant. "If the agency pedaling brides made inquiries? Well, let's just say that Seth and Jeb aren't the marrying type. No respectable work. No land. No home." Lily stuffed her small hands into overlarge front coat pockets. "Sweetie, you're just a means to an end. They don't figure you'll keep her. Not with all of the trouble they will cause you." Lily walked away.

Before she stepped from the shadows of the barn into the waning afternoon sunshine, she said, "Let's face it, you're more scrumptious than any of the other boys around these parts. You don't need a whore."

Justice shook his head and bent down to lift Charlie Horse's hoof. "I don't know what gets into that girl." He gently poked and prodded the sore foot. "He ought to be soaked before I nail shoes on."

I couldn't believe Justice was McKade's brother. Jack McKade was as bad as they come. Bad was in his blood. Lightning Jack McKade was a killer. I heard his father was holed up in the big house east of town. Like he was hiding out. I overheard some boys playing in the street say that the old man was all gnarly and pinched into a rolling chair. They say he took a bullet in his back. That he doesn't ever speak, but his amber eyes watch as keen as a cornered cougar.

"The sorrel has a loose shoe," I accused *Justice McKade*. I was angry. Angry that he was a McKade—bred bad like his brother and his father. Angry that I had liked and respected Justice. Angry because I'd thought he was one of the good guys. Angry at myself for trusting a man just because he was nice to me once.

Most of all, I was angry because I knew that I was of bad breeding too. Born a killer out of a killer. Angry for knowing firsthand about killing and running and hiding. I was angry because I didn't want to kill. I didn't want to run. I didn't want to hide.

"So, you saw the sorrel?" Justice stood to his full height, laying his hand flat to Charlie Horse's neck. "There was blood on the saddle."

Charlie Horse nickered from low in his throat, ending in a slow, long blowing through his nostrils. *Calm. Trust.*

But Charlie Horse was wrong on this one.

A buggy swung into the barn. It clattered down the aisle then jarred to a halt. As Rose drew in the lines to the horse, Sahara fretted with toppled packages.

"Seth and Jeb rode out to your homestead," Rose screeched. Her jaunty cap with its bright purple plume fell onto the bridge of her nose as the buggy settled. "They're out to convince Sahara to move into town. No telling what they'll do to your place." She grabbed Sahara's hand in solidarity. Sahara's fingers clutched Rose's, turning white.

Justice offered a hand to Rose and supported her elbow as she disembarked. Sahara scurried from the buggy.

I grasped the draped lines and hauled myself into the four-wheeled rig, staring down Justice, as if daring him to stop me. That had given Sahara time to climb up the back of the buggy and clambered over the bench seat to sit next to me.

"You're not going," I growled.

"I am," Sahara spat through clenched teeth.

If the circumstances weren't dire, I would almost consider her adorable with her tiny, tight jaw thrust forward in mad determination. "Suit yourself. But try to do as you're told or you'll get us both killed." I lifted the lines to the horse. "Hya! Getup!"

The buggy wrenched from the barn with the horse at a lope. We tore down Main Street. I was headed out of town, but there was one thing I had to do first.

The street had grown quiet. Not too unusual, but unnerving for a bustling, growing community in a mining, tent town. Especially since hours ago, the townsfolk had poured into the street in anticipation of a showdown. I noted the now closed doors and empty alleyways.

"Don't go in there. They'll kill you." Sahara's voice shook when she spoke.

The Watering Hole was a dark hovel. I waited with the saloon doors half swung inward until my eyes adjusted.

"Austin." Jack McKade greeted me from behind the daunting bar.

"Not too busy?" I asked.

"It's early. You get used to the stillness." He was swiping inside a glass with a filthy rag. Wiping any of them hadn't mattered. None of the grime ever seemed to come off. "You want a drink?" McKade slapped a kitten from the bar. He'd been teasing it with a string off his rag. Its little body thwacked the floorboards before I heard its paws scampering away.

I jerked a leather pouch of coins from my hanging satchel and bounced its jingling heft in my palm. The coins were all I had left. This was my saved stake for cattle or horses, feed or seed, in setting up a proper ranch. Who was I kidding? With Sahara at the homestead, I would have spent every coin before I got to the ranching. *I can't afford the extra mouth to feed.* Supplies were short. Winter was fast upon us.

There was no way to safely send her back. I clenched my fist around the pouch for a moment, then slapped it down on the sticky bar. *I didn't want her to go* "No. No drink. Give this to your boys. And tell 'em, paid in full."

I stomped from the Watering Hole. McKade barked, "That's not how it's going to work, Austin."

The sun headed to hide behind the butte. The temperature dropped. A cold breeze enlivened the buggy horse to a crisp lope. Sahara edged closer until the length of her leg was secure against my own. I felt her warmth and longed to lean into it. I liked the feel of her against me.

Her breath was a frosty fog. It smelled like cinnamon. I liked cinnamon. At another time, in another place, I think I could have really liked her.

But her silence made the frenzied chase into the darkening evening even more unsettling.

Sahara usually talked constantly, but never said much. Oh, sure, she commented on this and that. She jabbered away like a chipmunk scolding a nut thief. My eyes would glaze over. Maybe I didn't listen because she never said anything I wanted to hear? What did I want to hear? That she liked me. A little?

Steam rose from the tired horse. I reined in, gently coaxing him to a jog with the lines. Sensing my anxiousness, he pushed against the bit, wanting to run again.

It was getting dark. The hogan would have come into view by now if it was still bright daylight. If I strained, I could see the massive form of the rock backdrop standing against the gunmetal-gray sky. The slit of a moon barely cast any light.

Crack. A rear wheel splintered away. The horse spurred to a gallop. The buggy collapsed and dragged in that corner. Sahara was thrown over my lap. Before I could gain control of the scared flight animal, the other rear wheel tore off.

We thumped and bounced over the rocky ground. The horse bolted harder, like a spook was chasing his tail. I hauled on his mouth through those lines until his jaw gaped open and his chin touched his lathered chest.

When what was left of the buggy came to a jerky halt, I shoved Sahara upright. "Get out." I pushed at her, hollering, "Cut the traces."

Her fists twisted into my coat. "I don't know what those are."

I shoved the thick leather lines at her. "Hold him. Tight."

Knife in hand, I jumped from the wreck. The traces were taut to the singletree. I sawed them from it then slashed the leather loops from the shafts. The frightened beast jolted forward. I rushed to his head to grab him by the bridle.

Sahara let go.

A small critter rushed against my legs and yelped. My pup.

Sahara climbed from the smashed buggy and stumbled over. She reached for the dog. "She's shaking."

"Shh." I said, pressing a finger to my mouth. The gesture was lost in the darkening night. I stuffed a loose line of the horse's bridle at Sahara, lifted the scared pup to her, then disappeared into the near blackness without another word.

I had expected the cow to greet me when I scurried under the rock formation. Or to hear the soft, questioning nicker from the mustang mare in guarding her foal. Nothing. It was quiet. Too quiet.

An oil lantern sat on a jutting stone, shoulder height. I thought to light it. But I knew better. I also knew there would be nothing to see. My cow was gone. The calf, the mare, and the foal? All were gone. I didn't need a lamp to tell me that.

I slid my sweating palm down the leather shaft of my holster, flicking the loop from the gun's hammer. The revolver's butt filled my hand as I popped the weapon loose. I spooned the grip gently and extended a finger to caress the slim trigger snuggled inside its protective metal guard.

I crept to the hogan from its back side. There were no saddle horses tied as before. The door was left ajar. It was quiet within. The gaping hole was black. There were a few live coals in the fireplace. Not enough for light.

I steadied my breathing which had grown tight and quick. In doing so, I smelled the familiar scents of cedar, wood smoke, earth, wool blankets, horse, and dog. Sahara's scent, with her peculiar hint of lilac soap, laced through all of the others. But there was also the breath of alcohol. Not alcohol itself, but the pungency that's added with stale exhaling. And tobacco. Possibly tobacco. It was more like the spittle of chewing tobacco, old, fetid, and mixed with the rank body odor of men. Not just one man. Two. Each had his own stench. Both were familiar.

Their stenches drifted from the open door and wound around my head, alerting my senses. Had they departed? Or were they still inside, waiting? I'd have to enter to find out.

What choice did I have? There were always two choices. These choices were my pathway in life. *Flight or fight.*

I could wait. Do nothing. Cause nothing. Let whatever would happen happen. But that was still a choice. *Flight.*

Flight. I could run. I could gather Sahara and the pup and Charlie Horse, and run. We could leave to homestead elsewhere. But where? Where could I go that the same problems wouldn't follow. And Sahara didn't know. She knew nothing of any of it. I couldn't expect to take her with me. She wouldn't stay with me if she ever found out.

Maybe it was time to face my troubles, here and now.

I could *fight.* I could fight for what was mine, exposing my birth identity, my past, all of my secrets. I could fight for Sahara.

I crouched low at the doorway. I had made my decision.

With the flick of my wrist, I tossed my hat inside the doorway. Its landing caused a diversion as I rolled through the opening in a somersault, gun ready. Keeping my back to the shadowy wall, I slid along, watching, listening. All I felt was emptiness.

Seth and Jeb were gone.

The tired coals bit into the kindling I offered, devouring the small dried twigs and chips. The fire was ablaze in minutes, casting its warm, orange glow. Sahara would see it, but I hoped she would not run directly to it. I hoped Sahara would have more sense to wait for my return.

"Look at this mess." Sahara stood framed in the open doorway, one hand pressing fingers over her mouth.

"What are you doing here?"

"I live here," Sahara said as she entered. The sleeping pup filled her arms. She struggled to close and bar the door behind her.

I swallowed a word of disgust. Pulling the loop of my holster over the hammer of the revolver, I asked, "How were you to know it was safe?"

She placed the pup in front of the fire. "I didn't hear any shooting," Sahara replied, nodding and looking impressed with her own common sense. With a hand propped to her hip, Sahara then tilted her head to the side in an expression that was, no doubt, to make me feel like a scolded child.

I fed the fire a dried log. I would rather have used chips this early in the season, saving the wood for colder nights when a slower, hotter burn would be needed.

"Maybe I was taken by surprise. Hit over the head. Jumped and gagged. How would you know?" I reached to untie the holster's string around my thigh then glared at her.

Sahara didn't waste any time in spouting her reply. "No one would take you by surprise." She shucked out of her thick winter coat as if there was nothing more to be said.

I unbuckled my gun belt, the weight of which seemed to be heavier this past month.

Off the bar across the doorway, I hung my gun. It was difficult to restrain myself from throttling Sahara. I righted the table, bench, chair, and stool with too much vehemence.

The world wasn't as over-simplified as the spoiled, city-raised chit could attempt to arrange it to be. It wasn't good guys against bad guys. It wasn't the good guys always won and the bad guys always lost. Good guys didn't always win. Good guys weren't always good. Good guys could die just as quickly as bad guys. And in my estimation, good guys always got hurt, no matter the outcome.

The blankets were strewn around the room. I shook the dust from them. Potatoes needed chasing back into their bag. Done. Luckily, the sacks of beans hadn't split open. I restacked the sacks of beans, salt, flour, and coffee against a wall. And all the while, Sahara slumped in the middle of the dirt floor. Her personals were spilled. Her neatly arranged bundles from Percival's Mercantile were scattered. She looked deflated.

"My money's gone."

"What money?" I asked.

"The rest of my dowry."

"What?"

"Dowry." She didn't look at me. She seemed defeated. "You know, money that would go to my husband to help start a fine life. Money my mother had saved up since the day I was born. She wanted me presented properly." Sahara absentmindedly pulled at her collar and scrubbed her hand along the back of her neck.

She wore my necklace. The alternating beads of copper and turquoise twinkled from the firelight.

I took my gun from the wooden bar and unblocked the door. "The horse," I stammered. But she didn't look up. "I'm, um, going to the overhang...to take care of the horse." Still nothing. She sat crumpled on the floor. "I'll just feed and water the horse. Rub him down some."

I grabbed a short piece of rope from the wall and slipped out the door, leaving it ajar. With my gun belt hanging in two hands, I bumped my back down the logs, sliding until the cold earth met my buttocks. *She wore my necklace.*

Soft sniffling, turning into wracking sobs, emanated from the cracked doorway. "Mama, I lost my dowry." Sahara sucked on air like it was choking the life from her. "I'm living in a sod hut." She hiccupped uncontrollably. "Austin hates me."

Hogan. And I don't hate you. I don't. But you could never love me if you knew everything I am. And all that I'm not. I dropped the holstered gun to the packed dirt and scoured at my face with calloused hands. I was very, very tired.

At daybreak, the livery horse snuffled through my hair. He licked his lips and chewed in contemplation. His harness jingled and creaked. The horse blew dust from his nose, spraying gritty mist onto my ear.

I hauled myself off the cold ground and strapped my gun on. The fire inside had burned down. I added a log to the red coals. Sahara slept on the floor. Her arms wrapped around the curled pup. Tears stained Sahara's cheeks.

The fire snapped and crackled to life. As I left, I gently closed the door all the way.

The horse jigged and swerved as we approached the overhang. His nostrils flared. I stroked his neck and led him behind a hillock of rock to stand, watching. I had skirted wide around the worn path, wary of ambush. The horses skittish behavior signaled that my precaution had been wise.

I smelled it too. Blood.

The metallic tang tainted the biting breeze. Coyotes didn't howl. Owls didn't hoot. It was like the early morning was holding its breath but for the small, chill current of warning.

A buggy picked its way through rubble and boulders. I had built the hogan where there was only one way in. That meant there was only one way out. I would always know which direction danger was coming from.

As the rig plodded closer, I saw the brown cow tied to the back. Following on her heels was a staggering, weak speck. I did not clearly see the driver. They were slouched too low over the lines.

CHAPTER NINE

"Oh my God." Sahara ran at full speed toward the ambling buggy. "It's Rose."

I wrapped the short rope around the harnessed horse's neck, leaving him ground-tied, and stepped from behind the rocks.

Sahara was beside the rolling buggy, pushing at Rose's shoulder to prop her upright. Rose had been unconscious.

Stirring, Rose asked, "The cow? Is the cow all right?"

I slowed the buggy horse enough for Sahara to scrabble in.

"She's fine. Everything's going to be fine." Sahara put her arms around Rose's shoulders and flopped Rose's head onto her.

Rose's jaw was red and lumpy. Blood trickled from her nose and oozed from the cuts over her cheekbones. Her eyes were blackened and swollen. Her face was disfigured. Sahara dabbed at Rose's nose as the buggy bounced along the rocky debris.

Sahara swiped a sheen of sweat from her own forehead, smearing a line of blood across her wrinkled brow. She was beautiful. Now wasn't the best time to notice. But Sahara was fiercely beautiful.

A broken plume collapsed from Rose's cap. Her flouncy blouse, usually tamed by a corset, flapped loosely. The skirt running from her sculpted waist, over generous hips, to her buttoned ankle boots, was torn in slits. I wouldn't have recognized her if not for the particular fashion of her ruined clothes.

At the hogan, I lifted Rose from the seat. She wasn't light. I struggled to carry her. *Not what a woman wanted to hear.*

"Bring her in. Put her on the pallet." Sahara took charge in a manner I hadn't seen before. She set a pot of water on a hook over the fire to boil. She tore scraps from the hem of a cast off petticoat and shoved me to the side in her determination. "Who did this to you?" she asked Rose.

"Indians. But not Indians. They dressed like Indians. Only, they wore flour sacks over their heads thinking I wouldn't be able to tell." Rose waved her hand in front of her nose. "But Indians don't stink so bad as them."

Whites. But who? Barflies? Hired guns? And why hurt Rose? She was McKade's. Surely he wouldn't sanction this. If for no other reason, he wouldn't take the loss of income from her convalescence. "Was it McKade's men?" I asked.

Rose waved me away and tried to sit up. "I'll take care of it," she said. With a hand to her forehead, she continued, "But maybe I'll just sit here a moment first."

"I'm going after them." Someone had to make this right. Someone had to make them pay. "Bolt the door behind me."

"I have to get back to town," Rose exclaimed. "I can never stay away long. He'd never let me see her again. She's the only flesh and blood I have."

"Hush now." Sahara doted over Rose as I slammed the door.

I ran. As I ran, I dragged my thick coat on. The old buggy horse still stood in the rocks where I'd left him. I unharnessed the horse, dropping the leather webbing to the ground. I hoped he was broke to ride. All I knew was that he looked tired. Tired, worn out, and aged.

It was no trick getting on him. He lined up to a knee-high rock as if waiting for shafts. I swung a leg, sliding it gently over his protruding spine. So far, so good. He skittered away from my nigh leg, then hit the off leg. He was totally unfamiliar with a rider. His body bunched beneath me when he felt trapped between my legs. *Not saddle broke.*

I didn't have time for a rip-roaring deal. I held my legs off of him and drove him forward with my voice, like I was taking a summer buggy ride to a Sunday sermon. "Easy. Getup. Easy. Step up."

He'd seen better years. His whither sat so high and sharp, at best I was missing my saddle, at worst…I didn't need to think on the worst. Suffice to mention, I'd be rubbed raw in all the wrong places.

The first few steps told my body his spine was a ridge that shouldn't be ascended. But he was game. He settled to my weight on his back as we jogged off.

Rose's assailants didn't bother to hide their tracks. Six or seven men. Right where Rose described they overtook her. And they hadn't left more than two hours ago. Coals still glowed in a ring of stones. Dumped coffee turned the frost dark. Boots had scuffed the dirt where bits of ladies' lace littered the ground like fluttering tufts from molting quail. They had been Whites.

The gang was headed in the direction of town at a lazy lope. One of the horses dropped to a jarring jog. They weren't in any great hurry, but they were on a determined line. It surprised me when two of them split off toward Apache land. I climbed down from the exhausted buggy horse to have a closer look.

My trap line started in the low brush ahead. The tracks ran straight for it. I gently eased myself back over the horse's sharp spine, then pursued the tracks into the brush and mesquite bramble.

Snares were tripped. But anything could have done that. The snow had blown off and the ground was too hard here for tattletale prints. I slid from the buggy horse to reset the snares.

Deep within the mesquite, a twisted branch protruded from a small iron-jawed trap. A flour sack, limp and lifeless, was staked between rocks with a sharpened stick. I shivered inside my thick coat. *They know I'm after them. They want me to follow.*

The tiny hairs on the back of my neck prickled.

"Os-ten."

I spun. My Smith and Wesson leveled instantly at the intruder's gut.

"Whites." He waved a brace of rabbits, pointing to the snares. It rankled me that TwoFeathers never flinched when I drew on him.

I reset the trap with viscera and bits of rabbit fur. There were scrapes on stone from steel shoes. I trailed them. TwoFeathers followed without following. His path meandered parallel to mine, within sight and earshot. I didn't know if he was keeping me company or on his own mission.

The sun hadn't done much about warming the morning. I blew into my cupped hands. Now and again, I inspected hoof marks. I needed to discern all I could about the enemy before meeting up with them.

And we would meet up. Only time stood between us.

I recognized that one of the horses was unevenly shod. A new front shoe was paired to a worn one. Justice kept his horses shod. But it was too great of an expense for the common man of Molasses Pond. So, the horse was rented from Molasses Pond Livery. The worn shoe was rolled in the toe. That told me something also. It was particular to the individual animal's way of moving, which I recognized. *The sorrel.*

Seth.

The other animal was stout. Heavier. Shorter, by the looks of his stride. Horseshoe shaped scuffs from this animal drove more deeply into the rocky landscape. And slivers of potato peels were dropped as the horse walked. The peels were thin and precise, not chunky or butchered. *Jeb.*

The two of them followed my trap line.

"Why is it you never duck?" I growled at TwoFeathers.

"Os-ten does not shoot." He touched the tips of his fingers alongside his head then swiped the open palm in front of his face. That amounted to "brain" and "walled or blocked." *Brain blocked.* Thinking made me stop, or hesitate.

Hesitating would get me killed.

Pa's voice echoed in my mind, "Never pull a gun unless you intend to pull the trigger."

THE MAIL ORDER BRIDE

Trouble was, I was too fast. Too fast for my mind to keep up. Too fast to be sure that what I knew I'd hit was truly what I *wanted* to hit. I never missed. But I did hesitate. I hesitated because I wanted to be sure I was shooting the right man for the right reason. I smoothed my palm over my holster. I'd have to correct for that thinking.

Pull the gun. Pull the trigger. Pull the gun. Pull the trigger.

My next trap too, was sprung and empty.

Blood warmed the icy crystals on the ground around the closed metal jaw. It had caught something. Seth or Jeb had made short work of dressing the kill. Strangely, they had left the entrails discarded next to it.

I crouched to reset the trap. The viscera would make good bait—

Urine. They had marked my trap line like a dog pissing on its territory. I jerked the trap loose. Nothing would come near the trap now.

Grr. I slopped the bear claw jaw and chain over the horse's back. Then thought better of it. I took off my thick coat, and slid the padding between the trap and the animal's protruding spine. The tired buggy horse stood solid for this new invasion. Actually, he looked done in.

The next trap was devastated, raided, pulled up, with the stake rope cut. I slung that metal jaw over the animal's back too. The chains jangled, but a driving horse was used to a jingling sound.

Seth and Jeb were riding hard and spending less and less time at each of my traps. The areas were torn apart, ripped, and kicked. They were hell-bent for—

Sahara.

My line made a loop back to the homestead. And there was only one more trap between them and the hogan. Only one more pause between them and Sahara.

Panic blasted through my chest. "Sahara." I hollered, as if she would hear me.

A gun went off in the distance.

A yelp.

TwoFeathers disappeared into the bramble.

I ran, dragging the horse behind me.

The acrid odor of spent gunpowder carried over the distance on crisp, clear air. The stench heightened my sense of fear, making the old horse twitchy. I rubbed my palm along his neck and down his shoulder. Above his elbow, I felt dotted indents. The gelding wore rowel marks dotting his shoulders. The spur scars traveled the length of his barrel. His flanks had been chewed raw at some point in his life. Thick, gnarly skin bunched beneath the shaggy growth of winter's coat.

I couldn't think on that now. I had to get to the hogan. Fast.

My fear for Sahara infused the old horse with too much worry. His eyes rolled up until the whites showed. Sweat broke out around the base of his short, fuzzy ears. As I threw myself at him in a furious attempt to mount too quickly, the horse spun away.

I grabbed the bridle and dragged his nose close to my shoulder. We spun. The traps fell to the ground. The horse reacted like the lump of equipment would eat him. He leaped into the air. His white-ringed eyes searched for escape.

I kept a hold on him. We spun. "Easy. Sahara needs us. Whoa now. Easy. She needs us."

I needed her. *I needed Sahara.*

With the rope drawn across my midsection, I grasped a clump of mane, twisted it into my fist, and threw myself at the horse. Old Navajo trick.

When I was up, I held his head around to my leg hoping he'd settle. No such luck. And no time. I let the rope slacken through my hand. His neck straightened.

For a second, he stood.

With his next intake of breath, the pitching fit was on.

In a tug-o-war, I dragged his head to the opposite side, bending it around. The frightened horse spun his hind end in a futile effort to break free. I sat tall while he frenzied. As he settled into a spin, I reached to tie the end of the lead rope back onto the bit, once again having two reins.

When I let his head loose this time, he reared. I grabbed mane. Fistfuls of mane. It was all there was to hold onto. I had to be careful not to dig him with my heels.

His forelegs hit the ground solidly on his descent. The slam snapped my jaw closed. It felt like all my teeth had cracked. He bolted. The horse's hard-walled hooves clawed the crisp November earth. I hung on like a bloated tick.

Beads of perspiration swelled on my forehead. I leaned over the horse's shoulders urging him in his flight.

His hooves pounded the frosty soil in a maddened four-beat gallop. We whisked past a twisted sycamore tree. Its branch whipped my face, slicing my cheek over the bone. Blood gushed from the fresh cut. I felt the wind spread it. I hoped it streaked in red stripes, like war paint. Because I was riding to war. My wide-brimmed hat flew off. My hair whipped out to lash at my neck, as wild as the mane on that frantic horse.

The animal's nostrils flared crimson. His eyes ringed with white. Lather broke out over his shoulders and neck. I could feel the pounding of each hoof, the sucking of every breath, and the maddened pulsing of his heartbeat.

The hogan came into view. One man whirled astride the sorrel. Another was on the ground, bent over a smoky torch. The horsed man roped a corral post. He pulled it down with his loop, dragging the wood pole to whip it against the hogan's door.

A flaming torch was thrown to the hogan's roof. It festered and fought to grow.

I was still a distance away. There was nothing I could do but urge my frenetic horse on. I didn't have a rifle. My revolver couldn't overtake the range. I didn't have a shot.

Anger welled from within me, snuffing any fear.

I rode down on the scene, whooping and ki-yaying.

My war cry burst into the men's havoc, drawing their attention away from the hogan.

Sahara was nowhere in sight. Neither was the buggy Rose had arrived in. And the cow was missing again.

But the door to the hogan stood strong, giving me hope that the women were safe.

The frigid air bit my lungs as I sucked in vast volumes to steady my fury.

The fog, exhaled from the gelding's nostrils, misted around my head. It stiffened strands of my hair, freezing it solid. I must have been an eerie sight. I felt like a spirit warrior flying over the rough terrain on a spirit warhorse. An Apache spirit rider was untouchable. I was invincible.

Seth spun the sorrel, staring in my direction. The sensitive sorrel's eyes rolled into his head at the pain of his wrenched shank bit. Seth hollered for Jeb to ride. He waited only a split second for Jeb to retake his mount before galloping off.

The men booted the animals. Retreating legs flapped like birds with enough fervor to have taken to the air.

I reined up at the hogan, hauling on my mount's head hard enough to invert the animal's posture. He dove his front hooves into the ground, hopping to a stiff-legged halt that threw me from his back.

The door popped open as I gained my feet. Sahara slammed into my arms. Her red-streaked, puffy face buried into my chest.

"They're gone." I hugged her. Her smaller arms wrapped around my midsection in a vise-like grip. She sobbed.

"They're gone. You're fine." I pushed Sahara to arm's length in making sure. "You are fine, aren't you?"

Sahara twisted her shoulders away, turning from me. "I'm fine," she snapped.

I jerked the peeking handle of the lit torch from the roof and stomped the fatigued flame to nothing. Her back was still to me. "You can't be here." My voice croaked lower than it had ever been. "I never asked for a wife. I never wanted a wife. I'm not a man. You just can't be here."

When my anger burst, it rushed like an uncontrollable flash flood. "I can't feed the two of us. I can't work the trap lines or hunt or capture horses, knowing that you're here alone. Knowing that those men will keep coming for you."

I turned my back on Sahara with a finality I didn't feel. I wish I did. But I didn't.

I wanted Sahara here. I had grown accustomed to her presence. More like, I needed her here. Even though she was annoying.

I enjoyed her antics. She was funny. Maybe she hadn't meant to be... She was smart. Not a frontier wilderness survival smart, but she knew things. She was always surprising me. I looked forward to seeing Sahara every day, and she was the last thought on my mind each night.

Damn it. The girl had to go!

The lathered horse stood stock still. Exhausted and resigned. I took hold of his hanging rope and tried to act as if Sahara meant nothing in my life. "You're going on the next stagecoach," I said much more calmly, though my jaw was tight.

"I told you I can't. I won't." She screamed and cried at the same time. New tears flooded down her already streaked and swollen face.

I spread my arms and rotated. "There isn't enough of anything here to get us both through the winter. Look around." Posts and split rails were scattered as if a tornado tossed them. There was no livestock of worth. I had few tanned pelts. My traps were in ruins. My coin was spent. My coat... My hat...

"It's gone. It's all gone. And I can't let you stay in this territory. Not in this town—knowing what they'll do to you. And knowing I'm not a man. If anyone were to find out—men would come after me for the reason they chase you."

And all of that came out all wrong. It sounded self-centered. Insensitive. I didn't think I was either of those. Maybe I was.

I led the exhausted horse toward the rock overhang, leaving Sahara behind.

Being alone was hard enough. Being alone and a woman was downright dangerously impossible. And I wasn't a woman. I'd face any peril if it meant I could be with Sahara. But I wouldn't be a woman.

I'm a boy. My mind had always and ever been a boy's. I hoped to learn to become a man. I wanted to be a good man. Never a woman. I wasn't a woman. Not here. Not anywhere. Not for anyone. Not even for Sahara Miller.

Beneath the overhang, I rubbed the horse with scrub grass, fed and watered him. He was sorry looking. I tossed my woven wool blanket over his spiny back, just while he cooled.

The temperature was dropping fast. I kicked the cold coals inside the stone ring and built a fire that roared to life. It devoured the kindling and chips, then licked at a fat log.

"Here's your damn cow." Sahara flung the rope lead at me. It fell short, landing across my moccasins.

I didn't know what to say. *How?* I tied the cow next to the buggy horse and tossed her an armful of loose feed. The greedy calf poked at her empty bag. I stroked her brown furry neck and watched the calf, unable to look at Sahara.

My hair fell into my face. I prodded the strands to sit behind each ear. Blood had crusted on my cheek. I swiped my arm across the mess. The hide shirt scratched the scabs off. Warm, wet blood drooled from the wound again. And all I wanted was for Sahara to leave me alone.

If I ignored her, maybe she'd go away.

Fences needed rebuilding. I scooped water from the horse's bucket to dab at my face. *If I could gentle a colt to ride... If I could pack one behind Charlie Horse... I'd be able to ride my traps again, then spend next winter tanning pelts.* It felt like a step backward. But my trapping and trading had bought this land, my land. I could start over. I could always catch wild horses.

"When Rose insisted on heading back to town, I brought the cow to the sod hut and tied her just outside the door," Sahara said, breaking into my thoughts. "I knew I couldn't carry the bucket of milk that far.

"I had stolen milk when I was a kid so I knew how to milk her. I had the bucket filled and was going to bring her back. That's when those nasty men came." Sahara sniffled. "I didn't know what to do. I couldn't leave the cow and calf alone. They would have been scared. The calf might have gotten hurt." Sahara walked over to the heifer calf and placed her hand lightly on its tail head. "I led them through the door, shut it, then bolted it." Sahara dug through her pockets until she found what she was looking for and approached me.

She dipped a lacy handkerchief in the bucket of water then dabbed at my cheek. Her surreal eyes stared into mine.

"You can't stay," I said quietly. It wasn't without regret.

"Because you're not a man?"

"I'm a boy." I rubbed the back of my neck. "Inside…inside a girl's body." I could feel a tightness between my shoulder blades. "I've always known." Of a sudden, I felt chilled. I moved to the fire and squatted to prod it. "I think the Whites' God made a mistake when he put me in a female body." I stood.

Sahara stepped close again.

Absentmindedly, I pulled at the silk kerchief tied tightly around my neck, poking with my finger to scratch at the scar. "Boy. Girl. The Navajo believe it doesn't change my soul. It doesn't change *who* I am. And The People revere those of two spirits."

I stuffed three fingers under the neckerchief, digging at the damaged flesh. "I don't want to be revered. I just want to be a man, working my own land." When my skin was sore, I smoothed the hanging silk tails down my hide-covered, bound, flat chest.

"The scar on your neck? Is it from a hangman?"

I loosened the four tiny squares unified to create one large square. The knot symbolized the elements of earth, wind, fire, and water, coming together to create life. I allowed the neckerchief to slacken. Slowly, I slid it open, exposing the deformed mess.

Her eyes widened. Her hands flew to cover her gaping mouth.

Sahara screamed.

CHAPTER TEN

I twisted the silk back around my neck faster than I'd ever strung it before.

Thunk.

I spun my gun into action. TwoFeathers dropped to the ground, covered in blood. His .53-caliber Hawken crashed against the stone wall. The pup slammed into my shins. Sahara continued screaming like she would never run out of air.

"Os-ten." TwoFeathers held out a flour sack with holes.

"Sahara. The horse." I hollered through her piercing screams.

I slammed my revolver into its holster as Sahara scrambled toward the munching animal. The woven wool blanket fell to the dirt floor when she hauled him away from his feed. I shoved Sahara onto his bony back. The tired buggy horse came alive with a bug-eyed look.

"Ride to Molasses Pond Livery. Go to Justice." I didn't know anyone else. He was a McKade, but—

"What about you—"

I turned my attention toward aiding TwoFeathers. He had a sack in his grasp. It had slits for eye holes. I took it from him and shredded it to bandage his oozing bruises and staunch the flowing cuts.

"Austin."

"Ride." I snapped at Sahara, fishing tobacco from my pocket and pressing it into TwoFeathers's facial wounds. I saw the horror in her eyes as I helped him to the fire. I saw her disgust and fear.

I slapped the horse on the rump and sent him running into the dying daylight. The pup barked and nipped, keeping pace at his heels.

Sahara watched me as she clung tooth-and-nail to the galloping animal. She was chewing on her lower lip, but her eyes were squinted into slashes. She might have started to cry. The accusing look on her face broke my heart.

I hadn't told her about TwoFeathers. I thought she was too citified, too pampered, too weak. I thought she was too judgmental, too narrow-minded. I believed she was too White.

That look on her face said I had betrayed her. I hadn't trusted her. I had no faith.

I had too many secrets to ever let her in.

The sun had completely set as TwoFeathers and I crept around boulders and peeked down on the long-abandoned ruins of a rustlers' campsite. Below, a dilapidated fenced corral surrounded by looming saguaros and rattling tumbleweeds, was aglow from a huge fire of twisted mesquite and brambles. The angry flames lit the vicinity in a furious circle of blazing oranges and reds.

Apaches huddled in the corral, their hands bound. A daisy chain of hangman's nooses secured their necks to one another.

Of a sudden, my head pounded. I pushed at my temples with the tips of my fingers. The sun blinded me, but it was dark. I heard the harsh crack of a bullwhip but knew TwoFeathers's quiet breathing was the nearest interruption to this night's hush. And behind my open eyes, I glimpsed the long line of noose-tied Navajo dragged ahead of me.

I shook my head, clearing the flashbacks.

A man with a Winchester strolled the line of tied Apaches below us. He stopped to thump one Indian with the butt of his rifle, then kicked another. Three other Whites knocked a warrior to his knees and jerked his head back by his loose braid. His arms were cruelly held behind him with a pole thrust across the middle of his back, above his elbows. One of the Whites tipped a bottle of whiskey to his own lips before upending the contents over the Apache's mouth and nose.

The warrior stared at his torturers. The burning liquid splashed into his unblinking eyes. He didn't look away. Hate radiated from the Apache.

TwoFeathers plucked a copper ball and wadding from the pouch at his waist. He tipped a powder horn to the mouth of the barrel before packing in the wadding and ball. With a ramrod, he jammed the works down. I noticed his face had swelled. The cut on his forehead gaped from the growing goose egg underneath. The bruise on his cheek changed the color of his yellow paint to a sickly brown. And his lip hadn't stopped bleeding.

To the rhythm of gun blasts and rifle bursts, liquored Apache Indians stumbled in a dance around the beastly fire. A collapsed Apache laid in his own vomit. Spittle drooled from his mouth. Feathers woven into his hair had been shot short. He hadn't moved.

TwoFeathers rammed the wadding and ball and more wadding into the Hawken's barrel. He snapped at me. "Told Os-ten. The White man is the same. Our enemy is the same. White enemy man is the same."

I still didn't exactly understand. We didn't speak the same languages fluently. Until recently, we had managed fine. But yeah, there was always that something missing.

TwoFeathers thumped his chest with his fist after sliding the rod under the long barrel. "Told Os-ten," he growled in broken English. He fluttered his flat hand away from his body in a motion meaning time having flown by or time past.

The White enemy is the same. *But what does that mean?*

All Whites weren't the same. All Indians weren't the same. There was good and bad in every bushel.

With the barrel of that buffalo gun rested on a rock, TwoFeathers dropped a prime on its pan, and took aim. His deliberation was keen. His patience long. Just before he shot, he slowly exhaled his breath through pursed lips like blowing out a candle.

I covered my ears and crouched behind him, sighting over his right shoulder. My clenched fists brought out recollections of other brutal times, in past brutal incidences. Massacres. Murders. Those recollections of scenes came in horrid bursts of red. *Sharp explosions of gunfire ripped the oppressive heat. Indians rained down on lodged Conestogas. Running women collapsed midstride. Lost sunny bonnets fluttered on a stifling breeze. Blood spurt and splattered. Crying children climbed into wagons or clambered beneath. Fear. Huddling. Hiding.*

Horsed men shot rifles from high above.

Returning fire came from behind the wagons.

Indians circled, screeching their horrid wails. Spears were thrown. Bows plucked. Arrows hit their marks as deadly as any bullets.

I hid in the shadow of a boulder, slapping my tiny hands over my ears, crushing hard enough that my small head should have burst.

TwoFeathers squeezed the triggers. The report from his Hawken was deafening. It jolted me to the present in time to see the guard buckle from the smacking impact of TwoFeathers's copper bullet. He hadn't fallen off his horse.

I had seen a man fall dead from his horse once. He slapped the earth, limp and lifeless. I had seen scars of rope burns then too, on his bronze wrists and neck. I had smelled the whiskey from his last gurgling exhale. His open eyes stared blindly at me in apology as his killer sat watching from the top of the ridge. Only now did I remember these details.

TwoFeathers was up and running before that horse knew his rider slumped dead in the saddle. Screeching bone-chilling whoops, he ran through the camp. I trailed after him as fast as I could.

With impressive strength and proficiency, he reloaded the massive barrel on the run. I'd never heard of any White buffalo hunters capable of that feat. He cocked the hammer, smashed prime onto the pan, and set the rear trigger. The Hawken would blow on a hare's whisper.

Angry, cursing Whites attempted to muster as we wallowed into their string of tied, screaming horses. We cut every tether. The herd of saddled mounts high-tailed it toward town. Even the horse with its dead rider fled with them.

Bumped in their rush, I dropped my skinning knife.

I pulled my revolver. Flames coughed from its barrel as I shot the ropes binding Apaches to looming saguaro cacti.

TwoFeathers's Hawken blasted too closely behind me. Sound vanished that instant. I pounded at my ears. They felt full of wool. I was dizzy. I put my hands out to steady myself.

TwoFeathers wrestled with a bloody corpse that clung to his waist. The Hawken had exploded its head clean off. He was yelling at me. TwoFeathers was yelling, but I couldn't hear him. His lips opened and closed like a fish out of water, gawping for air. I shook my head and kept slamming my ears. I felt woozy. My sight grew fuzzy.

My eyes glazed.

Blinding sun. Hearty laughter. Shod hooves rang against stone. Gunfire. Navajo dropped in fleeing poses. Flames. Smoke. Gunfire. A blue dog's limp body draped over my arm as I hugged him to my chest. Gunfire. I tripped on bronze legs peeking from the fringed hem of a deerskin skirt. Mother. Gunfire. Her face was a bloody mess. Gunfire. She had had the most beautiful long, black hair. A rope snapped closed around my throat. I dropped my lifeless dog to claw at the burning noose jerking me from my feet.

I shook my head. The glimpses retreated. Tears gushed over my cheeks, though I'd sworn as a child never to cry again. TwoFeathers came into focus. His lips were drawn into a thin line. He reached out with a muscular arm to crush me to his broad chest. I struggled the huge Bowie knife from its sheath at his waist and pushed myself from his grasp.

He bobbed his head in a nod. I took off running.

In the split rail corral, I cut the ropes binding the wrists of an Apache. With freed hands, the Indian tore the noose from his neck. He jumped to release his brothers.

I sawed at the restraints of the next, then the next.

A warrior lunged toward me, his lips formed a feral grin. His teeth gleamed in the dancing firelight. I glanced at the Bowie knife in my gun hand and awkwardly yanked my six-shooter with the other palm.

I didn't hesitate. I grabbed at the trigger as the nose of the barrel cleared the holster. *Pull the gun. Pull the trigger.*

Click. The gun was empty.

The Apache warrior sailed past me, slamming his shoulder into one of McKade's men.

McKade's man. McKade.

I saw McKade now, atop his massive horse, flanked by hired guns.

It wasn't the first time I'd seen him murdering and massacring from the back of that big black horse. Clearer memories flooded my mind. McKade was the man on the ridge inciting the wagon train massacre. He had also orchestrated the murder of my Navajo tribe.

McKade, The scourge of the West. Lightning Jack McKade, the killer. Murderer.

White soldiers had laughed. They had made sport of chasing down the mothers, tormenting the grandfathers, and corralling the fleeing Navajo children. The soldiers set flames to our hogans, our crops, and our pampered peach trees. They shot our dogs, our horses, our sheep. Young boys and little girls were set to running for target practice. Older boys, not old enough to become warriors, were tied by the necks and dragged in a line like livestock.

I was in that line.

That huge man on his enormous black horse had ridden next to me as the hangman's noose ripped at my neck. The steel hinge of his braced leg had constantly squeaked with the motion of his mount. *McKade.*

I stared at him. His brace glinted from the fire's light. I was sure he was staring back at me, with recognition.

I pointed my revolver. *Click.* My weapon was empty.

One of his henchmen leveled a rifle at me. McKade pushed the barrel downward. He posed his fingers as a gun and dropped his thumb-hammer down. *Bang,* he silently mouthed. Lightning Jack McKade whirled his massive steed on its haunches, then launched toward Molasses Pond.

I blundered into the night, following his retreat. That's what it was: McKade's retreat.

Behind me, Apaches swarmed over the dead bodies of White gunslingers. They whooped and hollered in earnest. Shots sang in celebration. They had won this battle.

I plodded toward town. The night had grown as dark as a pocket. I stubbed my moccasin covered foot on a fist-sized rock. *Damn.* It had been hours of stomping in the dark. It would take me hours more. I no longer heard whooping or gunshots. But visions of shattered faces and torn flesh tormented my mind with every step.

I wouldn't let myself dwell on any one scene. I had no courage for horror. I only wanted to live a good life and to be a good man. First, I needed to survive—

I survived massacres. Survived losses. Survived deaths.

Killed to survive. Ran to survive. Ran from the memories of needing to survive. Always hiding.

I could never run far enough, fast enough. The memories overtook me anytime, anywhere. They taunted me in the dark, and harried me in closed spaces. I drew my gun, mindlessly twirling it back and forth on my trigger finger. The antler grip kissed my palm before whirling away, just to come back to a firm embrace, over and over.

There was one thing I was dead set on doing. I jammed the gun into its holster.

I would kill McKade.

My gun weighed heavy on the front of my thigh. I pulled it again and flipped the cylinder open. The casings had cooled. They ejected easily. I reloaded the empty chambers and slapped the cylinder closed. I spun the Smith and Wesson around once, then slammed it back into my holster.

"I'm coming for you, Jack McKade." I shouted into the vast nothingness.

I reached to tug the brim of my hat lower over my eyes out of habit. I'd forgotten that my hat was gone. A strand of hair fell into my face. I tucked it behind an ear. A chill wind bit at my deerskin smock. I shivered. My coat, too, was gone.

I arrived at the edge of Main Street. The crumbling Spanish-Mexican fountain in the center of town glowed by the light of too many torches.

"Psst. Psst."

I yanked my gun and cocked the hammer. "Step out."

"Okay. I'm coming out."

Squinting, I shifted my gaze this way and that. I couldn't make out any definition to the man. I aimed center mass.

"Don't shoot," he said.

That wasn't a given. I widened my stance and shifted my weight onto the balls of my feet.

Brush rustled. A twig snapped. "Ouch. Damn." He emerged. The white square at his throat beamed. "I was waiting for you," the pastor said. He swatted at the lower legs of his trousers. "I knew you'd come this way."

I stared at him, letting silence grow between us.

He took that to mean he should keep talking. "You can't go through the middle of town." He brushed his hands down his frock. "They're gathering a posse." He fidgeted with his lapels. "For you." The pastor displayed his open palms. "Could..." He pointed. "Could you lower your weapon?"

I did but I kept it handy.

"McKade's whipped up a storm about you killing the dead man who rode into town." He swallowed loudly. "He says you started an Apache uprising."

When I didn't react, he said, "We have to go. This way." The pastor scurried off.

I followed.

My senses were alert. I could feel the tension in the air. Crackling from lit torches assaulted my ears. Burning pitch sputtered rancid smoke into the cold air. I snicked my tongue off the roof of my mouth in distaste.

We skirted past the back side of the first cluster of tent establishments. Every split second, I studied each and every noise carried on the breeze. Businesses were closed in these early hours of predawn. Tents were still. Lanterns had sputtered out. But there was no obnoxious snoring.

Flickering light from the abundance of torches on Main Street reached through the alleyways.

If anyone came, I was sure to be seen.

A man floundered from a privy in his half-sleep. His suspenders were collapsed to his knees. The button fly on his holey breeches gaped. He wiped his nose on the faded red sleeve of his long handles then belched, smacking his lips like he'd regurgitated tasty chunks.

I slipped to the side of the outbuilding to wait. I had to grab my nose. *Foul.*

In a patch of darkness, the pastor waved me to him. There was no way I would chance it. The privy man might be half-asleep and drunk, but it would only take the one person to sound an alarm.

When the man staggered from sight, I dodged the fingertips of light that crawled between the tents to catch up with the pastor. I sneaked around one outhouse to the next then slipped, falling into a shallow ditch. At the bottom, liquid sludge engulfed me to the ankles. Stirred, the excrement alerted my nostrils to the furrow's use. When the privy shacks were occupied, miners copped a squat outdoors. I had landed in their overflow.

Bile rose in my throat at the stench. I scrabbled from the pit, racing to catch the pastor.

Past these tent establishments was the Watering Hole. *McKade's lair.* I'd have to be extra cautious. Men came and went constantly on a dull night. They trolled the alleys for dalliances with other men. And the stack of outhouses was busy busy busy because Jack McKade didn't allow open air fouling behind his saloon. On a dull night, it was treacherous. Tonight? I hoped the impromptu town meeting was occupying any extracurricular traffic.

"Kill the breed," a thunderous voice boomed.

I crept a little ways into the vacant alley next to the Watering Hole. Risky, yes. But fears of frolicking gold diggers and privy attendees didn't quell my curiosity.

"Kill the breed," a higher pitched voice echoed. I didn't see who shouted. There was a milling mass of rabble-rousers in the street. They gazed up at men standing on the boardwalk toward the far corner of the saloon.

McKade was orating like he was running for mayor.

Scant handfuls of men stood distant from the main murderous horde. Neckerchiefs wrapped around their throats, probably to ward off November's bite. I touched the silk encircling my own neck.

Voices took me by surprise. Several men rounded the corner into the alley. Glowing cigarette butts hung from their lips. They were deep in conversation. Their low hat brims narrowed their vision.

From behind, my shoulder was roughly shoved against canvas. A slender hand clasped over my mouth. I squirmed, attempting to cock the hammer of my gun, attempting to worm my way from the thin figure that pressed against my body.

"Who's there?" a gruff voice demanded.

"Hank, it's just the pastor." He giggled. "Atta boy."

They each chucked the pastor on the upper arm as they walked by.

"No more sightseeing," the pastor rebuked in a whisper. "Let's get out of here."

On his release, I coaxed my revolver's hammer open. *Click, click, click, click.*

We ran to the church as quietly as we could. The good thing about tent housing? It wasn't as solid as it pretended.

"Sahara's at the livery." *Charlie Horse. The pup.* Though I could see Molasses Pond Livery from where I stood, it was impossible to get there. Diagonally across the torch-lit street, the big barn sat too far to run to unnoticed. "I need to get word to her." Even as I said it, I knew there was no way. Not even a pastor would be safe darting across Main Street on this night.

I ducked under the low edge of the canvas to come up inside the church tent. "It wasn't me." That's what I wanted to tell Sahara. "What they're saying—it wasn't me. She needs to know that."

The Whites' nailed Lord was on his cross looking down at me. He looked peaceful and kindly. Except for his eyes. They followed me as I moved among the benches in the tight tent hall. I sat. Those eyes pierced me with accusations. But I knew them to be blind.

They were blind to what was happening to the Indians, the miners, Molasses Pond, the whole country outside of this tiny sanctuary. Did he see what happened to my White ma and my baby sisters? Did he care what happened to my Navajo mother and father...my Navajo brothers and sisters... Where was his divine intervention?

"Would you like to pray with me?"

"Why did you help me?" I rolled the cylinder, one chamber at a time, just to feel the smooth oiled action of the too familiar killing tool.

The pastor stared at the gun in my hand. He preached, "Thou shalt not kill." But his words weren't spoken in a direct manner to me.

Was it that I was gunning for McKade? Or that McKade was gunning for me? "The Whites' God? He makes little sense when it's the Whites who started the killing."

The pastor sat on a bench opposite me. He reached into the watch pocket of his trousers. I thought to see a silver timepiece with some pertinent godly inscription. He revealed a derringer. "I have my own reason to commit sin." He flopped the derringer around in his palm. The pastor was comfortable with its weight and familiar with its shape.

He stroked the floral-engraved surface of the frame with the soft pad of his thumb. "Vengeance is mine sayeth the Lord." The pastor stared at the tiny weapon, mesmerized, as if he didn't hear himself speak from rote.

I looked at him. I really looked at him. He was hurting. His heart was so greatly wounded that his Lord must be having difficulty repairing it.

His .22-caliber derringer was loaded.

CHAPTER ELEVEN

W hat's happening out there?" I asked as the pastor lurched into the church tent. The sun was shining brightly, near to its zenith. I must have fallen asleep toward dawn. I had slept right through morning.

"The town's quiet. A crowded posse is out looking for you." He squirmed onto a bench across from me. From an opened cloth in his hand, the pastor offered bread, cheese, and apples. I shook my head.

The pastor mulled the selection over like it was the most important decision of his life, then popped a bite of cheese into his mouth. After he swallowed, he said, "I stay in Molasses Pond to show McKade that he can't run me off." A hunk of bread had his interest next. He ripped the bread in half. "McKade took someone from me. Not much I can do about that. I'm not a fighting man. I'm not even a brave man. All I can do is stay to be a reminder of what he's done." His hand strayed to his watch pocket. "I stay. And I wait."

I stomped toward the front tent flaps, doubtful McKade had any care for anything he'd done. Never mind dwelling on one pastor's nuisance.

The pastor continued. "Nothing left he can take from me. Except my life. And he knows that." The pastor cut his teeth into the torn piece of crusty bread.

I chewed on the inside of my cheek until it bled. A gust fluttered the tent flap. I eased it open.

"You can't," he said, choking on the dry mouthful. The pastor flipped the cloth over his bounty and tucked it into his coat. "McKade's got men standing outside the Watering Hole. They can see clear down Main Street to here, and then some."

"I need to get to Sahara." I needed to see her. I needed to know she was safe. I needed to tell her... I wanted to tell her—

"There he is. In the church."

I burst from the tent, sprinting toward the livery.

A burly bunch of men gave chase. They wore six-shooters tied down. I could hear their spurs chink and jingle.

I was tackled and pinned to the ground. My arms were wrenched cruelly behind my back. I thought they would pop from their sockets. My face mashed into the mud as my hands were tied. My lower lip split. I tasted grit and blood. Their metallic tangs coated my tongue.

I didn't have to walk. They dragged me down Main Street. At the Watering Hole, my knees bumped the step up. The tops of my moccasins scraped and scuffed along the floorboards through the saloon, to a private room on the side.

"Where's the girl?" McKade asked as his men propped me in front of him. He backhanded me before I had a chance to answer. Not that I was planning to.

I spit a wad of mud and blood from my mouth.

He punched me in the nose. The crunch echoed in my head.

"I want the girl. Here." When he socked me in the gut, I fell to my knees.

Lily stood behind him, examining her nails. She looked quite bored as I gasped for each shallow breath, fresh blood dribbling from my mouth and nose. "What *I* want to know is where's the copper. Where is it?" She huffed and puffed like having to ask a question had really put a strain on her.

I struggled to breathe. "I noticed your men," I said to McKade, "don't usually let the debate of right versus wrong leak into their decision-making." I paused for a raspy inhale. "I can see how it'd get in their way." I sucked air in through my mouth, heaving with the spasms from that belly punch. "What'd you have to spend to buy their consciences?"

"You'd be surprised how little a man's soul sells for." McKade poured himself a shot of dark liquor and tossed it down his throat. "A swallow of whiskey." He saluted me with the empty glass. "Money dictates the law around here. I dictate the law." McKade smacked his lips and belched. "Gold diggers are a dime a dozen. None of them are worth anything unless they make a strike." He turned his back on me to pour another glassful. "Then, they're only worth killing."

McKade tossed back another shot of whiskey. "It's the hired guns I pay a premium for. Men like Seth and Jeb are worth the coin." He smacked his thin lips then squinted into my eyes. "You'd be worth my coin. I'd pay you well to stand at my side."

Lily sighed loudly. "Make him tell me about the copper."

McKade slammed his glass onto an ornate desk. "There's no sustainable copper strain. Just crumbles hammered into trinkets." He eyed me, watching for any reaction. "Long-term, the whore's worth more. That's where the money is. Working women and whiskey. You control a man's whore and their drink, and you control him."

He grabbed Lily's upper arm, escorting her from the room. "What did I tell you about being in the saloon during business hours?" he said.

Rose scuttled through the door like a June bug scrambling from under foot. "Let me have a look at you." She pressed a wet cloth to my lips and nose, clearing the blood and grunge.

I was still heaving for breath when she pressed her hands over my torso.

"Oh," she gasped. Her hands slid down to my lower ribs and pressed again. "I don't think any are broken."

"Are you going to say anything?" I asked.

"You don't know what they'll do to me if they find out I haven't told everything I know. You can't imagine what he's capable of."

I had a feeling I could imagine. I couldn't blame her if she did tell. Information was worth gold...or life.

"I'll try to keep your secret. After all, I think we both know it hasn't been that much of a secret between us." She dabbed at my lip and nose once more with the damp cloth. The cuts and bruises coloring her own face had yet to heal. Splotches of dark purple were turning green. The outer edges were ringed with yellow and brown. "There's something you should know—"

Thudding boot steps echoed just outside the office room.

Rose jumped. She scurried out, leaving the door ajar.

I looked long and hard at that opening. But there was no escape. McKade's hired killers were standing guard. Still, I struggled against the ropes binding my wrists. The twists bit into my flesh. Even slick with blood, the restraining rope was too tight to wiggle from.

"—was holed up with the pastor." *Seth.* "That weren't no problem. I explained it real nice to the preachy man and he was happy to oblige me with information." He giggled. I hated his weaselly giggle.

I sat my butt to the floor and worked my tied hands under. Then, I squeezed each leg through my bound arms.

"Boss, the girl's at the livery. Justice won't give her up." *Jeb.*

"Locked and barred tighter than an Army fort in an injun raid," Seth said.

I shoved myself to standing. A groan leaked from between my clenched teeth. I felt my heartbeat pounding in my sore ribs. My nose throbbed like it was swelling and stretching to ten times its size.

"We've got us a solution," Jeb snickered. His heavy boots thunked over the wooden floorboards. The saloon doors swung with a complaining creak as he exited.

McKade burst in to find me upright. I grabbed at my holster for my gun.

"Looking for this?" He plucked my revolver from his belt. "Smith and Wesson. Old, if I'm not mistaken. The condition is fine, belying its age. And the action is too smooth." McKade spun the cylinder then sighted down the barrel at me. "I'll bet she's fast."

"Fire. Fire." A triangle rang in alarm from Percival's Mercantile.

Townsfolk poured from hiding. Smoke billowed through Main Street like a slow moving fog.

McKade socked me with a roundhouse to the side of my head. The torque crackled my neck. I dropped.

"Austin. Austin." The voice sounded distant. "Austin. Wake up." My cheeks were patted. I felt my limp head waggle from side to side but my brain wasn't keeping up. I scratched at the wooden floorboards, using my calloused fingers to grasp for consciousness. The last thing I remembered was standing in McKade's office.

"Who?" It was all I could form for words with a swollen, cracked lip, blurry eyes, and a fuzzy brain.

"It's the pastor. Come on. You have to get up." He tugged at my listless arms. "We have to get out of here."

Was he helping me? Or was he reminding McKade he'd stay underfoot? The pastor came into focus. Red handprints marked his pasty cheeks. A bright pink egg blossomed in front of his ear. The pastor wore a black silk neckerchief, doubled and tied, obliterating his white collar.

"My gun."

"It's here. C'mon."

The pastor left me at the backside of Molasses Pond Livery. I checked each chamber in the cylinder of my Smith and Wesson. Empty.

Flames burst from the gambrel rooftop. Boards splintered and popped. Beams moaned. Horses hollered. Steers bawled. Waves of heat shimmered and danced, blurring the huge livery. Thick smoke billowed from the open back barn doors. Cattle busted their pen rails in escape and scattered in frightened disarray.

I saw a way in. *Would there be a way out?*

"Smoke signal." TwoFeathers pointed toward the fire with his rifle. "Men on horses come." He had appeared from nowhere like an apparition. "A man is inside. A big man." TwoFeathers laid his heavy Hawken on the cold ground. He stripped from his great coat, pulling pouches off his shoulders and over his head. "Osten's woman is inside. Charlie Horse."

"And the pup," I said, more to myself. I plucked the one and only bullet left in my belt and slipped it into the cylinder. My thoughts were on the raging fire. It was probably like an oven inside. *Could they still be alive?*

Horses screamed. The fire roared.

TwoFeathers ran in. I was at his heels.

The smoke was thicker than the shaggy winter coat on a bull elk. I waved my hands to try to move it aside. More smoke filled the momentary gap. I coughed, lurching my way deep into the inferno. Charlie Horse's white rump with its bright egg spots pierced the smog like a beacon. He was tied in a standing stall.

I climbed toward him, waving at the smoke again in another futile hope of clearing my sight. My eyes watered. My lungs burned. I'd never appreciated the crisp, clear autumn air over the wide-open land as much as I did at this very minute.

My toe caught. I tripped and fell forward with my hands out. There was a whole lot of hairy white in front of me. I slapped Charlie Horse's rump, leaving sooty prints smearing downward as I fell. It was his sparse tail that rescued me from hitting the ground.

Sahara was huddled beneath Charlie Horse, tugging at his knotted rope. I clawed my way to her in the close confines of the standing stall. The horse's back was singed. A spittle of smoke wafted from his winter coat. And though his eyes were wide with fear, he stood stock-still.

I twisted the back of Sahara's coat in a fist and yanked her from beneath Charlie Horse. She let go of the tug-o-war to hug onto me.

The butt of a big Bowie knife jammed into my palm. Its pommel felt cool from November's sharp air, though the inferno was intent on baking that welcome chill out of it.

TwoFeathers tore off his pale yellow skirt, ripped a piece from the hem, and tied the bulk around Charlie Horse's head. The quill design weighted the flimsy cloth to hanging over the animal's nostrils. TwoFeathers handled Sahara like he had Charlie Horse, firmly, taking control to tie a mask over her face. He stripped off her coat, throwing it over the horse's blistered back, then tossed her on top.

The Bowie knife sawed through the thick rope. Charlie Horse snapped backward. TwoFeathers grabbed the dangling end of the cut lead. They bolted for the door.

The pup whined, or I wouldn't have found her. She was huddled in a front corner of the standing stall, burrowed deep within dry straw. Her scorched, black nose poked from the deadly shelter. With Charlie Horse's absence, falling embers glowed around her. When straw burst into flames, she cried. Her screeching was horrible.

I lunged to the floor, slapping her in extinguishing the flames. The pup's shaking body became a puddle in my hands. I ran from the barn with the terrified little dog in my arms.

TwoFeathers held Charlie Horse at a safe distance, out of sight. Townsfolk formed a line on the street side, futilely passing buckets to battle the inferno. They might as well have spit at the fire. The splash of their buckets made no difference.

Molasses Pond Livery was a total loss. Justice—*Justice!*

I looked at Sahara crumpled astride Charlie Horse, attempting to avoid sitting on his wounds. Her face, blackened from the fire's filth, was wet with sweat. She shivered in the cold November air. Her store-bought boys' coat was over the horse's burns. She said nothing. Her eyes were red and swollen. I didn't know if that was from smoke irritation or tears.

I slid the scared, singed pup in front of her. "Go," I said to TwoFeathers.

I charged back into hell-fire.

Horses bugled in terror. They thumped and kicked in their stalls, attempting to escape. I threw open their doors while searching for Justice McKade. But the animals frenzied in circles inside their boxes, slamming against the outside wall in trying to bust through. I doubled back with a torch of twisted straw, spooking each from their trap. Horses bolted into the smoke-filled aisle, milling until one animal spied a way out. *The sorrel.* He looked at me and beckoned. I waved my hands to flag him away. He ran. Taking the horror-filled herd with him.

A stout bay blundered by, dodging sideways to avoid hitting me. His rush blew the air clear for brief seconds. In that clarity, I saw Justice pinned by the flames walling the mouth of the disintegrating barn. He struggled to cut the harness off of his old buggy horse. A slice across his brow dripped blood into his eyes. He staggered, but his deft hands sped over the harness releasing buckles and unsnapping lines.

"Sahara?" he hollered over the inferno's roar when he saw me.

"Safe." I climbed a fallen timber that pinned the harnessed horse. "It's no good. We've got to get out of here." A loud crack sounded above my head. A shower of embers fell. The buggy horse's thick hair began to fester in flames. The old gelding screamed the likes that would haunt me for ages.

A rafter split from the roof and collapsed. Justice was struck with debris. He lumped, unconscious, across the frantic animal.

I whipped my revolver from its holster and—hesitated. I hesitated with grief. I hesitated over my decision. I hesitated with too much weight of responsibility. I hesitated, not wanting to do what must be done. I hesitated.

The trapped horse kicked and thumped, wallowing in his web of leather. His flailing hooves sliced the thick air too close to Justice while I stood numbed with indecision.

I shot the animal.

Tears dried to salt instantly on my cheeks. The struggling buggy horse went limp.

My lungs burned from hiccupped breaths of searing smoke and heat. I climbed over the sizzling carcass, and struggled to haul Justice from the burning barn. He was too big. Too heavy. But I wouldn't leave him.

TwoFeathers burst through a wall of flames, dousing us in buckets of trough water. He jerked me to my feet then shouldered Justice. The big blacksmith's head lolled sideways. Arms hung the length of TwoFeathers's back. We lumbered from the disintegrating livery.

Gray skies opened with a torrential downpour. Burnt wood sizzled. Steam rose to mingle with smoke. Townsfolk scattered as if they would melt in the rain.

TwoFeathers left Justice on the ground and spirited Sahara away.

Men collected Justice, hustling him down the street.

I limped slowly home.

At the homestead, the three of us silently washed black grime off our faces and hands. I was too tired and sore to peel off my filthy clothes and too wet to care. I dipped a bucket into the well, sharing a cold, clean drink of water.

Sahara scurried into the hogan with the pup.

I straggled to the overhang with Charlie Horse in tow. Thank goodness TwoFeathers had never been a talker. Silence felt more comforting than struggling with glib banter.

He slathered Charlie Horse's burns with a thick salve then tossed me the pouch of goo. I used a generous amount on my wrists, fearing they would become a patch of gnarly, scarred skin if unattended. The copper band slipped from beneath my sleeve, sticking in the salve. Its turquoise eye glared at me. I smoothed the pad of my thumb over the oval stone.

"Look into my eyes," TwoFeathers demanded, jerking my chin toward him. He wanted me to know about my future by staring into his eyes. A man could see his own death if he stared too long into the eyes of a shaman.

"No." Maybe I should have cared about a foretelling, but I was scared. Scared of what I'd see. Scared I was soon to be taken from this world when I wasn't finished here. Scared I'd leave Sahara before I could tell her… I sighed. "I'm going to kill McKade." And I didn't know if I stated that to distract TwoFeathers or to distract me.

There was a lot I had to do yet in life. There was more I wanted to become. There was so much I wanted to say to Sahara. And then there was McKade.

"Look." TwoFeathers held up his hand, pointing fingers at his eyes.

"No." I didn't want to see my own death. When he pointed those fingers at me, I crushed them in my hand, shoving them away. "No."

TwoFeathers jerked the front of my sopping buckskin tunic in his fist and grabbed my chin. "What does Os-ten see?"

"Nothing." I struggled against his firm hold.

Wait. What? I peered again into his deep, dark brown eyes. They were like endless, mesmerizing pools. For a second, I thought I saw something. I shook my head. *Nothing.* "I see nothing."

He thrust me from him. "Not Os-ten's time." He squatted to stir the tired coals to life. "Os-ten is not-woman woman. Man-woman. Like TwoFeathers woman-man man." He waved in front of his face as if clearing the air, then fluttered his hand upward. *Of nothing. Means nothing.* "Os-ten is a good man. Strong man."

I dropped dry, twisted mesquite branches onto the coals and prodded them with a green stick. Flames erupted. Their wicked tongues licked at the brush.

TwoFeathers jabbed my shoulder. When I looked at him, he pointed to the fire then grabbed a fist of his hair. *Sahara.* "Woman wants Os-ten man."

"You must be hungry." Sahara carried a steaming cook pot. She plunked it inside the stone ring of the firepit. Her cheeks were rosy. She had scrubbed the soot and dirt from her entire being no doubt. If nothing else, she was fastidious.

And she wore her green dress under the heavy boys' coat. "I hope you eat stew, Mr. TwoFeathers." She stuffed her hands into large coat pockets. "Well, I didn't mean that you don't have stew. I'm sure you eat anything." She procured tin plates and spoons from her pockets. "Well, I didn't mean you'd eat *anything.*" Her rosy cheeks turned scarlet red. "For all I know, Indians have discerning appetites. Not that you wouldn't. I didn't mean that either."

"Sahara?" She was absolutely adorable squirming under TwoFeathers's benign stare. But I couldn't take her discomfort for much longer. "Can I have a spoon?" I had trouble suppressing a grin.

She was pale and feminine and all things beautiful. She hid her strength, but it was no less powerful for being subdued. Sahara was everything I wasn't and never could be. I wasn't girlie. I couldn't forgive easily. And I wouldn't change.

"It's gorgeous." Sahara blurted. She stared at a copper band in TwoFeathers's outstretched hand. A smaller, similar turquoise stone to mine stared back at her. "Where did this come from?" she asked.

He pointed to the crevice between the shifted stone walls. His belongings sat at the base. I hoped she thought he was pointing to those. I toed his deerskin-covered leg and shook my head.

"TwoFeathers makes the hammered bands after smelting copper ore." I tried to draw her attention. Sahara was too smart for that. And too curious.

She moved toward the back of the overhang and placed her hand flat to the cold stone. TwoFeathers went with her, shimmying into the crack. He brought out two bagfuls of raw copper and several large chunks of turquoise.

Sahara clasped her hands over her mouth. Her eyes opened wider than a night owl's.

"Oh my God."

Chapter Twelve

Thunder rolled, echoing off the distant butte. Lightning illuminated the barren, rocky landscape in a quick flash.

It was difficult to discern the time of day except to say it was morning.

Sahara brought me a pot of freshly brewed coffee.

TwoFeathers had quietly left, per usual. He took one of the sacks of copper. The other sack leaned against the base of the wall, apparently taunting Sahara.

"This isn't going to go the way you're thinking," I said. My aches had settled into complaints through the night. If I didn't move, they didn't register...much. My chest binding had slipped down around my waist yesterday from sweat. It had tightened as it dried. I could feel its gagging grip over my pained ribs.

Sahara set a bucket under the cow. She hunkered down to milk. It was a chore *I* did each morning, but I wasn't jumping up to knock her out of the way. My ribs hurt. The sh-sh-sh-sh from warm streams of milk hitting the wooden bucket might have been soothing if Sahara hadn't had ulterior motives for doing my work.

She sloshed the bucket next to me and went to turn the heifer calf loose with her dam. I dipped my cupped hand into the fresh milk and scooped a splash for my black coffee. It was rude. I was feeling fractious.

"All of your talk of not having enough and you're sitting on a copper strain."

"You know nothing, Sahara Miller." The skin over my ribs complained as I grunted at her. "That strain is played out before you even start pecking at it. Then what? The attention it will attract on a small hope that there might be more underground? It would get us killed."

Sahara was a pretty girl, without the scheming. Last night, I almost thought I liked her. That was before she found out about the copper strain. *Before* she went instantly money mad. Before she stuffed thoughts of riches ahead of my own dreams, my own welfare, the life *I* had already started to build here, on *my* land *before* her.

Absolute wealth corrupts absolutely. Pa had said that.

"You could buy them off." She tossed feed in front of the cow. "Pay them to leave you alone."

I wasn't about to answer her absurdity. I propped my back against a stack of cut wood and flipped an errant branch into the ring of fire with the toe of my moccasin. The slight movement sent stabbing pains throughout my side.

Sleep hadn't offered me any company, so I had brooded all night. The moaning and groaning as I shifted must have kept TwoFeathers awake. But he never let on.

I raised my tunic to pull off the binding coiled around my waist. Even in the low light of the fire, I saw the dark purple bruising leaking throughout my left side. Deep breaths were impossible. I wrestled out of my wet hide clothing and into my Sunday-go-to-meetin' shirt. The cotton shirt was dry but scratchy to my irritated skin. It certainly couldn't hold a candle to the comfort of my buckskins. But dry was warmer than wet. And in the coldest part of the night, just before dawn, I had pulled the worn, woven blanket over me. Warmth seemed to ease my screaming soreness.

That first hot, creamy coffee of the day went down in a few gulps. Its heat surged through my body. I came instantly awake. There was something I had to do.

I struggled to my feet by clawing the pile of firewood.

"What are you doing?" Sahara rushed over. "I can get you what you need."

"I need to get up," I snapped. Then, I felt bad for being gruff. I pointed to the small stash of untanned pelts with a smaller pile of cured rabbit skins. "I need that wrapped bundle. Please?" The Whites always needed their niceties—please and thank you.

On top of the stiff pelts sat the crush of exquisitely soft rabbit furs. It was the six-shooter wrapped inside that I wanted. I hobbled a few steps closer. My feet tingled. They were numb and clumsy. I gently stamped. *Gently* didn't wake either one up. Stomping set my bruised side to screaming.

"Ooh." Sahara crooned as she caressed the fluffy skins. "Oh," she startled from the gun. Sahara picked the heavy revolver up by its trigger guard with her thumb and forefinger and walked it over. She carried the gun at arm's length, as if it would bite.

I rescued the dangling weapon. "The holster is beneath the furs. Please." She went in search of it.

There was a question in her eyes when she returned with the matching leather holster. Since she didn't ask, I didn't say. "Thank you." I took the holster and went about my business.

Two guns once again hung from the fat belt slung low beneath my hip bones. I'd have to leave the cross draw behind. I needed speed, not convenience or disguise. I needed complete accuracy. And I needed both guns.

Gingerly, I prodded the cuts and contusions on my face with my fingertips. A flock of hens must have used my head for a laying box. There was an egg above the cut on my lip, an egg over my crooked nose, and another egg swelling my eyelid near to closed. I winced.

My hands were damp with sweat. I rubbed my palms down my thighs, they scraped the leather holsters alongside my upper legs. I had missed them. The guns, that is. They ran heavy and solid at my sides. They felt like family. They felt like home. Dependable. Reassuring. Safe.

I had adopted lazy habits when the second revolver came off. First and foremost, I totally quit shooting left-handed. Lefties stood out.

Second, two guns was a sure sign of a lucrative business. I wasn't in the business of killing. So I learned to affect a frontiersman's coarseness and fumbling with a single weapon.

Third, I had adopted a cross draw of late, seating the holster on the front of my thigh. That made it easier to employ the handgun to pound nails or crack nuts, using it as a ranch tool, not a weapon.

Lastly, I hadn't practiced with my left. Bullets cost money. Not to mention that I'd rather not drag my past around, especially on a fresh start homesteading.

I popped the right-hand gun from its holster and twirled it around my trigger finger. The friendly familiarity boosted my confidence. I flipped it into the air, caught it, then thumped the gun home. *Excellent.*

When I jerked it again, I blasted three thin branches from a stilled tumbleweed lodged against a distant boulder. My shots were clean and precise. The brush never moved a whisker. Arrogance was swelling my head. I puffed my chest, though the movement hurt. *I've got this.*

Like all gunslingers, I had a tell—that little behavior just before squeezing the trigger. A *tell* was every fighter's Achilles' heel. My tell? I held my breath. Simple. Small. Actually, very minuscule. But it was totally wrong for shootists.

The best gunmen breathed through their shots, letting the air steady their hand.

It didn't always matter what the best did. What worked for me was most important.

Best? I wasn't the fastest. I wasn't the deadliest. I was accurate. My aim had always been true. I'd hold my breath on purpose, as if suspending my breathing would give all my life force to that one single moment in time. A beautiful thing if it weren't so lethal. And I was good at it. Too good.

Riding that confidence in my craft, I slapped leather to draw with my left hand.

I didn't find the revolver's handle without an exhaustive search. When I did grab hold, I tipped the barrel up as if to fire from my hip, too soon. It caught. The gun hadn't cleared the holster.

Not a problem. It was only a snag. One time in a million. Just a little rusty. I've got this.

I slapped the grips again, and made sure to twist the gun high enough to clear. I bumbled the action. My brain got in the way of my work. Thinking wasn't always a great thing. Not if it jammed the process.

More determined, I gripped it and ripped it. Too tight. Speed was affected.

I drew again. Too loose. The barrel canted to the side. No accuracy.

Again. My wrist was straight and locked. I'd feel the jarring percussion in my thumb and down through my palm, numbing my successive shots.

Sweat broke out on my brow.

I propped my gun loose in its holster, shaking my hand out at the wrist. With a jostling of my shoulders, I tried to loosen the growing tightness. My side screamed in stabbing pain that made me buckle. *Breathe. Just breathe.*

Practice was all I needed. The trapper who had taught me said I'd build muscle memory. And I had. I'd have to now remind those muscles of what they'd forgotten.

The rainy day waned on. Sahara came and went. I was no better for the practice. My arm ached. My ribs grew too tired of complaining and decided to settle into a constant screaming pain instead. My breathing ran fast and shallow with exertion. Little blisters bubbled over my palm.

I pushed at the pustules but didn't pop any. Burst blisters meant open sores that festered and rotted. I did what I thought TwoFeathers would do. I poured whiskey onto them and loosely wrapped a cloth around my hand.

I took a sip of the smooth brown liquid. It burned. My throat clenched. I coughed and coughed. That was a big mistake. The hacking jarred my ribs to striking back. I chastised myself, but was in no mood for the rebuke. So I gulped several mouthfuls quickly without tasting the toxic brew.

Now I really did cough, finding it hard to breathe again. My face scrunched into contortions at the singeing flavor left in my mouth. Heat washed across my cheeks and forehead. Sharp inhales were answered with fiery stabs of pain. But the smoldering warmth from the brown liquid sliding along my insides was surprisingly comforting.

Rain poured down outside. I hunkered by the firepit and took a pull on the whiskey bottle. The sky grew dark. Flash flooding whooshed in the not-too-distant distance. I wrapped my lips over the mouth of the bottle again and again throughout the night. Much like a lover's kiss. I giggled at the thought. *A sloppy lover.*

The next morning, I stood in the rain again. My head felt near to splitting. *Someone, pull the ax from my skull.* I shoved sopping strands of hair out of my face. Ratty limp ropes of it fell back over my eyes. Rainwater dripped from the ends onto the revolver in my open palm.

I stared at the gun. I was no good any more.

My left hand was tender. My arm complained from the weight of the gun. The steel was cold. The antler grips were coarse. And the cold rain poured down.

Huddled in my sodden cotton, store-bought shirt, I squeezed off shot after shot. Missing.

"You can't go after Jack McKade." Sahara wrapped the woven wool blanket about my hunched shoulders and tugged it tightly around me. "Look at you. Soaked and shivering. You're going to catch your death."

"Sometimes it's about doing the right thing, not the easy thing."

She rolled her eyes. "Sometimes staying alive should be the *first* thing."

I plucked the bottle from the mud. Sahara walked off.

I took a swallow before emptying the spent cartridges from the cylinder and shooting again. My aim might have improved with the whiskey. I know my pain had subsided when I drank enough.

The sun hadn't peeked through the gray overcast all day. At night, the stars couldn't gouge their way past the clouds. This was the wettest November I'd ever remembered anywhere. Prickly pear cacti happily gorged on the water when they should have been hibernating beneath frost. Everything else was miserably drowning. I passed the night huddled by the fire attempting to feel dry.

In the morning, it was still raining. And cold. Three days of drenching torrents. I had started drinking coffee through the day. More so than whiskey, but then I started combining the two. In this type of weather I saw the appeal that I'd never understood in the past. Coffee with a nip. Warmth crept over my tongue as I sipped the hot beverage before stepping into the deluge.

I wiped at my eyes. My lashes held water, giving the landscape an ethereal look around the edges. It was fitting. My nightmarish visions had come back in force. I had once-upon-a-time thought they'd leave for good when I took off my guns and put my silver dollars on land. They hadn't. The vivid memories constantly haunted me, as if trying to disclose some truth I absolutely couldn't live without.

I raised my left hand and fired at the slumped targets on top of a flat boulder I had set up yesterday.

Crack. Crack.

My mind's eye took me back to a man in Durango.

A sickness churned in my gut. My knees felt like they'd buckle.

Two bullets slammed into his chest, a split second apart. A jaunty bowler hat kicked from his head on impact. Blood spurted from each hole. His gun was out, but it hadn't leveled. He went down. He fell and fell and fell. His shoulders hit the dry street with a thud. A cloud of dust burst from beneath his inert body. The nose of his gun with its overly raised sight smacked the ground and jumped loose from his grip.

Dirty blond curls sprung around his face, outlining ruddy cheeks, a button nose, and a delicate chin. He was slight for a grown man. Angelic. Cherubic.

He was dead.

A solid blast of thunder from a Hawken jolted me out of the nightmare. The entire line of targets went down like toppling dominoes.

I gagged, heaving until whiskey burned my throat, ten times more caustic on its way back out.

The gun in my left hand drooped as if it had swooned from exhaustion. I stuffed the weapon into its holster. I hissed through my teeth as a blister splayed open. The raw stinging crept through my palm. I grabbed the whiskey bottle from the muck at my feet.

A big paw wrapped around my skinny wrist. He was usually gentle. At present, he was unusually rough. TwoFeathers flipped my hand over. He extricated the bottle from my fist then dropped it into the mud. Rain pelted oozing blisters. I squirmed under the stinging barrage. TwoFeathers held me firm.

He slapped salve into my seeping palm, then wrapped and tied it in a clean bandage.

I yanked my hand from his fierce hold and shoved him away. I didn't need TwoFeathers. I didn't need anyone. All I needed was that whiskey to soothe my pains away. And the bottle sat upright, neck deep in mud, waiting for me to rescue it. I did. When I did, I pressed its mouth to my lips. He pried it from me.

TwoFeathers walked off.

I tried to follow, reaching for that bottle. Mired in mud, I fell to my knees. "Damn you, injun. Damn you to hell." I dropped fully into the slurry and spanked the mud with my right hand as if it had insulted me. The splash rained back. Grit landed in my mouth to lodge between my teeth. It was gritty. "I hate grit! Grit! Grit! Grit! I hate grit. I hate mud. I hate hate hate! Hate!"

I rolled around like a newborn calf, unable to gain my feet. After a while, I didn't try. Why should I? This wasn't the life I wanted to live. I had had dreams. My dreams had been derailed. Derailed by Sahara Miller. Everything revolved around Sahara Miller. I never asked for the girl.

A big pair of moccasins stomped beneath my swollen nose. He lifted me by the middle of my back in one meaty fist, then lugged me over the mud. My wet, stringy hair hung like a heavy theater curtain. My knees bogged, plowing furrows a farmer would envy. Still, TwoFeathers hauled me onward.

I quit struggling. *Let the McKades of the world have the place.* I stopped fighting TwoFeathers's grasp. *Let the Indians and the Whites battle for the land. I'll find my place between their worlds as always. Alone.* I gave in to being dragged. *Let Sahara love her copper and her rich men, if money is all she wants.* I gave up. It was too hard. Life was too hard. It had always been hard. Every day, I struggled to find my way. It was complicated. I was complicated. I didn't fit in. I didn't even fit me.

Dumped by the fire in a sorry state, I curled into the fetal position and rocked my wounded body well into the dark afternoon. At some point, sleep overwhelmed me.

Waking in the night too many times was disorienting. The rain hadn't let up. Its monotony pounded inside my brain. I heard the fat drops pattering the hard ground in a slow drum roll. I'd heard the onslaught gush in foul torrents, flooding rushing runnels. The rain had been the sole noise in the blackest darkness.

In the morning, gray skies tattled that the foul weather wasn't planning to stop. Maybe ever. The fire was near out. Smoldering coals weren't to be coaxed to glowing in the frigid dampness. And the pot coffee was a cold sludge.

By the dim light of that squelched dawn, I tripped over TwoFeathers's long, outstretched legs. *Strange.* I expected Charlie Horse to laugh at me, in the way horses do, as I stumbled on numb feet, intent on milking the cow.

"Horse is gone. Woman is gone." TwoFeathers glared at me accusingly. The whites of his eyes were pinched with squinting, but they still pierced the dimness.

A fresh bucket of milk sat in Charlie Horse's place. The heifer calf poked and prodded her dam's drooping udder.

Gone?

I blundered from the overhang, running toward Molasses Pond.

By the time I reached town, the skies had lightened. Main Street was a slough of mud. There was no wagon traffic. The sludge was impassable for wheeled vehicles. Even saddle horses labored to lug each hoof from the sucking muck.

Sitting rainwater soaked into hoofprints even before hooves moved forward. Fetid odors hung thick in the drenched air. Saturated leather steamed on sweaty, straining horses. Soaked canvas tents sagged. Sopping men in soggy clothing hauled their hat brims to the bridge of their noses and scurried for cover. Overflowing privy pits washed through alleyways into the road. Wet dogs hid under dripping boardwalks. Stale, sodden stenches mixed in the most foul ways. The entire town was rank.

I skirted around the main street until I got to the alley between the land office and the burgeoning bank. When I plunged into the slow moving sludge on Main Street, my neck itched. I scratched at the uneven patches of scarred skin beneath the silk kerchief with my cold fingers. My neck only itched when something was unsettling to me.

Townsfolk moved from my path but lingered in my wake. They wore neckerchiefs, doubled and knotted. I had never thought myself the height of fashion before. My clothes were practical. I didn't own a leaky parasol or stained white gloves. I didn't have silver spurs with jinglebobs dancing on the rowels.

"She's in there." Justice chucked his chin toward the Watering Hole as he stepped in front of me.

Panic ripped through me with those three little words. *She's in there.* My eyes slid to the front of the saloon. Ropy strands of dripping hair fell into my sight. Charlie Horse was tied at the hitch rail.

I tried to shove past Justice. He held his ground, clutching my upper arms. "She came here for you."

I settled in his grasp.

"She had a sack of copper with her," he said.

I wretched, grabbing my belly.

Justice had the good sense to let go of me.

I puked. The bile stank of stale whiskey. "If she had a sack of copper then she came for herself." I swiped a forearm across my mouth. "I want my horse."

He stepped from my path. "A man's got a right to his horse."

I thought I saw disappointment in his eyes. I thought his shoulders slumped a little more than the cold, wet rain had called for.

What did he think? I could save her? That I could save this town? Hell, she didn't want me to. She'd made up her mind.

Seth sauntered from the Watering Hole. Thumbs in his pockets, he leaned against the shingled wall. "The girl done told the boss that's all there is. One sack." He spit a wad of tobacco. Spittle drooled from his bottom lip. "Now I don't care about your copper. Yet." Seth picked at the calluses on his hand. I briefly wondered what he'd get calluses from. I never saw him actually do any work. "I'm gonna have me a visit with that girl first," he said, "then I'll get real interested in your copper."

"You got at least a day to clear out. My business could take longer though." He ran his tongue over tobacco-yellowed front teeth, then licked brown spittle from his lower lip.

Flight or fight. There was only, ever, those two options.

"Oh, that's right," he said over his shoulder as he turned to slither back into the Watering Hole, "almost forgot." Seth spit a slimy dollop onto the boardwalk. "We got us a friend of yours inside."

CHAPTER THIRTEEN

B ullets."
   The clerk looked at me like I was a spook with two heads. He prodded his wire-rimmed glasses higher up his narrow nose, then smoothed his bow tie against his throat. His engorged Adam's apple bobbed from a huge swallow.

I was dripping onto his counter. A puddle accumulated, threatening his scratch pad and stubbed pencil. "I do have money on account," I said.

He shook himself from his staring stupor. "Yes. Yes you do, Mr. Austin." Swooping his pencil and pad into his petite hands, he said, "I'll get those right away. .45-caliber?" He scuttled off before I answered.

The clerk dropped the box to the counter like it was weighing him down. "Can I get you anything else? A coat? Or a hat perhaps?"

I have a coat and a hat. Somewhere between my hogan and the Apache lands. "Whiskey."

"Mr. Austin, we don't sell spirits here. You'll have to go to the Watering Hole for those."

I crushed my fist around the paper-wrapped box and slid it from the counter. A brightly swirled stick of peppermint candy looked too enticing to pass up. I plucked one from the jar. "And this." Before the clerk nodded, I had the peppermint stick clenched between my teeth.

"Color me pink and put me in a pig pen. It's Austin."

Lily. Lily often chirped ridiculous sayings that belied her true nature. I used to think they were cute. I used to think she was pretty. I turned toward her, making like I was tipping my hat to a lady. "Lily." Leaning my buttocks against the counter, I peeled open the box of bullets, drew one of my revolvers, and methodically loaded each chamber.

She spun on her buttoned boots and pattered from Percival's Mercantile. The bells above the door jingled with her passing.

"Now, Mr. Austin, I don't want any trouble in here."

I shifted the peppermint stick to hang from the other side of my mouth then slipped the first gun home. The bruise over my ribs complained, but I was beginning to ignore it, for the most part. I plucked my second weapon and began to fill its empty cylinder. Rose shuttled in. The bells jingled. The red plume from her hat brushed them as she walked beneath. "I saw Lily. She's in a rush. I knew there had to be something gossip-worthy in here." She bobbed her head in a polite manner. "Austin."

I clicked the cylinder around, listening to its smooth ratcheting and feeling for any hitches in the well-oiled action. "Rose." Her face looked strained. Her lips pursed, pinching her cheeks inward.

She squinted her eyes ever so slightly. "They have the pastor."

"What's it to me?" Which wasn't fair. It was something to me. He was something to me. He had saved my life.

"You listen here, Austin." She spun into my face with the speed of a much younger woman and the ferocity of a poked bear. "Jack McKade will take everything you love. He'll hold it just out of reach to taunt you, to torture you, and finally, to break you. If you don't break, he'll dance you like a puppet on strings until your life is nothing. He enjoys destroying others."

Rose sat back on her high heels to regain her composure. "Your fight is up here." She tapped my temple with a gloved finger. "Use it. You're a smart boy. Think first. If you go blundering in with guns blazing, you're only doing exactly what he's goaded you into. Don't." Her cap fell onto the bridge of her nose. The plume dusted my face.

She pushed her hat to the top of her head and patted her hair. When she turned to leave, she pulled her cloak to her earlobes.

Minutes passed. My stomach rolled. I was beginning to feel my toes again, but they were angry knives stabbing my feet as they thawed. The clerk anxiously tutted over the water I dripped onto his counter. He wasn't likely to ask me to leave, but I knew he'd cheer after I had.

I walked to the door and cracked it open to peer outside. Before making a move, I closed the door of the mercantile and contemplated my options, as Rose eloquently suggested.

A crate of fireworks collected dust beneath the front window of the mercantile. Leftovers from a long forgotten Fourth of July celebration. I pressed the barrel of my Smith and Wesson to my lips as if I were to kiss it, and shushed at the clerk. He nodded in an overexcited fashion.

I propped my second revolver loose in its holster for the ready. A plan was coming to mind. Into my baggy cotton shirt, I packed firecrackers and cherry bombs. I jerked a calculated length of dynamite fuse from its spool and stuffed that into my drawers, briefly scanning for the dynamite. None.

Rain came down harder. I stepped from the warmth of Percival's Mercantile. It was going to be a long journey around Molasses Pond to get behind the Watering Hole unnoticed.

Men gathered as I tromped the boardwalks of the mercantile and past the bank. Women collected their children from my path. When the boards ended, I dropped into muck and scurried from the crowds, losing any followers in the alleyways.

Sewage burbled from beneath the privy sheds. Ditches overflowed their waste in gushing streams. The cold, drenched air calmed the stench, but it was still definitely ripe. I coughed, gagging more than once while splashing through the crap to circle around the outskirts of town.

The sky opened up to loose another torrential downpour.

I kept a blistered palm over the fireworks as I ran. My shirt was soaked. I rounded my shoulders forward to keep it from sticking to my chest. I hadn't replaced my wraps, or the trouser prop. If I looked down, I'd see the budding female body that didn't align with my boy's brain. *Don't look. Don't look.* It was repulsive. A hideous reminder that I didn't fit anywhere—even in myself.

The Watering Hole's outhouses came into sight. Caution wasn't necessary. A man running to a privy wouldn't usually get interrupted. A man running to a privy in torrential downpour that had lasted for four days, was probably on the verge of lunacy and shouldn't be harassed for any reason. I trotted directly to the sheds and slammed into the middle of three.

The floor felt unsteady, as if it was floating. It most likely was. But the roof was tight, making the inside dry. I fished the fireworks out and set to work, dribbling the long fuse in circles around the shed's hole. I plugged the cherry bombs on the line in succession, then rigged the firecrackers to spark off after the initial booming explosions. Dynamite would have been better.

It took me several matches to light the damp fuse. I was surprised when a wet sulfur tip finally burst into a minute flame. I coaxed the match to burning before stabbing it at the fuse.

The length of line crackled to life, akin to a sparkler's starburst. I shot from the privy on a dead run. Hot sweat beaded on my cold forehead, mixing with the rivulets of rainwater sluicing down my face. I swiped the back of my hand over my eyes to clear the dousing, only to cause moments of blurry vision.

At the corner of the Watering Hole that began the alley between it and the bathhouse, I looked back, praying the fuse hadn't gone out. I had calculated a length correctly to the amount of time needed. I think. Probably. I mean, I took my best guess.

I charged through the alley then climbed onto the boards at the other end. Even though they were wet, they creaked under the shifting load. I held my breath and crouched against the wall, waiting.

The window to McKade's office was directly above my head. The fireworks in the outhouse still hadn't blown. I popped my head up to peek through the office window. A gun-tough sat inside on the sill, plucking at the cylinder of his six-shooter. Beyond him, I caught a glimpse of Sahara pacing the length of the room. The pastor was collapsed on a braided rug.

Bam. Bam. Bam. Crack. Crack. Crack. Crack.

The hired thug ran from the window.

Crack, crack, crack, crack.

I smashed the glass. "Sahara. Get the pastor."

Crack, crack, crack, crack, crack.

She spun around and hugged the slumped pastor under his arms. I attempted to climb through the broken glass while Sahara struggled with his weight. She couldn't lift him. Dragging his listless body also failed.

My shirt caught on the jagged points, snagging me from tumbling in. The bruise over my ribs shrieked. I shoved my hands onto shards and felt the searing slicing as I pushed to tear myself loose.

"Austin." Sahara screamed.

Shots fired. The glass over my head rained down like hail. Sahara pushed at my shoulders, knocking me back outside to the wet boardwalk.

I grabbed her wrist, trying to pull her with me.

She ripped from my grasp.

A revolver thrust through the broken window and fired at the boards. I rolled to the alley and made my escape beneath the bathhouse boardwalk.

When the rain was a blinding curtain, I crossed Main Street behind the fountain and took refuge against the solid side of the bank. *Now what?* I should have gone with the direct approach of guns blazing.

"Austin. I know it's you. I know you're still out there." Jack McKade's voice boomed over the roaring downpour.

I stepped from the protections of a solid wall, and its darkened alley to walk down the middle of Main Street. The deluge lessened to a nagging drizzle. My sodden, moccasin-covered feet mired in the crud, making sucking sounds with the pull of every step. If I had to run, I couldn't. *Flight or fight.*

It was time to make a stand.

McKade's men were already lining up on the boardwalk in front of the Watering Hole. Sahara was crammed through the swinging doors. Jack McKade muckled onto her arm, forcing her to walk ahead of him.

Lily leaped around them. "This isn't all there is," she shouted at me. Lily held up the flour sack filled with the copper ore. I expected steam to come off of her, she was so heated. In her other hand, Sahara's necklace and bracelet dangled from her tight grip. "No matter what Sahara wants us to believe, this isn't all there is. I want it all. All of it. Do you hear me, Austin."

There was a handprint across Sahara's left cheek. Blood smeared her sleeves. Her red hair sprung from a tangled bun to hang in her eyes. My heart sank into my roiling gut at the mussed sight of her.

"There is no more." Sahara shrieked at Lily. She squirmed in McKade's tight hold. "I don't love you, Austin. You'll never be a rich gentleman. I'll throw my lot in with Mr. McKade. The Watering Hole is where the money is." Her speech was stilted. She sniffled too loudly.

I didn't know if she was trying to fool them, or trying to fool me.

"I'm tired of living in a sod hut," she hollered.

Hogan.

"Don't rescue me, Austin."

"It's McKade I'm here for now." I regretted it as soon as I said it. Sahara seemed to shrivel into her delicate green dress. I wanted to run to her. I wanted to put my arms around her shoulders. I wanted to tell her I didn't mean what I said. I needed to tell her—

I loved her. I loved Sahara Miller.

Seth and Jeb hammered through the saloon doors dragging the pastor's beaten body between them. "We got us a friend of yours," Jeb said. "Says he knows nothin' 'bout no copper strike. But I'm not likely gonna believe him. You two was thick as thieves in that tent of his."

Seth jerked the pastor's head up by his hair. "He's still alive if you're interested in trading him for your strike."

"We didn't agree on that," Jeb said to Seth. "You said I could kill him."

"Well, now I'm saying we could get us a claim," Seth retorted.

"No. No. You said I could kill him."

"Well, now he's worth more in trade."

"No, no, no, no." Jeb punched his knife into the pastor's gut, punctuating each no. The pastor collapsed onto the boardwalk, snatching at his stomach.

Sahara lunged to put pressure on the belly wounds. The pastor came alive with the deadly pain. He clutched at Sahara's hands and fussed with his watch pocket. A glint of steel passed between them. Sahara tucked her hands inside her skirts as McKade's men yanked her away.

McKade's shotgun blasted the air. He kicked the hound dog scurrying from the saloon with its tail already tucked. "Jeb. Get your mess off my property."

Jeb twisted his meaty claws into the frock coat, lifting the pastor from between the shoulder blades. He drudged the pastor through the muck to deposit him in the slurry that was center Main Street.

He danced a jig back to the Watering Hole, hooting and hollering like it was a holiday celebration. Before Jeb climbed the step to the boardwalk, he cut the reins that hitched Charlie Horse to the rail.

Seth plucked his revolver, exploding several rounds into the air, spooking Charlie Horse out of town. He leveled his barrel on me.

I trudged a few steps forward, dropping to my knees in the cold mud. Blood saturated the pastor's coat. I shoved his hands away. Not only blood, but ingesta gushed from the knife wounds. I jerked the pastor's clothes apart and pressed my hands to the ragged holes.

"Kill him for me." The pastor clawed at me with his gore-covered fingers.

I looked at McKade. He pushed on the barrel of Seth's Colt Navy revolver, lowering it. With his fingers forming a mock gun, McKade pointed at me, dropping his thumb hammer down. *Bang,* McKade silently mouthed.

"Kill McKade," the pastor begged.

"I will. I'll kill him." That was a promise.

His throat gurgled. A fat tear escaped his eye to roll across his pale cheek. "I loved Jamie. I loved Jamie McKade. I followed him here from back East." He choked on a swallow. "His uncle, Jack McKade, drove us apart. 'Unnatural,' he had ranted."

The pastor tried to sit up. I held him down. "He took Jamie from me." Tears ran from his bloodshot eyes. "McKade took Jamie on his murderous spree. Away from me."

"Hush," I said. "Easy. It's okay now."

His eyes stared at my face, but he no longer saw me.

"Jamie wrote me every day. Then the letters stopped." He coughed. His heaving expelled more vital fluids from his belly. "I know Jamie will come back for me one day. I know it." His throat burbled with blood as he sobbed. "Tell him I love him. Tell him. Tell him I loved him to my last breath."

"He knows." Blood pumping beneath my palm dwindled until its beat was gone. "He knows, but you'll tell him yourself." Red trickled from the corner of the pastor's mouth. With the pad of my thumb, I smeared it across his bottom lip.

The rain stopped. A sliver of sun poked through the scurrying clouds.

Jack McKade stood tall and proud on his boardwalk. "Austin killed Jamie McKade," he shouted. "Austin gunned down the young man in the streets of Durango. Jamie was just a city dandy celebrating his twentieth birthday."

Sahara's hands flew to cover her mouth. Her eyes grew wide with horror.

"He's a killer." McKade hollered, pointing at me.

It was kill or be killed. I had no choice. I didn't know who he was. It didn't matter who he was. It mattered that he called me out and pulled his smoke wagon. I didn't have to accept his invitation to the gunfight, but I'd have been shot in the back if I didn't. At least I'd had a fighting chance in a showdown.

"Austin's a cold-blooded murderer," McKade shouted. "Who will be next?" He was intent on whipping the crowd up like a politician on election day. "You." He pointed to a panhandler. "You?" He thrust his hand toward a woman in the doorway of the assay office. "You?" McKade's eyes scanned a huddle of men in knotted neckerchiefs.

The men coughed and guffawed, shifting their stance.

I swiveled my head around looking for Justice. I wasn't a killer like McKade. I had regret. A dead man was always someone's nephew, or cousin…or son. *Justice?*

Those men in neckerchiefs lifted the pastor's body from me. They carried his dripping carcass to Percival's Mercantile and laid him out on the board walkway, folding his hands across his chest.

With a jerk of McKade's shaggy head, he signaled for Sahara to be taken inside. The hired guns followed, escorting Lightning Jack McKade safely back into his lair.

Rooted in the muck, I shivered, wondering what it was all for. I had journeyed to the edge of the frontier to be alone. To work a living on my own land. To become a man.

Lost in self-pity, I hadn't heard the Indians until they had already descended. I hadn't seen them until they had wanted to be seen. It was their way. They fled past me. Their hands touched my wet shoulders and sopping hair. *Counting coup? No. I wasn't the enemy.*

A feather with one side painted yellow fluttered to the mud in front of me.

Apache warriors rampaged through the tent housing. Their fierce whooping and painted faces inspired denizens to flee in fear. Wooden facades offered no protection against the angry band flailing knives and hatchets. But there was really nothing here for them.

With four days of pouring rain, Molasses Pond was buttoned up. There were no wares on display outside. No doors gaping open in invitation. No mule trains with provisions had come through the pass in a month.

The Apaches would have known. They watched. They listened. They waited. It was unlike any tribe, even in desperation, to raid without purpose and planning.

Gunmen emptied from the Watering Hole in pursuit of the Apaches. They shot their handguns with no worry to accuracy, smashing glass windows and splintering wood.

A woman ran from the bathhouse, her little girl hanging limp in her grasp. Blood blossomed over the girl's pristine dress. Red smeared the length of the woman's apron as the unconscious girl slipped from her grasp.

McKade hunkered inside, beneath the broken front window of his saloon. The tip of his double-barrel poked above the sill as he reloaded. Behind him, Sahara pulled her coat onto her shoulders then wrung her hands together, pacing the office again.

Rose stood framed inside the open doors of the empty saloon. The plume of her hat drooped over her forehead.

I could hear the whoops and shouts and gunfire from around the burned out livery. The skirmish wouldn't last long. Every Indian would fade into the landscape as easy as ghosts.

Rose waved, pointing to the end of town. She was telling me to go.

CHAPTER FOURTEEN

I hit the thickets on the outskirts of town. Smoke billowed in the distance too far away to be the waning skirmish at the livery. I would bet buttons to silver dollars that that smoke signal called the Apaches off. Single shots of gunfire pecked at the stilled air only now and again. It was over in minutes.

For years to come, the Whites of Molasses Pond would, no doubt, inflate stories of fighting off an Apache raid. I twirled the painted feather between my fingers as I left town.

Townsfolk were silently picking up ravaged canvas tents and strewn lumber. A gathering huddled around the little girl who had been struck in the shoulder by an errant bullet. Panhandlers and diggers crept from hiding. A dog padded its way across Main Street. And Jack McKade flailed that sawed-off shotgun around on the boardwalk of the Watering Hole, shouting orders.

A twig cracked. The brush rattled. A blur flew at my chest.

Caught by surprise, I hadn't cleared either gun from a holster. A jolt of adrenaline tore through me, but the heightened alert calmed with the scent of her lilac soap. "Sahara."

Her warmth permeated my cold body as if springtime sunshine blistered through a heavy snow cover. I ate it up.

"I thought I'd never see you again," she said in a breathy whisper.

I buried my face in her neck. My eyes blurred with welling tears.

"Bles-sed me." Rose emerged from the brambles. "I left a shoe back there in that muck." She lifted her leg and grabbed off the remaining one. "I know buggies were invented. What I don't know is why I have to suffer walking."

Thank you, I mouthed silently.

Rose winked. "Okay, you two lovebirds, I need to trot back down to that wreck of a village."

Sahara loosened her hug, beaming a smile toward Rose, but she was already cussing her way back to town. "It's my gift to you," Rose said in a singsong shout. "Don't squander it."

Sahara's piercing eyes focused on my lips as if it were the first time she'd noticed them. She ran her fingertips over my mouth, brushing ever so softly that I shivered. Her eyelids fluttered closed. She shifted to her toes, replacing fingers with her mouth in a delicate caress.

Her warm breath whispered over my lips. Her insatiable mouth teased too gently, too timidly. I wanted more. I needed more.

I entwined my hands in the silky mass of her fiery red hair and deepened our first kiss. When I sunk my hungry mouth onto hers, I thought she'd pull away. Maybe I hoped she'd pull away because I couldn't help myself. I couldn't stop. I nipped and sucked on her plump lower lip until she yielded, opening for our tongues to entangle.

It felt as if our souls had made promises. It felt like there was nothing more right than the two of us together.

Sahara returned my fervor. Her kissing became feral. Her hands found the small of my back, pressing me to her until the rising heat burned between us.

Her palms roamed up my back and down my sides. My skin tingled. I needed to feel her flesh on mine—

"It won't work," I said as I tore myself from her.

"It will." Sahara reached for me.

I steeled myself against her. "I'm not a man. You deserve a man."

I walked off.

It was eerily quiet on the journey home. I listened to the pitter-patter of Sahara's feet behind me. Once in a while, I heard her sniffle.

We parted ways at the hogan. She went in. I went to the overhang.

The cow moaned. The heifer calf stretched like a lazy house cat as she climbed from beneath her dam. I fluffed dried grasses and brush in front of them, not having the heart to put the calf in her pen. I heard the pup yip. She would be dancing and jumping around Sahara's legs in frenetic circles of happiness.

I stirred the coals to life then fed them kindling until the flames were strong enough to devour chips. Empty whiskey bottles littered the ancient stone floor. Brass casings were scattered in a haphazard trail through the cavern. A tall pile of manure mounded ever higher at the far edge, waiting to be taken to the garden. Even my few personal things were disheveled, as if ransacked by a rampaging bull.

First things first. I untied my neckerchief and gently crept from my sopping shirt. A shiver ran through me. Now that the rain had settled, the cold air turned crisp. Gooseflesh pimpled my skin. I rolled the length of my binding about my chest, snugging each pass across the front. A sigh of relief escaped my lips.

The coloring over my ribs had dulled. The dark purple bruise was encircled by a thick ring of pale green. The pain wasn't as sharp as it had been. I prodded the center and winced. *Still sore, but workable.*

Using a bucket of rainwater, I doused my head, scrubbing my hair with a bar of soap as well as torturing my underarms. My teeth chattered uncontrollably. If I clenched my molars to still the quaking, my entire body shook.

I shimmied into the scraped buckskin smock, hung my wet button-down near the fire, then began to clean up. The mess kept my mind occupied. If I stopped to think, I thought about her.

I envisioned her face so easily. The way her eyes were greener than lush prairie grass. The countless shades of red in the strands of her thick hair. How her tresses shimmered with the touch of the sun, or in the glint of firelight. Her button nose was sprinkled with freckles. And her gap-toothed smile was caressed with a quaint awkwardness.

And that kiss. I'd never forget her kiss. Sweet like candy and salty like pork beans. *Perfect.*

The calf suckled her dam's udder. The noises reminded my stomach it hadn't been fed. I stirred the bucket of cold milk, dipped a cup in, then gulped long swallows. Next, I rummaged jerky from stored packs. With my hands full, I went to the fire and sat down. The heat of the flames and a full belly made me drowsy. At some point, I let myself drift into an exhausted sleep.

"I know you're going after Charlie."

Charlie Horse. And I don't care how much I fancied her. Anyone screeching at me early in the morning, before coffee, was on my dislike list.

"And I brought you coffee."

Forgiven.

I cracked my eyelids to slits, shielding myself from the bright morning sunshine. My body complained as I stretched for the coffee. I swear Sahara was moving it out of reach. The cup floated back and forth in front of my narrowed sight. I growled and made a lunge for her legs.

She evaded my grasp with a squeal. Coffee splashed onto my head. "Oopsie," she said. "Sorry."

She didn't sound apologetic.

Her screams of giggles broke the pleasant morning stillness.

"Coffee," I grunted.

Sahara stuffed the scalding cup into my hands. I jostled it from one to the other until I found the handle. With the open weeping blisters and oozing cuts, my palms smarted from the hot heat. I didn't know whether to blow on the steaming liquid or at my re-bubbling blisters.

"I'm going with you. For Charlie. I'm going with you. And I won't let go this time. Not unless my very life depends on it. And even then, I'll really try to hold on tight." She bounced on the balls of her feet with too much enthusiasm for early morning.

I think I used to be a morning person. Once upon a time.

"I'll be your faithful sidekick," she screeched, clapping her hands together. She clearly read way too many dime novels.

Sahara was dressed for the part. Her boy's chore coat gaped to show a buttoned shirt over long handles—*one should never refer to undergarments in polite company.* Her pants were tucked into the tops of her high Wellington boots. The redness of her right cheek, turning purple, definitely completed her rough-and-ready persona.

Moreover, there was nothing to be done about the fact that she was safer with me than staying alone. I rolled to my feet, tied my hair back, and picked up a lariat. "Let's go then." I swallowed the rest of the coffee in two gulps.

An hour later, it was painfully obvious this wasn't going to work. Sahara talked incessantly. She galloped circles around me in a childish, loping stride, yelling "yeehaw." She pantomimed throwing a lasso, then pulled twin finger revolvers. To top it all off, she constantly asked if we were there yet. About now, I'd pay a mountain lion a sack of copper ore to come sniffing at her toes.

I was losing my mind. Worse, I was losing my patience.

"Stay here," I barked. The flash floods had carved steep walls into the arroyo. Water was flowing along the bottom, but it was easy enough to climb down and cross. There were small areas of flat ground inside the walls, cut when wild torrents had swelled, eroding the banks. One of these sites would make good cover for Sahara to wait, if she could remain quiet.

Sahara had no *way* about her. Not for out here. When she needed to be light, perceptive, and wary, she stomped around like a bull in a china shop. When she needed to be silent? *Don't get me started.* Sahara chattered like a rabid squirrel with a mad on. Ceaselessly.

Her face scrunched. "But—"

"Just stay." I clambered over the top of the banking, disappearing from her sight. I had been tracking Charlie Horse all morning. It was near to noon now. The herd often milled at the bottom of the butte just over the rise.

Charlie Horse stood in a thicket of brambles and branches that were twisted and stacked together by the recent flooding. I zigzagged toward him so he wouldn't feel threatened. As I got closer, I thought it curious that he wasn't moving at all. He usually greeted me politely before bunching to leave in a cloud of dust. It was strange he didn't even turn his head in my direction.

He startled as I got too close, but remained standing like a statue. Charlie Horse bugled through his nostrils, straining to look. His ears swiveled frantically. Sweat glistened over his neck and shoulders.

He was trapped.

If I hadn't blatantly tracked the horse, he might have starved to death tied in the twisted wreckage. Or, more like, gotten attacked and killed by a large predator.

Speaking Navajo to him, I approached. Charlie Horse settled.

His leather headstall was hooked by a thick branch. I rubbed his neck, then ran the lariat over his head before unbuckling the bridle. As soon as he was loose from the headstall, he scrambled backward.

The loop tightened around his throat. His smallish eyes went wide with fright. I fed him line so he could bolt from the brush.

Charlie Horse calmed once he was clear. I fashioned a nose band, then clawed my way back through the mangled scrub for the hanging bridle. It was useless with the reins cut short. I tied the contraption behind the seat, then checked the saddle's cinch and mounted. We rode quietly to where Sahara was waiting.

The sound of singing perked Charlie Horse's ears forward. I huffed in exasperation and clucked the horse to a jog.

"Sahara?" She climbed from the ditch as I stepped from my horse.

"Charlie."

When I handed her the rope haltered horse, it was with the confidence that she couldn't possibly lose him this time. I gave her a stern look anyway.

"I promise," she reiterated in a monotone, "I won't let go this time. Not unless my very life depends on it. And even then, I'll really try to hold on tight." She ended the rote speech with a huge smile. "Cross my heart." And she did cross her heart.

I told Sahara to stay put, then took a coiled lariat from the saddle horn. The herd still milled in the area where I nabbed Charlie Horse. The band had been chewing on brush. They hadn't been bothered by my presence. It was an opportunity.

I needed to rope another saddle horse. One more horse wouldn't begin to cover my losses, but it was a start. One more horse could mean the difference between life and death on the frontier.

With two saddle-broke horses, Sahara could ride along as I set a new trap line for pelts. I could hunt, knowing that Charlie Horse would babysit her. Eventually, she might learn to help, or at least stay quiet.

Several loose wisps from the tie in my hair danced on the brisk wind, telling me which direction my scent carried. I stayed down wind. When I crept close enough to take a head shot at one of the branded strays, I shook out a loop and lifted it in a slow, lazy fashion. If I didn't get hurried, the horses wouldn't become alerted.

When my hand came forward in its rotation, the skin stretching over my ribs complained. But the loop felt perfect. I released.

A piercing scream ripped the air. The herd spun as one, charging into flight and kicking clods of mud out behind them. My throw went to the ground. The loop was empty.

Déjà vu.

Angered, I gritted my teeth, grinding the molars. It wasn't the first time Sahara had foiled my efforts, but it might be her last. I clenched the tail of the limp rope in a fist.

When I reached to coil the length, strangling the twisted strands, grit ground into my oozing blisters. Cuts bled onto the waxed coils. "Sahara." My jaw worked back and forth. *I've had it. When I get my hands on her—*

Charlie Horse whipped past me with lightning speed. His recessed pig-eyes flashed with surrounding sclera. Hair was scraped from his nose. His lariat's loop rode loose around his neck, down to his chest. "Charlie Horse." *Damn.*

I ran for Sahara, swearing with each pounding footstep that she had better hope a snake actually bit her this time. No weak threats from the slithering ghoul. No kidding. If the varmint hadn't already killed her, I just might.

"Sahara?" I didn't see her as I came over the rise.

"Sahara." Maybe she was hunkered in the arroyo.

"Sahara."

She was gone.

I gulped for air, sucking as if I'd been deprived for far too long. "Sahara?" I buckled over at the waist and attempted to catch my breath. "Sahara."

"C'mon, Sahara, quit fooling." My panting calmed. "Yes, I'm mad. But hiding is just going to make me madder." I slapped my leg with the coils. "Damn it, Sahara."

I searched the ground for clues to her hide-and-seek.

There had been a scuffle. Three horses. All shod. Three different sets of prints. Charlie Horse made one of those sets.

There was only one set of human prints; small, petite. *Sahara's.*

"Sahara." I shouted into the vast rocky terrain.

The marks in the wet earth headed west, to town. The flood plain was like quicksand after days of rain. It couldn't be crossed. Riders would have to go around the butte. They'd have to run Apache Pass.

That's where I'd catch them.

The rocky ground blurred beneath my feet. My breath consciously steadied as I timed it with my footfalls. *In-one-two-three. Out-one-two-three. In-one-two-three. Out-one-two-three.* My Navajo childhood prepared me to go a distance at a jog. With discipline, I could cover the ground like a gazelle, swift and untiring. My bruised ribs were not signing on for the adventure though. They nagged for me to stop.

A familiar game trail led high along the steep butte. It was too dangerous to ride. Charlie Horse had led me on a chase, traversing the trail, several times in the past. The footing was like walking on glass marbles. One wrong step, one shift to imbalance, one lapse in concentration, any impertinence to the spirit of the butte, a stray thought, a mindless gesture…one indiscretion and down, down, down in a hail of merciless rubble.

But even in treachery, the trail had its beauty and benefits. I had climbed it many times to watch foals clamber on stilted legs, or to survey the miles of outstretched, rocky land from high above. I had hunted here too, following prey to the sheerest heights, but never reaching the top. And the sunsets were most spectacular over the butte. I'd run the thin trail just to chase the sun around to the other side as it sank.

Now I was running and chasing again.

I meant to race the mounted riders to the pass, where I'd cut them off from their homestretch to town. *Seth-one-two-three. Jeb-one-two-three. Seth-one-two-three. Jeb-one-two-three.* A steady beat. Steady footfalls. A blistering, steady pace.

Screams echoed off the canyon walls from far below. "Sahara." I lost my rhythmic count at the thought of her. For a split second, I had lost respect for the complexity of the butte. *Sahara.*

I lost my footing.

Stumbling, I skidded over rocky ground on my chest, skinning my face. My heart thumped wildly. My breathing came quick and choppy. Down I went.

I slammed to a sudden stop as my right shoulder smacked into a human-sized, red rock.

A groan escaped my tight lips. I grabbed my right arm, crushing it to my body. Pain washed over me. My head grew woozy. Bile rose to burn in my throat.

I propped my back against the boulder and remained still, hoping the sharpness of the agony would subside. It didn't. *Long breath in through my nose. Blow out through my mouth as if cooling hot coffee. Long breath in through my nose. Long breath out through my mouth. In through my nose. Out through my mouth.*

Sahara screamed. My breath choked.

I tried to climb to my feet. Dizziness knocked me back to the ground. I retched.

A muffled scream made me swallow bile.

I clawed my way to standing, clutching at the tall rock like a toddler hanging on its ma's apron.

My head grew woozy. Down I fell. *I can't.*

I rolled to sitting then rested my forehead on my bony knees. My sight was misty and blurred. I wasn't crying. Maybe it was the pain. Or specks of gravel had gotten in my eyes from the fall. But I wasn't crying like a little girl.

I clenched my midsection low at the waist of my buckskins, steadying the injury. *Ugh. My shoulder.* The ball had popped from its socket. It was sitting in a tight, horrid lump on the front of my chest. I violently vomited. The acrid coffee was twice as powerful coming up. My throat felt seared as if from the white flames of a blacksmith's fire.

Sahara? What did she matter?

She needed me. I couldn't let her down.

She didn't need me. She managed well enough on her own.

I'm responsible for her.

Really? Was that all there was to it?

I love her. I need her.

She makes me feel weak and vulnerable. She makes me question who I am—what I am. And she knows. The girl will get me killed with her friggin girly ways.

But that kiss...

Gathering my wits, I tried to get up—half-sitting, half-kneeling, half-huffing out of breath. I waited for a wave of nausea to pass. The world was spinning out my control. My eyes crossed in the back of my skull.

Another scream urged me from self-pity.

I used the rock to steady myself. If I had my bearings correct, I was above and ahead of the riders. I could descend from here and still catch them in the pass. That bolstered my will.

The descent was perilous. I felt every ragged stone through my moccasins. The balls of my feet bruised with each step. Gravel, sand, and rocks slid, racing me down the twisting trail. Inevitably, my feet flew from under me. My rump hit the landslide of moving earth. Dirt spit into the air.

Rockslide. I bounced and rolled with the rubble that was swiftly escaping the steep butte. Down. Down. Down. The speed was frightening. I jounced and twirled out of control.

Nearing the bottom of the butte, I jammed to a halt on a solid boulder. *Snap.* A sudden sharp pang ripped through my shoulder. The ball had plunked back into its socket on my sudden stop. Vomit exploded from my mouth. My chest was awash in fatigued burning.

Through a gap in the jagged landscape, I spied Jeb on the bay, riding ahead of Seth at a considerable distance. Seth rode the sorrel with Sahara slung across its withers. She struggled against Seth. Her writhing was driving the sorrel into blind flight. He swerved and swayed dangerously.

Sweat trickled down the middle of my back even though the chill autumn air bit at my buckskins. I tugged on the kerchief wrapping my neck. I had to stop them. There was no choice this time. *Flight or fight.* Fight was the only answer. Fight for Sahara. Fight for what was right.

I climbed from the strewn rubble to search for the perfect spot. I'd halt Seth and Jeb in their tracks. Sahara would have to have enough sense to get herself safe when I did.

A single gunshot ripped the air. *Seth? Or Jeb?* I couldn't discern who fired off the gun. It was a small caliber. It could have been either one of them.

A grunt, a gasp, then a weak scream carried on the sharp autumn air from below.

Sahara went silent.

CHAPTER FIFTEEN

I lodged my back against a sturdy boulder, wedging my bruised feet to push a fat, round rock. My head spun in dizziness as pain shot through my shoulder. Sweat broke out over my forehead.

This side of the butte was steep. Clear of any vegetation. It formed one wall of a pass that ran between two mountainous ridges. Apache Pass was like running a gauntlet on a quiet day. Creating a bottleneck in the pass, which I intended, would make it downright deadly any day. *Not my deal.*

Seth heeled the sorrel. The horse's belly buckled with each powerful blow. Blood from the raking rowels dotted the sorrel's sides. The animal was wild with fear and pain. His bloodshot eyes glowed red. White lather covered his neck and shoulders. Under his doubled load, he couldn't keep up with the bay. That didn't stop him from trying. And Seth wouldn't have let him slow regardless.

The sun was going down. The temperature was rapidly dropping with it. I wouldn't think on what any of that meant in the coming hours. *Can't do anything about it.*

I grit my teeth, clawed for purchase with my fingernails, and shoved with my legs. The rock shifted. *I could do this.*

I grunted through my clenched jaw and thrust with all of my might. The rock teetered on the verge of taking the plunge. Encouraged, I prodded it farther. Slowly, too slowly, it began to roll. With one last push, my legs flattened straight. Not even my toes could reach the round rock now. But that had been enough.

The rock was rolling. It picked up speed quickly, then plummeted.

As it went, it banged into other rocks and off larger boulders. It hopped and jumped and crashed its way into a monumental landslide. The roar was deafening. The entire side of the butte shook as the writhing mass of stone surged toward Apache Pass.

The trembling ground loosed rubble all around me. Tremors spit gravel from higher up threatening to rain scree onto my head. I slid a few feet, grasping for purchase. It was no good. The ground squirmed too much beneath me. Down I went.

The colossal butte came apart. I nose-dived toward the pass. My body was tossed like a rag doll in a dog's mouth. A shrill, unbearable bleating of pain screamed in my brain.

The riders below charged full-bore at the closing pass.

A high-pitched squeal pierced the rumble of the avalanche as Jeb hauled the reins of the bay too viciously. Open-mouthed, the animal screamed and fought, shaking its head from side to side. Jeb pulled harder. The horse twisted its neck in half, folding in an abnormal position. The horse crumpled to the ground.

Jeb was thrown clear. He waved his arms for Seth.

I came to an abrupt halt at the floor of the pass. For a moment, I lay there, afraid of what the slightest movement would bring.

The sorrel pulled up hard. His butt tucked to mark an eleven into the hardened earth. Seth braced himself in the saddle as the sorrel popped his front end in a series of hops that kept him upright. He stopped short of the piled rubble.

Sahara's limp body flipped into the rocks. My breath caught in my chest. I wanted to run to her. I wanted to scream out her name.

Seth flew off to land on his feet.

Slowly—cautiously—I stood.

A veil of dust rode the wind. As it cleared, I was exposed.

"No, Jeb," Seth hollered.

"Stay out of this, Seth. I'm tired of taking orders from you. Austin's time's been coming."

"You can't beat him." Seth made a grab for the sorrel but missed. The sorrel spun away, three-legged lame.

"What do you know," Jeb growled at Seth, never taking his eyes from me. "His gun arm's stove up."

"He's strapped under two guns. Leave it be."

"Don't mean nothin'. Anyone can wear 'em. Two guns ain't nothin' if'n ya can't use them." He spit a glob of mucous without turning his head away.

If he had a *tell*, I didn't know it. I didn't need to know it. Jeb was clumsy and slow with a handgun. His forte was knife throwing. Could he kill me with a throw of a knife? Not at this distance.

Time held its breath. My surroundings came into keen focus. Initially, I watched both men, because there was no way one moved without the other.

The whites of Jeb's eyes were riddled with jagged red bolts. Sweat beaded on his forehead, though the temperature was dropping with the waning sun. Greasy hair hung like oiled ropes onto his shoulders. His heavy coat was soiled at the bottom from dragging its draped length as he walked. The long coat was tucked open behind his holster, where the massive hogleg hung too low. Its hammer loop was off. The gun rode perched. Jeb took a wide, solid stance on his bowed legs.

Seth's arm hung relaxed. His palm brushed his leather holster in flipping off the loop. The strain of indecision lined his face with tension. He wouldn't dare pop the gun loose from its holster's tight grip, lest his actions get mistaken. Seth wore the short, waist-length coat of gunslingers. It was meticulously clean at the wrists. His gun hand was manicured. His hair was short and slicked back beneath a wide-brimmed hat. His eyes were well shaded from the sun. As he readied for business, I heard the excitement in his breathing.

"We was there when you kilt poor Jamie," Seth said.

"You'd have shot me in the back if I didn't go when he called me out," I answered Seth, but I decided to watch Jeb's every flinch. This was to be Jeb's kill.

"Jamie needed to get his feet wet. We thought you'd be his first. We thought he'd take you. You were a sorry looking runt strapped under a cannon. Pullin' that revolver shouldn't have been possible."

Jeb wiggled his meaty fingers like dangling sausages. He waited for me to glance Seth's way. *Wasn't happening.*

"Ya know, we didn't even knowed it was you. Not til the boss recognized a wanted poster that had come in on the very same stage as that sweet little whore you stole from us. McKade knows who you are now. You're wanted for killin' and rapin' and pillagin' and such, breed." He spat a dark stream of tobacco. Thick drool oozed down his chin. "McKade tried to clean out all you injun mongrels when he was scoutin' for the cavalry. You was like rats in a barrel. Makes no sense the cavalry kept a few of you alive."

"McKade and I seem to go way back," I said. "Maybe even further than he realizes."

Jeb dropped his stance ever so slightly over his rooted feet. He was committed to the draw.

Seth's eyes crinkled at the corners in delight. "Oh, you two do go way back. He knows it now. He's got it all figured out." He swallowed, struggling to get a lump down his throat. That was his *tell.*

Seth pulled first.

Blam. I shot the Colt Navy revolver from his hand.

Jeb yanked at his big weapon but was still lugging the over-long barrel from its holster when I turned. I blasted him in the chest. *Blam. Blam.* He blew backward as if a ram had butted his midsection.

Seth bolted. He was out of sight before Jeb's body finished twitching on the ground.

"Sahara?" There was dried blood at the back of her scalp. My fingers came away sticky with the goo. I smoothed her tangled hair from her face then patted at her cheeks. Sahara's eyes fluttered open.

"Wha…Where am I?" She tried to sit up.

"Shh. Lie quiet until you've had a moment to remember."

"Mm. My head." Sahara's fingers searched her skull, settling on the lump. "Oh. He hit me." She gingerly groped for other injuries. "He told me to shut up. I shot him with the pastor's gun. He squeezed it from my hand. Then he hit me with it."

Her body jerked at the memory. She whirled around. "Where are they?" The slight motion made her grab at her forehead.

"Gone. Jeb's dead. Seth ran toward the opening at the end of the rockslide." We had to head in the same direction. I hoped Seth wasn't planning an ambush.

"Wait here." I climbed through the debris looking for the bay. He lay among the littered boulders, bathing the dry earth with his sweat and blood. Three of his legs had broken when the rockslide broadsided him. He paddled the floppy limbs in a futile attempt to get up. Past that, I didn't want to know.

This was my fault.

He snorted at my approach, lifting his head and thrashing his fractured legs. Sweat had darkened rings around his eyes and ears. Blood trickled from his flaring nostrils. His soft, velvety muzzle oozed a pink froth. Huffing and puffing in gasps, he labored to breathe.

I shot him.

Of all the animals, two-legged and four, that should be put down, he hadn't been one. Sniffling, I took a moment to remember the time he busted loose under me and how he came around to be as gentle as a lamb. He had been rugged, tractable, and steady. It was a shameful waste of a life.

"Austin?"

I climbed from the rocks, scrabbling back toward Sahara. Seth's weapon was on the ground between us. I plucked the revolver from the rubble. The handle of the gun was shattered. There was blood on the splintered grips. Seth had been wounded. Echoes of Pa resounded in my head, "Wounded bears come back enraged."

"He'd need a gun first," I said aloud.

"What did you say?"

"Seth's gun is no good." I emptied the Colt Navy revolver, pocketed the bullets, then tossed the broken weapon aside.

Even dazed, Sahara was pretty. She was the combination of a fiery sunset and fresh buttermilk. And she was sweet like that molasses bread. I really liked her. I thought I even loved her. It was unnatural, but I couldn't help my feelings for her. To me, what I felt for Sahara was the most natural thing in my entire being.

"I'm dizzy. I think I have the vapors." She fluttered her hand in front of her face. "I just need a minute."

I stood next to her and petted on her shoulder like I was calming a frightened horse. It wasn't like I'd had a lot of experience with women.

"What will you do with Jeb?" she asked.

"I can't bury him. I won't bury him. Not my deal. That's for him and hell to decide."

Two holes in his chest burbled blood. My mind threatened to flashback on killing Jamie McKade. But this gun-scum was no wet-behind-the-ears dandy like Jamie was. I had very little regret for this death. And at the moment, I had other worries. *Staying alive.*

With a struggle to roll his dead weight, I liberated the gun belt from Jeb's holster and strapped my injured arm along my side. Jeb wasn't going to be using his outfit any longer. I know he'd begrudge me the use of it, though I couldn't see how he was about to make that clear now.

Bullets? Coat pocket. Rummaging through his long coat produced a stench. I'd heard of last gases passing on death, but I was sure Jeb stunk this bad when alive. Opening his coat had released his foul body odor. *My knife.* I had dropped my skinning knife in the melee of fleeing saddle horses that night TwoFeathers rescued the captive Apaches. I thought I'd lost it for good. Just goes to prove, things come back around.

Sahara picked up Jeb's Colt Dragoon.

"What do you want that for?" I asked as Sahara lifted Jeb's revolver with two hands.

"I want a gun." She stuffed it in a holey flour sack that was fluttering on the breeze nearby.

"You won't be able to shoot it. It's too heavy for you." I took the huge hogleg from the sack and flipped the cylinder open. I made sure it was fully loaded. "Don't shoot yourself." I handed it back.

The sorrel nickered as I approached. He pressed his forehead to my chest. I scratched beneath his jaw. The horse's head grew heavy against me. When his eyes drooped, I bent and lifted the injured leg. "You'll be all right." Dried lather caked his exhausted body. "If you can make it to town, you'll be all right," I whispered to him.

"How does it look?"

"The leg's not broken. Bad, but not broken. Bowed the tendon and I don't know what else." I gently lowered the leg and pushed my face to his neck. He smelled of everything horse, everything good and decent, and wholesome and kind. His steamy breath smelled of mashed oats. His body of lathered sweat. There were scents of oiled saddle leather and fired steel from the blacksmith's forge. Most of all, he smelled familiar, like home.

"We're not going to move fast. We might as well take the horse as far as he can go." I couldn't leave the sorrel. I knew what fate awaited him out here, injured and alone in the vast wilderness, with the blackness of night fast approaching.

Sahara smoothed her coat and slapped at the accumulated grit on her trousers while awkwardly gripping the massive gun in its holey sack. "At least you've captured a horse today."

I rolled my eyes and scooped up the hanging leather reins to the sorrel. "I did."

Sahara tested her feet, stabbing one toe forward then the other. She moved timidly at first, as if she were checking for thin ice.

The walls of Apache Pass loomed high above, casting deep shadows over us. We plodded around the settled boulders. The sun descended. Darkness threatened. The wind picked up. The temperature continued to fall.

Sahara dropped back. A gray pallor settled across her face as she silently walked behind the three-legged beat of the struggling sorrel.

Snow fluttered on the wind once we were free of the pass.

Sahara began to hum. She had a lovely voice. Most everything about her was lovely. I hadn't taken notice at first meeting. Like any boy, I had crushed on the dazzling girl with the painted face, parading the latest fashions. *Stupid me.*

As Sahara hummed, the tension in my back eased. The striking pains throughout my body settled into a dull, throbbing soreness. And the whirling jumble of thoughts in my head calmed.

Pa had played the same tune on his harmonica each night. "Foolish Pioneers." Folks had jigged around the campfire after the wagons were circled and the stock had been bedded down. When not in use, Pa's harmonica rode in his breast pocket, ready to stave off long hours of boredom, or soothe the soreness at day's end.

Blood had drooled over the harmonica after turning the gun on himself. Its shiny steel had once glinted in the sun. Steel glinted in the sun. Steel glinted from high on the ridge from that leg brace of McKade's. I shook the apparitions from my head. I wouldn't think on that now.

"Where'd you learn that song?" I asked Sahara, tugging at my neckerchief to take apart the knot.

At my question, Sahara trotted to catch up. "Back home. It's about the gold rush of California, when everyone back East packed up to move their families West. It's called 'Foolish Pioneers.'"

I slipped the kerchief from my neck and wrapped it around my wrist. Then, I looped the twisted silk through my gun belt riding low beneath my hips. Jeb's belt, securely fastening my upper arm to my body, had already eased the pain in my shoulder. But my swinging lower arm sent strikes like lightning into it.

"What are you doing?" Sahara asked.

"I need to tie this."

"Here, let me."

She smelled perfectly wonderful as she leaned in to knot the kerchief at my wrist. *Lilac soap. How does she always smell spring fresh?* Her fingertips fluttered on the back of my hand, like a butterfly caught on a gentle breeze. When she was done, her eyes stared into mine. Their green was so vivid I could feel them to my toes. She licked her top lip, then ran her fingers along my ragged scar.

Shivers shuddered the length of my spine.

"You never told me about your scar," she said.

"Nothing really to tell." But I would tell her anything she wanted…if she'd just touch me like that forever and always. I cleared my throat and put a little distance between us.

"Do you know the words to that song? My White pa played the tune on his harmonica."

She sang the words softly beside me.

There's gold on the plains, gold in the hills.
But the gold you would find is only for thrills.
Go, foolish pioneers, go West and begone.
There's gold for the taking if you don't wait over-long.

There's gold in the mountains, gold in the streams.
But the gold you would find is only in dreams.
Go, foolish pioneers, go West and begone.
There's gold for the taking if you don't wait over-long.

When Sahara abruptly stopped singing, I looked at her. She was pale. The sickly complexion stole her unique creaminess. The gray pallor had blanched, creating a worn, deathly appearance that the moonless night couldn't hide.

"Austin, I don't feel so good."

The wind blew. Snow flurries blustered. The temperature couldn't possibly get any colder. We had to keep moving.

Sahara dropped to her knees and vomited.

CHAPTER SIXTEEN

S ahara's face turned the color of uncooked dough. I'm not sure if it looked better or worse than the gray pallor. Both were frightening. She knelt on the cold ground, doubled over, and hurled. Her retching continued even after her stomach was emptied of its contents.

As the gagging calmed, Sahara attempted to stand. "I-I can't." She clutched her head. "It feels like someone's stabbing knives into my eyeballs."

"Stay down." I'd seen this before, when a Navajo boy fell from his horse. Hours after, he got sick, his eyes went wonky, and he babbled nonsense. Days later, he was dead.

I leaned into Sahara's face. One pupil was larger than the other. Panic gouged its way up my gullet like acidic bile. "Can you lay flat?"

Sahara giggled. "I've never seen eyes so blue. They're like a clear summer sky that's cooled off after a fierce, hot downpour."

Keep her with me. Talk to her. "My White ma used to tell me that." I buttoned Sahara's coat, snugging her collar around her neck as she lay back on the cold, damp ground.

"Well, she must have been a smart lady." She rolled to her side, clutching her arms over her chest.

"Truth is," I scratched at my scar, "I couldn't really say. Don't know. When my baby sisters were born, I was already old enough to trot around with my White pa. Ma didn't seem to have a lot of time for me."

Sahara yawned. Her eyes fluttered with the strain of forcing them to stay open.

No. No. No. I couldn't let her sleep. "My ma doted over my sisters' light-colored, long, straight tresses, filling them with ribbons after tying them in braids. She'd have loved your hair. My hair was too unruly for Ma's brush." I tried to keep Sahara focused. "Now you. Talk to me."

"Your father must have had a dark nest of hair." Her sentence ended in a drowsy whisper.

I shook her shoulder. "No. It wasn't like mine, I don't think. He kept it shorn. And wore a hat. I actually can't remember. I know I didn't exactly look like either of them. Do you look like your ma?" I gently shook her shoulder again. "Sahara? How are you feeling?"

"Fine now. Just sleepy. I'm fine. I can stand." She looked around confused. "It's so dark." Her fingers clawed their way up me like she was rock climbing the steep face of that butte. I steadied her ascent.

Sahara stood erect. She blinked once then swooned into my arms.

"Sahara? Sahara." I tapped her pasty white cheek. "Sahara." Blood soaked the collar of her coat. A laceration on her crown bled profusely. The jagged wound was riddled with grit.

I lowered her to lie flat, then ripped the hanging tail off her shirt and tied a bandage around her head, pressuring it with my palm until the bleeding slowed.

I left Sahara on the cold ground and started for the pinions. The sorrel offered to follow. I rubbed his neck. "Stay here. Look after Sahara." I slipped his reins into Sahara's limp fingers, making him stay put.

A coyote howled. His lonesome note was echoed in the distance by another. They were hunting.

I ran to the stand of short pines. It took precious time, too much time, to cut two poles. I could have chewed through the saplings with my front teeth just as well as carving them down with a skinning knife. I'd needed a hand ax. At least Jeb had kept my knife's blade honed.

After I dumped the poles near Sahara, I unsaddled the sorrel, taking account of how very little equipment there was to work with. Using the upturned saddle and anything I could pillage from it, I set to building a drag. If I stayed busy, I wouldn't have to think.

I tossed the string cinch aside. While lashing the latigos of the upside down saddle to two poles, thoughts wormed their way into my head. The very act of surviving McKade's massacres was why he hunted me. I rubbed at the scarred skin of my neck. But he wasn't ready to kill me. Not yet. He was still in the mood to toy with his prey. That gave me time.

McKade loved a public demonstration of his power. And he always figured out how to avoid responsibility for his murders. He had planning yet to do where I was concerned. But I was planning too. It might cause the death of me, but I would get Sahara safe from McKade's evil clutches. Somehow.

I loaded Sahara on the drag. Her skin felt cold to the touch. I tapped at her cheeks.

"I'm tired," Sahara said. "I'm so tired."

"I know. But you have to stay awake."

The sorrel's reins slipped. I handed them back to her. "Hold on. Don't let go."

"I promise…" she answered in a whisper. Her eyelids fluttered, losing their battle to stay open.

"Sahara?"

The travois was heavy. I struggled to hold it up, only long enough to drag it a few steps.

"I promise," she whispered again. "I won't let go. Not unless my very life depends on it. Even then, I'll really try to hold on tight."

"That's right. Hold on tight." *Don't leave me. I beg you not to leave me Sahara.* "Stay with me."

My right shoulder and arm were useless. Straining sent shooting pains through me. It's no wonder tears trickled down my face. I sniffled. I wanted to give up. I wanted to sit on the cold ground and quit. Life was too hard. Too much struggle. Too much suffering. I was tired of fighting.

"Hold on tight," I heard her whisper.

I retrieved the discarded cinch and laid it over my good shoulder to diagonally cross my chest. After I notched the poles' ends, I hooked the string girth's large metal rings onto each.

When I leaned into the girth, it pulled forward. This time, the rig worked.

Every step took me nearer to the homestead. The thought of getting Sahara warm and safe in the hogan kept my feet stomping in that direction. I was tired. Pained. And I was seething.

I'm going to kill you, McKade. You've been a plague on my entire life.

My heart pounded. Every breath slammed my lungs like I had been gut punched. Every step was a battle. I sulked on anger to spur me forward.

That all-consuming fury drove my feet to plodding. Even in the dark. Even as the moonless night shrouded us in blackness and spooks howled their hunger.

I'm going to kill you, McKade.

The horse was the first to quit. As it balked to a standstill, the reins slid from Sahara. I didn't know whether he was done in, or if he recognized the fork in the path. One direction jogged on to the road leading to Molasses Pond. The other went toward my homestead. Town was closer.

I lowered the travois and trudged back for the stalled animal.

"Where are we?" Sahara's voice was weak, like the whisper of a frightened child.

"We can turn here for town."

"No. I'd rather die at home than live in Molasses Pond under Jack McKade's reign."

Home. She said home. "You're not going to die." I rubbed on the sorrel. He leaned into me.

"Austin? Would you bury me by your garden? I love to garden. I'm good at it. Rose was going to bring me cacti blooms in the spring."

"I'm not burying you. You're not going to die."

"But if I did. Please. By the garden."

"In town, I could get you help. Rose, maybe."

"No. They'll kill you." I thought I heard her hiccup a sob. "They'll keep me. Please don't take me to Molasses Pond."

I hauled on the sorrel. In his three-legged hop, he moved with me. I kept his reins in my hand and hoisted the travois, trudging homeward once again.

Of course they'll kill me if they've seen the wanted posters. I killed Jamie. Justice McKade's son. Justice is well respected and well liked. No doubt the civilized folk of Molasses Pond will come for me. They're too afraid to go after the real evil in Molasses Pond. They're too afraid of Jack McKade.

I stewed into the night, until the sorrel pulled back. If he quit completely, I'd have to leave him.

I'm sure his muscles were burning like mine. His lower leg had swelled to twice its normal size. Sweat sopped his neck. He was done in. Horses lived in the present. His here and now was forever. He couldn't pep himself up with flowery future promises. In exhaustion, his self-preservation was waning.

My own body ached in places I hadn't known it could ache. My arm was near to numb. I was losing this fight too. It was a battle of my mind now. A battle of will. And I had Sahara that I was responsible for. I had to see her safe before I could selfishly quit.

"C'mon," I encouraged him. "C'mon." He hopped, leaning farther onto his shaking haunches to lift his front end. He hopped.

Right, left, right, left, right, left. I kept hauling Sahara, scolding my feet to move forward.

But I was tired too. Too tired.

Riigghhtt, leeeeeft, riiiiiiggghhhtt—

The horse stopped, snapping the ends of the reins from my hand. "Darn it to hell." I collapsed to the ground in a defeated heap.

The sorrel barely remained upright. He swayed in a puddle of exhaustion. He leaned onto his nose for support.

Sweat soaked my buckskins. The cold air quickly chilled my stilled body. Tears welled behind my dry eyes. I choked on an intake of breath.

There was no time to wallow. I needed to get Sahara warm and safe. I needed to kill Jack McKade, ending his tyranny of terror.

I coaxed myself to stand then approached the horse for what might be our last moment together. I gathered his reins then stroked his slick neck, speaking in the low, soothing, guttural tones of the Navajo. His eyes watched me intently. His ears twitched. I should free him from his pain and spare him from the torment of predators.

I slid my hand to my sorrel's poll and gently slipped the bridle from behind his ears, careful not to let the heavy hardware bang his teeth. The long-shank bit fell to the hard-packed ground with a resounding clank.

I thought of my revolver. I thought of the shame it had been to make this animal suffer a long, agonizing walk just to come to the same conclusion I should have made at the outset. I should have shot him in Apache Pass.

I thought about the fact that his lameness was repairable with time and attention. Time. Time I didn't have to get him home to where he could lay up and where I could afford him the proper attention.

And I thought it would be nice to pretend that if I left him, he could now run free and live happily ever after, herding with one of the wild bands that roamed the territory. The trouble was, I knew the truth of it. The grain-fed animal wouldn't survive the night. He'd be taken down by that pack of coyotes circling us. They'd spill his intestines over the ground, causing a slow, terror-filled death.

The sorrel pressed his forehead to my chest. My breath caught in the back of my throat. *Love made decisions more difficult.*

I ran the cold tips of my fingers over the grips of my gun. If Sahara hadn't needed me…

If I hadn't been saddled with a bride I never asked for…

If I had never come to the ruthless frontier in search of Pa's paradise…

If I hadn't survived the massacres…

If I had never been born…

I flipped the loop off the hammer and eased my revolver free of its holster.

I stepped away from the sorry animal and cocked the hammer.

The sorrel watched my every move with questioning eyes. I wished he could run from me.

He gimped forward, reaching to nuzzle my leg.

I stepped back. Turned. And fired. The report of the gun echoed throughout the landscape. The kickback nearly jerked my fatigued left arm off.

There was a yelp in the dark.

"What?" Sahara asked in a voice as weak as an orphaned kitten. "What happened?"

"Coyote. It's been following us. I nicked it to give us all time." I flicked the cylinder open by rote, replacing the spent shell. "We need to get out of here."

"Your sorrel?"

"I'll come back for him." I raised the travois and towed. The horse attempted to follow at its own pace, but was too slow to keep up.

In the distance, coyotes barked and screamed and squelched and howled in epic proportions. The pack attacked its own wounded, as was their way.

I dragged Sahara toward the homestead with renewed strength of mind.

"Do you think Justice will forgive you?" Sahara asked.

"No." There was no way he would. How could he? I killed his son.

"Maybe you underestimate him."

I hadn't yet forgiven myself.

I saw the horror in their eyes. The townsfolk so easily believed I was a cold-blooded murderer, where moments before, they had looked to me to be their savior from Lightning Jack McKade. No. There was no way Justice had any forgiveness. Toward me, he was now likely to be deadlier than his brother.

At some point, I recognized the overhang's looming backdrop. It was a daunting black shape in the blackness of night. "We're home." My voice wavered with too much relief.

There was no reply.

I kicked at the door to the hogan. When it burst inward, the pup lunged at my legs, knocking me to my butt. I would have stayed there forever under warm, welcoming licks to my frozen skin. I didn't think I had the strength to pick myself up one more time. I hugged the pup to me and buried my face in her short, soft fur.

Don't think. Do.

Rose was right. My fight was in my head. Over-thinking and second-guessing continually got in my way. *Pull the gun. Pull the trigger. No thoughts. No hesitation.*

I hauled the travois directly to the fireplace. The fire caught quickly. Its flames devoured the kindling and chips, eagerly tasting the fat logs. There were blankets on the pallet. I wrenched them over to Sahara and swaddled her, travois and all.

TwoFeathers. I needed him now. Something must have happened to him. He would have known about the rockslide in Apache Pass. He would have heard the gunfire. TwoFeathers would have discovered it was me. He was always watching. I rubbed the hammered copper band around my wrist, swiping the pad of my thumb over the large turquoise eye. That's what he had meant. The band was his symbol that he watched over me. He had given one to Sahara too.

TwoFeathers had always been at my rescue.

But not this time.

And even as Sahara slept nearby, even with the fire crackling to life and illuminating the inside of the hogan with lively shadows, even with the pup nudging at my hand, I had never felt so alone.

Sahara's hand touched my leg. She smacked her dry lips, grimacing. "Tea. Can I have some tea?"

Tea?

"In your basket. There." She pointed at the wicker basket Rose had given me a month ago. It was full of labeled bottles and cloth-wrapped packets. There was a tall bottle of sorghum syrup. Smaller bottles of iodine and oil of clove. Packets of thyme and catnip. There was comfrey and rosemary and sage. And a bar of lilac soap.

"Catnip tea, please," she said in barely a whisper.

I shifted the bottles and wrapped packages, uncovering other packets and bottles. *Laudanum.* I knew what that was. A quarter-pint bottle of laudanum.

"Did you find it?"

"Have it here." There was a notebook. I dipped a mug in the pot of water that continuously hung in the fireplace. As the tea steeped, I flipped through the pages of the book looking for a certain dosage.

Sahara blew over the surface of the hot brew when I handed the cup to her. "Mm. Thank you."

While she sipped, I studied by the firelight.

"I'm glad you didn't go to Molasses Pond." She fussed with the blanket, smoothing the top and tucking the edge under her armpits. "You are not going to Molasses Pond? Right?"

What could I say? I didn't answer.

"Austin, promise me."

I reluctantly said, "Yup. Sure."

"Say it. Promise me."

It felt like I should cross my fingers behind my back. But that would be childish. And obvious. I crossed my toes instead. "I.

Won't. Go. To. Molasses. Pond." I hoped she'd forgive me the lie. It was for her I was going. And that was only a half-truth. I was going for me. I was going to kill Lightning Jack McKade. Because he needed to die and because I was the only one in the territory to get the job done.

What I didn't need was Sahara mixed up in the killing. I needed her to stay right here. I needed to know she was safe.

I freshened Sahara's tea with hot water, adding a splash of sorghum syrup. "This should taste better."

"Mm. Nice. Thank you."

I had also added six drops of laudanum.

She was out like a blown candle and had a smile across her lips.

What I needed now was to get gone. I had already hung around too long. The sun would be up soon. It was light enough to travel easily. I grabbed jerked venison and a short hunk of rope at the door. The copper band on my wrist caught my attention. I plucked it off, turned back to Sahara, and placed it on her wrist. "I love you, Sahara Miller." Loose hair had fallen across her sleeping face. I pushed it behind her ears then kissed her forehead.

She really was beautiful. And good and gentle and kind. I laid the loaded Dragoon on Sahara's belly and folded her hands over it.

The pup whined, snuggling into Sahara's hip. "Take care of her, girl." I tossed her a venison strip.

I didn't know why I was reluctant to leave. Something just felt wrong about it.

I gently closed the door, stuffed the painted feather in it, then scurried into the dark night.

When the threat of dawn seared pink streaks across the sky, I had finally arrived at Molasses Pond with the lame sorrel in tow. I draped the limp neck rope over the hitching post outside the bank. Someone was bound to find him come sunrise. Justice would find him.

The sorrel had meant a lot to me, but I had let him go once before. It had near to broken my heart. I lifted his head in my hands and pressed my forehead to his. His body relaxed. "You're safe now." With a last stroke along his neck, I left him again, fading into the dark alley.

Molasses Pond was still asleep. Main Street was empty. The boardwalks were barren. A few tent flaps were just now lazily lifted to greet the streaked dawn. A bell jingled over the mercantile's door, admitting that it was open for business. But the rest of the town couldn't be bothered as of yet.

Wanted posters with my likeness were nailed to every wooden facade. Rubbing blue fingers of my tied hand, I watched Main Street from the alley. It was quiet. Too quiet. But Molasses Pond was always too quiet too early.

I jumped onto the boardwalk and secreted into the mercantile, forgetting that the bell would betray me.

"I need some strong liniment, bandages, smelling salts, and more of the laudanum." I needed one of his boys to fetch Rose from the Watering Hole. But I'd gauge his reaction to the sight of me first. "Could you put that on my account?"

"No, Mr. Austin. You need to leave. You have no credit here." He began sweating profusely. His wire-rimmed glasses slid down the sheen on his narrow nose. If he hadn't been dusting and tidying, he would have escaped me through the back door.

I didn't say a thing. I glared at him.

"You had credit, yes. But you don't. Those fireworks you took used the rest of your money." He adjusted his bow tie which had already been perfectly straight, then rubbed a palm over the back of his neck.

I said nothing.

"If you'd like, I can fetch the tally sheet to show you. But I'll have no foul business in this establishment." Like a skittering bug on hot sand, he peddled backward for the false safety behind his counter.

The clerk winced as I reached just above my gun handle into a pocket. I slapped the .53-caliber copper ball that TwoFeathers had given me onto the counter's top. "Will this cover what I need?" I needed to get a message to Rose.

The door slammed open, jangling the bell. A maddened mob rushed inside. Not one of them was properly heeled, but one of them carried a rope, which made the mob dressed for a lynching party.

I weighed my options. *Flight or fight.* There were way too many of them.

The clerk made himself scarce.

The bell above the door complained again. Justice walked in. The days hadn't been kind to him. Stubble darkened his jaw. Brown bags drooped beneath his eyes like a hound dog's jowls. His shoulders rounded over his large, muscular physique. I thought his hair was more gray than black now. It was definitely unkempt, where it had been clean-cut and brushed flat previous. His small eyes were steely gray, from their usual vivid blue. They darted from one man to the next.

When his cold gaze landed on me, Justice looked much like his brother, Lightning Jack McKade.

CHAPTER SEVENTEEN

J ack McKade has everyone believing you killed my boy," Justice said. His eyes were red. He might have been crying. I couldn't imagine it. A grown man crying. "There's wanted posters substantiating Jack's claim." Justice's haunted look said he hadn't slept.

"It's true. I killed Jamie McKade." I didn't stand any taller over it. I did look him in the eyes though, without wavering.

"And that's all you've got to say?"

What else was there to say? I was called out. It was kill or be killed. If I had to do it all again, I wouldn't change a thing. I didn't know Jamie McKade. Even if I had, I wouldn't want to be dead in his place. He called me out. Being dead was his deal.

I was sorry Justice was heartsick. I'd never wanted to hurt a man like him. None of that changed anything.

Justice stared at me. The rabble behind him quieted to stillness.

I couldn't apologize for something I wasn't sorry for. And I wouldn't do Justice the disservice of lying about it. I did it. I killed his son.

A man coughed. Another sniffled. The waxed coils of the lariat rattled as they jostled in a fidgeting grip. Shuffling boots scuffed at the floor. Coats rasped against one another in the close confines. These were the upstanding businessmen of Molasses Pond. The boot maker, Sven, stood elbow to shoulder with the coffin builder, Edgar, and the banker—I didn't recall his name.

The government man from the land office was flanked by his counterpart from the assay office. The owner of the hotel rubbed against the sketchy man who ran the opium den. Both looked like they'd rather be elsewhere. The butcher, I'd sold deer and elk to in the past, blocked the doorway with the mule driver from the last freight wagons to have arrived in town before the snows covered the mountains.

They were all here—ready to hang me. It's a shame they wouldn't grow a spine between them to stand up to Jack McKade.

Justice faced the assembly. "Go home. There won't be any gallows dance today."

The gathered men mumbled.

"If anyone has the right to hold the boy accountable, it's me. Go home." Justice turned from them. He looked me in the eyes as he waited for the crowd of men to disband.

"Now hold on, Justice. We don't want his kind—"

Justice pivoted. "Really? Really. Then I suggest you haul yourselves down to the Watering Hole and start cleaning out this town from there." His crimson face was invaded by encroaching purple. "And who are you, Lester? Shall we peek into your past? Are you hiding anything you'd like a fresh start from? Are any of you? Most likely all of you are, being this far from nowhere." The boom of his roar could have shaken the walls down, if the escaping townsmen hadn't nearly destroyed them in their scramble to leave.

Men ripped kerchiefs from their necks to throw them on the boardwalk. Muddy feet trampled the scraps of their fickle solidarity.

Justice wrenched my buckskin smock in his fist and hauled me out of Percival's Mercantile and through the middle Main Street. I didn't resist. The tied sorrel snorted as we passed. He whirled on his sound foreleg, swinging his sweat-lathered hind end. Men lined the boardwalk in front of the hotel, across the street, refusing to align themselves with either of the McKades. The sun was climbing to its zenith. The days were too short this time of year.

Jack stepped from his saloon doors to watch Justice parade me past. Jack McKade was heeled. A huge hogleg crept along his thigh. It was an Army Colt. The original grips had been switched for what looked like carved, polished bone. His wide, black gun belt was studded with silver spots that might have taken an entire silver mine to fashion. And the bottom of his holster was tied down tight to his good leg.

At the end of the road, Justice halted abruptly. Behind me, a privy door creaked, then slammed. A cough echoed through the stillness. The rumbles of voices were a distant hum. My small world hesitated to even draw a breath.

"You didn't kill Jamie."

I thought I hadn't heard him correctly.

He plucked a derringer from behind the belt buckle at his generous midsection. Tracing its floral designs with the pad of his thumb, he said, "I had given this to my boy. Before he left."

I recognized the weapon. *But how—*

"You didn't kill Jamie, son. Jack McKade killed my boy when he wouldn't accept him for who he was and convinced him to be someone he wasn't." He gently slid the small gun into the palm of my bound hand. He closed my fingers over the ornate derringer before letting go.

It fit my grip perfectly.

"There's work to be done," Justice said with a nod of his head. He left, slopping back through Main Street.

I sidled off the road at the edge of town and waited. "We have to stop meeting like this," I said to Rose as she climbed through the brambles. I had been listening to her unsteady steps approach.

She looked around, keeping to the brush. "I can't stay. I can't go with you either. And don't bring Sahara into town."

That didn't leave me with a lot of options.

She swung a bulging pair of saddlebags at my gut. "I heard what happened at Apache Pass. Seth's version of what happened. I dug a .22 slug from his thigh and gave Jamie's derringer back to Justice. It wasn't Seth's to hold on to."

I closed the derringer in my tight fist until I felt the pain of squeezing it run all the way to my shoulder. Did Rose know I had the tiny gun?

"Nothing I could do about his hand." Rose was acting surly and standoffish, as if I had kicked her dog, but she didn't want to come right out and accuse me of it.

I set back on my heels and took her upset like a man.

"I can draw my own conclusions." In a knee-jerk reaction to her eyes landing on my ugly scar, she pulled her knitted shawl higher around her neck "What you need to settle Sahara's concussion is in there. Keep her warm and quiet. Lots of rest."

I had that covered.

Rose wiped at her nose with a white-gloved hand. "Tell her I'm thinking of her."

She headed back toward town on high heels. Her ankles rolled and wobbled. It was a wonder she hadn't broken one yet. I heard her sniffle. She stopped and doubled back. "I don't have a right to say it, but you've disappointed me, Austin."

That hurt. For all of the injuries I'd suffered of late, I think that one hurt the most.

"I can't help you in your intentions." She hesitated as if she were choosing her next words too carefully. "I cannot help you kill the father of my daughter. No matter how much he deserves to die."

Whoa. Back up the stagecoach.

"I couldn't mother Lily. That was the deal with Jack McKade. He would raise her to be a proper young lady. And I could watch her grow up as long as I did whatever he said. But she was never to know that she's the daughter of a whore." Rose drew a handkerchief from her sleeve to dab at her eyes. "Jack McKade always gets what he wants. No matter who he ruins. In fact, destroying folks is his pleasure."

Lily was her daughter?

"He wants you dead at this point. He wants your Sahara." She checked over her shoulder, peering down the road. "Austin, there's things you don't know that aren't mine to tell." Rose stared me in the eyes, pressing her lips into a strained, thin line. "You cannot kill Jack McKade," she finally said.

For the time it took, I watched Rose dodder into town, skirting the worst of the muddy slog. I watched her climb the step of the Watering Hole. I watched her. Hoping she would change her mind about me. Hoping she would turn, give me a wave or a smile.

"You're late," I snapped at TwoFeathers as if I'd expected him. "You missed the lynching party." He didn't understand the humor. He probably hadn't understood the words. It's not like he truly wanted to embrace the White's language.

TwoFeathers held up the painted feather I had jammed in the hogan's door. He held a rope to Charlie Horse in his other hand. My hat and coat were hanging on the saddle horn. He took the set of bags from my arm and tossed them over Charlie Horse's loins, tying them behind the saddle.

TwoFeathers wore a splint of split limbs and rawhide around one of his lower legs. He moved in a stiff gimp but showed no twinge of pain. His wrists were raw and bleeding. A swollen, purple cheek made his face look lopsided.

He stepped reluctantly, using Charlie Horse as a crutch. I winced for him as he hobbled on an obviously busted limb. The horse stood patiently. I took down my coat. He helped me into it.

My coat was dry. It warmed quickly. Familiar scents of wood fire and horses teased my nose. I had forgotten its comfort. I had forgotten its welcome, weighty embrace about my shoulders. I had forgotten the feelings of safety and security and courage that it lent me on cold days.

I had forgotten I could stand tall, be proud, and command my own destiny through sheer will, hard work, and seeing a job through to the end.

I had forgotten me.

I stuffed my hat on then pulled the brim low over my brows. TwoFeathers shoved the painted feather into its narrow band. I helped him mount Charlie Horse.

When TwoFeathers settled in the saddle, I led my horse from the wheel-rutted road onto a less conspicuous deer run. It was a long walk to the homestead. TwoFeathers fell asleep in the saddle to the horse's swaying.

I propped my collar around my neck. A storm was coming, but it wasn't on the winds.

I wouldn't ask for TwoFeathers's help. The Apaches were running and fighting and hiding from the US Cavalry. He had his own troubles. Besides, Jack McKade was all mine.

In the hogan, TwoFeathers stretched on the dirt floor, along the front of the fire. The pup wrapped herself in the crook of his powerful arm. His splinted leg extended past the stone fireplace. His breathing was low, long, and steady. I'd never seen TwoFeathers sleep so soundly.

The pup got up when I crouched to poke at the coals and throw a log onto the prancing flames. I let her climb halfway into my lap and was rewarded by a lick of her warm, wet tongue. I pressed my lips to the top of her head. She smelled faintly of Sahara's lilac soap. My eyes closed. My insides came alive. I thought about every little thing that was Sahara and worried about even more.

I set a stew to bubbling over the fire. The aroma that filled the hogan made my stomach grumble. "Try some of this." I served Sahara a bowlful. She glared at me. She hadn't said one word since I'd gotten home. I dished some stew to the pup then sat alone at the table to eat. When I finished, I kicked my feet up onto the bench and squirmed my butt around on the wooden chair, attempting to find a comfortable position I might sleep in. It was no use.

"You can sleep next to me," Sahara whispered loudly. She pulled back the covers to invite me under.

"I'm okay."

"Don't be silly." She let the blanket fall back across her hip. "There's plenty of room on the pallet for both of us."

It was an uncomfortable decision, filled with dread if I did and dread if I didn't.

I went over to her and lay down.

Rolling to face away from Sahara didn't prevent the heat of her body from consuming my mind.

She draped the edge of the blanket on me. Her arm pressed along my spine as she jostled to get comfortable. I was aware of her every breath. I swear I felt her opening and closing her eyelids in fighting off slumber.

"Can I touch it?"

I jolted. The exhale of her question wafted across my ear.

"Your scar? Can I touch it?"

I nodded.

"He absolutely adores you, you know."

"Who?" I didn't know anyone who adored me at the moment.

"TwoFeathers," Sahara replied as if I were being intentionally thick.

Oh, right. "I'm not his type." I needed to sleep. Tomorrow, I intended to call out Jack McKade. "If anything goes wrong… If I don't come back…"

"What are you talking about? Where are you going?" She shimmied to sitting upright. "Austin, what are you up to?"

"Take as much copper as you can. TwoFeathers will help you. I'll turn the cow and calf loose in the morning."

"Don't you dare turn Buttercup loose." Sahara hissed.

Buttercup?

"I'm going to make yogurt to sell in town. But I've thought to make cheese. And I've already made soap. Not that I think soap will be a big seller in Molasses Pond. But believe you me though, those people need some soap."

I broke into her litany. "Justice will come for you." He would. If I died, he'd come for Sahara. Hopefully, he'd do so before his brother did. "You can trust Justice. No one else. Do you hear? Don't go to Rose." I didn't turn toward her. I didn't want to see her face. I didn't want to read disappointment in *her* eyes.

"I'm not going anywhere and neither are you." Fury rolled from her like a bank of dense fog moving over the land. "Do you hear me, Austin? You will not leave me here alone again." I felt her turn away from me. As she scooted lower under the blanket, her bum bumped against mine. "I'm your bride. You ordered me."

And she knew I hadn't. But didn't we all want to be wanted? Didn't we all need to be needed?

"We *will* live happily ever after."

She was asleep in minutes. More like faking it.

I waited in the dark, unable to settle. Flickering light cast shadows on the log walls. Mesmerized, I took account of my aches and pains. The bumps and cuts from McKade's beating were healing well enough. The bruises had changed to pale green. Their edges were already yellowing.

My split lip had recovered completely. The swollen eyelid was back to its normal size. My nose would probably remain crooked, but I could breathe fine. My ribs were still tender, but I had bigger worries.

New, pink skin replaced the rope burns on my wrists. The salve from TwoFeathers had been a boon. Blisters on my palm had dried and filled in. And the cuts from climbing through the broken glass would scar, but made for a good story. Hopefully, I'd get to tell it one day. *All good.*

Lying to myself wasn't going to work. I was never so ill fit for a gunfight.

But I had to go. Not just for me. For her.

Sahara would never be safe around Molasses Pond with the likes of Jack McKade and his henchmen running the town. No one was safe from McKade's reach.

At some point, Sahara's breathing became deep and steady. I couldn't lay quiet any longer. If I did, I might never leave.

"I love you, Sahara Miller," I whispered.

In her sleep, Sahara had rolled to face me. She snuggled into me as if we were two halves of a whole. I felt her soft breath caress the back of my neck. Her curves pressed perfectly to mine. And I swear she sighed in contentment.

I eased myself flat then stared at her lax face. Sahara was a rare beauty. I wished I had realized that from the beginning. I wished I'd had time to tell her now how she'd wrapped herself so completely around my heart.

My eyes played connect-the-dots with the sprinkle of freckles over her nose. A tendril of hair fell across her closed lids. I brushed it back and pressed my lips to her sleeping forehead. It felt like I was saying good-bye forever.

Without waking anyone, I rolled up and secreted through the door.

A limb with a Y poked from the stack of uncut firewood. I took a minute to jerk the sturdy stick from the pile then chopped it to the length of a crutch for TwoFeathers. I should have done more for him. He was my friend. He was my brother. I propped the crutch against the log wall of the hogan.

The stiffness in my body loosened as I walked to the overhang. Immobilizing the injured shoulder kept it from complaining. But the arm was useless while tied to me. At least I'd only need to holster one gun. Losing half the lugged weight beneath my hip bones would feel freer.

I hadn't ever been parted from Pa's Smith and Wesson. I wasn't about to be now. I shifted the 1855 revolver to the left-handed holster, then emptied the cylinder of the newer gun. At the back of the overhang, I bundled it in rabbit pelts.

As predawn yawned across the sky, I saddled Charlie Horse and mounted.

TwoFeathers gimped in under the overhang on the crutch I had cut for him. His splinted leg was hidden beneath a skirt fashioned from the faded green dress Sahara had arrived in about a month ago. He scrutinized me in his unnerving way.

I squirmed in the saddle like a child caught poking a finger in a freshly baked pie.

I wasn't going to discuss it. My mind was made up.

"I'm going alone."

CHAPTER EIGHTEEN

Charlie Horse reached the edge of Molasses Pond and was reluctant to go any farther. I couldn't blame him. The center of town was a churned, muddy mess. He twitched his ears furiously before raising his head and stiffening to bolt.

"Quit," I grunted. I dropped the reins to his neck and flicked the hammer loop from my gun then slowly drew it out. Of course it was fully loaded. An unloaded gun was of no use. Still, I rotated the cylinder one click at a time.

Dawn was too early in the morning for Molasses Pond to be fully awake. I dismounted to walk Charlie Horse alongside Main Street, in an attempt to avoid the deepest slop. The street might have appeared deserted, but eyes watched my progress.

Tent flaps were closed in the squatters' area. Snoring emanated from more than several makeshift shelters. Campfires were long cold. My hide-covered feet sunk to the ankles in crud, leading me to briefly wonder if the men inside those squatters' hovels wallowed like piglets in the mud.

Half-constructed buildings and newer wooden facades promised that Molasses Pond was growing. But the abandoned wagons mired in muck, with lumber and barrels still in their beds, proved that the work had stalled.

Without shingles hanging, it was difficult to discern what goods or services were offered inside each tent establishment. A Chinaman tossed dirty water from a wash bucket into the street.

When he saw me, he scurried away. I heard his melodic muttering from beyond the alleyway.

The Watering Hole was open for business. That, or they had never closed the night before. Its swinging doors hung still. The full-length blockade door hadn't been shut, even against the cold. I didn't see any movement from within.

At the fountain, I filled my hand from the dribbling water to rinse my mouth. Charlie Horse sloshed the pooled water's surface for a long drink. The gray sky was fast changing to a vibrant pink. The sun would be over the rooftops shortly.

In front of Percival's Mercantile, I unsaddled Charlie Horse, tossing his rig onto the boardwalk. I eased the headstall over his ears and took a moment to say good-bye before turning him loose.

The shade was drawn over the mercantile door's glass. I climbed onto the board walkway. At the end, I jumped down to duck into the alley between the land and the assay offices. Across from the Watering Hole, I waited.

I jerked the skinning knife from the back of my belt and concentrated at scraping the calluses off my trigger finger. Then I trimmed my ragged nails short. A professional gunman didn't want anything between him and the cold steel of that trigger. It was an intimate relationship I never truly understood, until now. Cleanliness increased sensitivity, which increased control—speed and accuracy.

I rolled a cigarette and lit it up to affect calm, cool, collected manliness. To let whoever watched know exactly where they could find me, I blew a thin stream of smoke from my pursed lips.

When I stepped from the alley, I leaned on the hitch rail in front of the assay office to further survey the town of Molasses Pond. Main Street ran from south to north. The Watering Hole was on the east side. The rising sun would soon blind me to the details of the comings and goings at the saloon. That was a detriment.

I didn't smell any coffee brewing. Unmolested chickens were still silently roosting. Tent flaps remained tied closed. Even the light breeze was too lazy to bother jostling the tight ties.

As I studied the quiet town, Death came to mind. The fourth Horseman of the Apocalypse. Missionaries loved to tell their Bible stories. I remembered the Horsemen. I liked horses. *Behold, an ashen horse; and he who sat upon it had the name Death; and Hades was following with him. To kill with sword and with famine and with pestilence and by the wild beasts of the earth.*

Obviously, he didn't have a six-shooter.

I didn't have a pale horse.

It evened out.

Seth sauntered from the Watering Hole to take a leak off the side of the board walkway. Something McKade wouldn't have tolerated. So Jack McKade wasn't awake yet.

I cleared my throat.

Seth looked. His holster was a gaping hole yet to be filled with a new piece of iron. He fumbled at his open drawers and tripped over his spur rowels as he paddled backward. There was a clean white cloth wrapped around the palm of Seth's gun hand. Rose was taking good care of him. I didn't know if that fact niggled at my anger or my hurt worse.

I stood from leaning on the hitch rail, chucked the butt of my smoke to the mud, and smashed it as I walked forward. "I've got no quarrel with you, if you stop pursuing Sahara. It's McKade I'm here to see."

"McKade ain't had his coffee yet. And I do have quarrel with you." He continued toward the swinging doors. I noticed the potbelly stove's pipe on the roof coughed smoke. Someone else had awakened.

"I don't want to kill you," I said. Seth would be difficult to kill. He was fast with a gun. He was sly and given to slight-of-hand tricks. Seth also had a lot of practice at killing.

No one lives forever.

"You killed my brother." Yellow-brown spit sprayed from his lips. Drool seeped over the scraggly whiskers on his chin. "You killed Jeb. He was my brother."

"Jeb set up to draw on me." My long strides had me in the middle of Main Street before I finished chatting. "You pulled your leg iron to distract me. Seems it's lucky you're not dead too."

"He warn't no gunslinger like you. Jeb warn't handy with no gun."

Flight or fight. Kill or be killed. Choices. Always choices. I stood very, very still. "Jeb had made his choices."

I unbuttoned the top of my coat to open the collar. It exposed my scar. "You've made your choices too. But right now, you can choose to walk away from this. I'm here for McKade."

"If you want him, you'll have to go through me first."

"Don't be stupid. You're not heeled."

"Take my gun, Seth." A steel revolver poked through the swinging saloon doors. I couldn't see who encouraged him. It wasn't McKade's six-shooter. The revolver had stock wooden grips.

Seth grabbed hold of the weapon like it was a life preserver thrown to a drowning man. He spun the cylinder in checking the load.

When he dropped it into his holster, he had made his next choice.

Seth propped the gun loose. Then jammed it in. Propped it. Jammed it. Propped it.

"I haven't got the entire day for you to court her," I said.

He bent to tie the strings around his thigh. His eyes darted anxiously, taking in his situation. When they became keen on me, he struggled on a swallow. That was his telltale sign. He'd committed to the draw.

"Huh-uh." I interrupted. "Won't work." My palm itched. "I got you dead to rights." I flexed my fingers alongside my holster. "Let's make it a fair fight."

Seth spit the wad he'd churned on. "Fair. I can do that."

I doubted it.

He moved toward the step carefully while keeping a watchful eye on me. "You gonna let me set up, ain't cha?" He cautiously dipped a toe over the edge as if testing the water for a swim.

I reached to tip my hat, bobbing my head at him. It took my gun hand a long way from my six-shooter. I wanted him to know I wasn't worried. I wanted him to know I had this—calm and cool like. I was in no hurry.

Though, on another note, I was. I wanted this business over and done with. I didn't enjoy the killing, like some did.

He stomped into the mud. "This won't take Lightning Jack." The street ran deep with sludge. "It'll be my pleasure to kill you." Sucking sounds followed Seth's every step. He wasn't in any rush now. Regardless, the slurry wouldn't have allowed for haste.

The morning was cloudless. A bright sun peeked over the two-story roof of the Watering Hole, blinding me to the happenings at its door. I wouldn't put it past the hired men inside to take a shot at me. But maybe they'd stick to some bad-guy code about who gets to shoot whom, when. I hoped they'd at least wait for Seth to drop dead first. I stood a better chance without dividing my concentration.

The glint of steel from a Winchester repeating rifle caught my attention. But it came nosing through the cracked door at the assay office. McKade's men hadn't had time to circle around town. And I didn't think the government men would side with a notorious gunslinger.

The crackle of a cocking sidearm alerted me to a man in the alleyway between the two offices. Another man belly-crawled beneath the floorboards.

Opposing, there was a rifle on the roof of the saloon, behind its wooden facade. A green shade rolled up from the broken corner window. And the orange tip of a cigarette glowed over the swinging doors.

Guns surrounded me. I couldn't tell where that left me, except for the obvious—right smack in the middle of an impending battle.

I hadn't come here to start a war. Me and Jack McKade. That's all I'd wanted.

Seth's arm hung loose and relaxed as he faced me. Without a coat on, I could see he was thin from living on too much whiskey and not enough solid food. Dirty shirttails waggled in the slight breeze. His over-large Adam's apple protruded from the front of his scrawny chicken neck. His hat roosted too high to protect his sight from the glaring sun. He hadn't exactly been dressed for business when he came out of the saloon.

I honed in on him. I could see the excited rhythm of his fast breathing plump his chest up and down. I waited for his tell.

My senses heightened. My adrenaline surged. My muscles grew tense with both anticipation and restraint. I was itching to cock my gun on the draw. Desperate to hear that *click, click, click, click* of assurance that the moments following would come together in split seconds of deadly clarity, speed, and accuracy.

Seth swallowed.

His palm scratched leather, but I was already leveling my barrel from the hip. *Pull the gun. Pull the trigger. No hesitation.*

Blam. Blam. Two slugs slammed into him at the same second he turned his gun on me.

His eyes went as wide as saucer plates. His mouth opened in an O. His look of horror said that he didn't believe I'd beaten him on the draw.

Seth flew backward to splash into the cold, muddy muck at the edge of the Watering Hole's boardwalk.

Guns began to blaze from every direction.

Molasses Pond was now at war.

My feet stuck in the deep mud. I couldn't move. Standing too long had cemented them in place. I couldn't run. I couldn't even walk. It was useless to duck. A shot pinged beside me, spitting a filthy, wet spray.

That everyone else had better cover didn't deter me. I crouched and took aim. The man on the roof rolled down, flopping into the alleyway between the saloon and the bathhouse. A woman screeched. Shutters on the bathhouse facade slammed closed.

There was no alternative, if I wanted Jack McKade, I would have to fight my way to him. I fell to my rump and pried my feet loose. Once freed, I skittered over the top of the slop too fast to possibly sink. For a second, I thought I'd make it into the Watering Hole. But bullets rained down around me, splashing fountains of muck into the air. I tumbled, slamming my injured shoulder against the step.

It took me a minute to remember how to breathe. Pain struck through my body like lightning. I heaved. My gut turned inside out, attempting to climb past my tonsils.

A shotgun blasted from within the saloon. Pellets peppered the swinging doors, harassing them to motion. *McKade.*

A chill breeze picked up. The gunfire died down.

Trampling boot falls scattered from the Watering Hole like rats abandoning a sinking ship. A single shot knocked a man into the mud beside me. Too close for comfort. I aimed my revolver at him. But an open wound in his throat gurgled blood in reply. He was already dead.

I scrambled up the step then squatted against the wall, just to the side of the swinging doors.

"Austin. Hey, Austin." McKade rumbled. "You out there? Come on in. I won't shoot you, son."

I couldn't see into the darkness.

McKade lit a long-burning match on purpose and held it to a fat cigar. He clunked the sawed-off scattergun onto the top of his brass-edged bar. I could see by the glow of his cigar's tip that he had moved away from his shotgun.

He was heeled. I knew he was heeled. But I took his forfeiting his favorite weapon as a relatively safe invitation. At least he'd let me in the front door.

Slowly, I shoved one of the swinging doors open. I hung onto it while my eyes adjusted.

McKade flicked a shade up at the front of the saloon. It sprung so hard that it flapped as it rolled, slapping the window frame repeatedly before settling down. With the opening of the next shade, bright light flooded the room.

In the midst of it stood Lightning Jack McKade, as bold as a weasel in a henhouse.

I walked, tall and straight, into his lair. My gun was aimed at his gluttonous gut. The door swung loose from my grip, waggling to a stop behind me.

He laughed, puffing his cigar to glowing. McKade took the smoke from his thick lips in a lazy fashion. He was mixed in with the solid, round tables and scattered chairs. "You going to kill a man just like that?"

I thought about it. It seemed like a good idea. "You killed my father," I said.

Jack McKade chuckled. "I am your father."

"Lie." I shouted, cocking the hammer on my Smith and Wesson.

"I knew your ma, shall we say." He held his hands in the air. "Fancied her. Even courted her." Ash fell from the stump of the cigar protruding from his fat fingers. Smoke rose from it in a dense cloud. "Put your gun away, son." He sneered the word *son* like he knew it wasn't true. "Aren't you man enough to draw in a fair fight?"

I was man enough. I was more man than him. Goaded. I thumped my six-shooter into its holster. I moved my hand from its grips, but not before propping it loose.

"She ran from me before we could marry. Bet she never told you that." He stuck the cigar beneath his full mustache and puffed. "Nah, you were too little when you last saw her. How could she have told you anything?" His lips wrapped around that plump cigar and his mouth filled with smoke.

"But you've seen me before. You know you've seen me before. When you were still clinging to your ma's apron back East, I came around, checking on your ma. Before the whole wagon train heading west crap. Before the Austin fellow took her away from me."

McKade lowered his hands.

I flexed my fingers in the ready, moving them closer to snatching my revolver.

"Whoa now. Easy, son."

"I'm not your son."

"Yeah, maybe not my son, but I am your father." He seemed too relaxed. He seemed too in command of this situation. McKade continued. "It was a couple of years later when she took up with that Austin fellow. He married her. Sired two kits on her."

"There were three of us." My eyes followed his every move. Watched his slight shifts. Keened on his gun hand. Surely, he had an ace up his sleeve.

"You were born before that Austin fellow had come along. You were considerably older than his two daughters. And you didn't look anything like them. Did you?" He took another drag on his smoke and waved it in the air with the pompous overconfidence of someone who thought they'd always had all of the answers. "You, with your nest of wavy black hair."

Hair meant nothing. I didn't look like Jack McKade. He was thick and ugly.

"I kept a watch on her. When they packed a Conestoga and headed west, I followed just so I could kill him and take her back." He shoved chairs out of the way and edged toward the bar. "Pity," he spat, like it hurt him to say it, "that Austin fellow killed your ma, just so I couldn't have her." At the end of the bar, McKade plucked a bottle and ripped the cork out. He proffered the brew toward me. "I thought my liquored injuns killed you. No one among the wagons survived they'd said." He poured himself a healthy drink and tossed it back.

"Your ma was wearing a blue dress covered in tiny flowers. She was huddled in the boot of that wagon with her two little girls."

He was there. I'd already figured out he was there. Him admitting it angered me more, if that were even possible. But it proved nothing about my parentage.

"I had thought there was something familiar about you when you prowled through the bar at times. A kindred killer, I assumed. I only recognized your face when I saw the sketch on that wanted poster for Jamie's killing. You look so much like me when I was your age. You got the McKades' dark hair, but you're built slight like Jamie and Lily."

I remembered Jamie. I knew Lily. We did have the same slender build.

"And you were under my nose all this time." He poured himself another generous swig.

"I don't believe you."

"Yes. You do. I can see it in your blue eyes. Same eyes as your half-sister and your cousin."

"No."

"You're a McKade. I thought to lure you into the family business. But you barely came around town." The neck of the near-empty bottle chinked against the lip of the stout glass. "And you were too set in your ways. Too quiet. Too *good.*" He sneered the word good like it had a bad taste. "When I realized you couldn't be turned, you had to be killed." He raised his glass in a salute. "No whelp of mine is going to defy me." McKade swirled the whiskey in his glass.

"Your bride? She's a fringe benefit I'll profit from. The town? Serves me. Lily?" He saluted with his drink again before belting it down. Sucking on the burn of it, he smacked his lips. "Ah, Lily is what I've made of her. She's my prodigy. She will be greater than me, with her extraordinary ability to manipulate and destroy without a gun. She uses whispers as weapons.

"You, my *boy,* are like me in bullying with that six-shooter."

"Don't flatter yourself. I'll never be anything like you." My palm itched. It was sticky with sweat though the air was cold.

"I've realized that." He gave a slight nod with his head. "You haven't got the steel in your spine." He roared with laughter, like thunder from an angry sky. "You haven't got the lead." McKade moved from the bar with intent.

My breath held. *That* was my tell.

"You can't kill your own father. Your flesh and blood."

I yanked my revolver.

CHAPTER NINETEEN

*O*of. Seth slammed me from behind. I went down. *I thought he was dead.*

My hat tumbled from my head. The gun flew from my hand. Grit coated my tongue as I hit the floor. I tried to crawl from beneath Seth's pinning weight.

Foul breath hissed from his mouth. His limp body gurgled then farted.

I clawed the floorboards to pull myself free.

Not forgetting Jack McKade, I whipped my head around in search of his whereabouts. I couldn't see him. And I couldn't escape the crushing weight of Seth's dead body. I stretched for my revolver.

A black boot landed on top of the gun. *McKade.*

His meaty paw gripped my coat's collar, hauling me from beneath Seth's lifeless body. Seth was really dead this time. A dry, gray haze glazed over his open eyes. I shivered.

"Make Austin tell me where the copper is before you kill him," Lily said. She whisked past her father, filling a carpetbag with money and deeds from the cash register. Her hair was perfectly coiffed under a fashionable hat. Her white gloves flashed as she shifted papers into a cloth bag.

The clip, clip, clip of Rose's footsteps echoed through the room. "Jack McKade. Lily. What are you doing?"

"Mind your own business." McKade growled low in his throat. He tossed me like I was no more than a handful of empty clothes.

"Stop it at once." Rose wrestled the high heels from her feet to throw them at McKade. They bounced off his massive shoulders. He turned toward her. She fled through the swinging doors.

Gunfire continued outside. The battle was blazing again. I didn't hear any screaming so I assumed Rose hadn't been shot on her hasty exit.

The air hung rank inside the Watering Hole. Fetid body odor, overripe whiskey, and stale cigar smoke hovered like a petulant fog. Not to mention the dead Seth added a whole new tang to the rotted atmosphere.

I pushed myself up from the rough-hewn floorboards then scratched my way to standing. Blood rushed too fast to my brain. Its pounding filled my ears until I heard nothing else. My knees weakened. My head grew woozy. Pain flooded my body but I stood straight and tall.

McKade backhanded me. I spun, doubling over the bar. Breathing became difficult.

"Where's the copper strike?" Lily demanded through clenched teeth.

I coughed. Bloody spittle drooled from my lips. I felt its warmth on my chin. I tasted its metallic tang as I forced a swallow.

Lily clawed my head. Her nails abraded my scalp. "Where's the copper?" Her fingers yanked my hair. "Useless. Kill him," she grunted in exasperation, cramming my swelling face to the bar.

Run, Sahara. Run. I can't protect you. Run.

I love you. I should have told you over and over.

Jack McKade wrenched me to look at him. "Any last words?" He shook me when I kept silent.

"I might trade your life if you had a copper strike like Lily believes."

I mumbled under my breath.

Jack shook me like I was an empty flour sack. "What's that? What are you saying?"

I quoted his words back to him. "'None of them are worth anything unless they make a strike. Then, they're only worth killing.'" I glared at McKade through swollen lids. "You won't trade my life for copper. You like the killing too much."

"True enough," he replied.

Bang. I squeezed the trigger on the derringer secreted in my right palm.

Lily screamed.

Lightning Jack McKade grabbed his gut. Blood oozed from between his fingers.

Crack. Glass smashed. The shards rained down around my ears. My last thoughts were regrets. *Sahara.*

The Watering Hole went dark.

The next thing I knew, my body bounced and flopped. I couldn't get up. Couldn't open my eyes. The bright sun glared through my closed lids. Sharp pain jolted my shoulder. I heard the snort of a horse and its jingling harness. Hooves slapped in a constant rhythm. A woman's shrill. A man's rumbling reply.

I gave in to oblivion.

The aroma of fresh coffee. The crackle of a warm fire. The firm pallet beneath me. A scratchy woven wool blanket over me. *Home.* I was home.

I didn't know if it was real. I didn't try to open my eyes. Opening them might dissolve the illusion. Then what? Where would I be? What would I be? I listened to the voices around me.

Sahara.

Rose?

I startled at the thunderous tone not a breath away from me. *McKade.*

Scrambling, I attempted to lurch from the bed. Screams of pain ripped through me. My body was sluggish and weak in response. My mind was fuzzy. I couldn't open my eyes even though I had desperately tried to.

"Settle. Settle." McKade's forced monotone had an edge of alarm. Meaty hands pressed me down. "He's awake."

"Austin?"

Sahara? I didn't dare utter it out loud. I stopped struggling against McKade's hold.

"We're going to take the bandage off your head," Sahara said. "Sit still if you can." I felt Sahara's small hand on my cheek. It was warm and smelled of lilac soap. I knew it was her. I pressed into her touch. "Okay, here we go," she said.

I nodded. At least, I think I nodded.

In seconds, the wraps slackened. Warm air caressed my face. My hair pulled. Pain stabbed. The fabric of Rose's flouncy sleeve brushed my nose before she jerked the bandage away.

Even the dim light inside the closed, dark hogan stabbed at my eyes. I winced.

"Go slow. Let your eyes adjust." The stiff pallet shifted as Rose got up.

Sahara filled the vacant space. She pressed close. I ached to wrap my arms around her. *Sahara. I thought I'd never see you again.* When I saw her through the slits of my eyelids, my heart leaped like a feral cat. Tears burned their way to leaking from the corners of my puffy lids. Words caught in my throat. I thought to never see her again.

Her gentle embrace gingerly wrapped around my shoulders. "Welcome back," she said. Her warm breath caressed my ear. She pressed her moist lips to my lobe.

"I missed you," I croaked. I hauled her tightly to me with one arm and clutched the fabric in the middle of her back as if I'd never let go. I never wanted to let go again.

"Jack McKade? Is he—"

Sahara moved out of my grasp. "You shot Jack McKade." She was animated and excited and disgusted. I couldn't exactly tell which she favored most.

Justice cleared his throat. "Well…first, you shot Seth, in the middle of Main Street. *That* ignited a town-wide war." He fidgeted.

I noticed Justice wore a sidearm. The gun was plain. The steel was dull. An over-large bucket holster swallowed it. The make and model were difficult to discern. It looked cumbersome and slow. I wondered if he'd ever actually shot the revolver. He didn't seem the type. But life had a way of forcing folks into living something they're not.

"I was almost too late," Justice said. "I don't know how Rose found me in the fray without getting killed. She commandeered a team and wagon and bolted along the back side of town, screaming and hollering my name. I'd never seen the like of it." He looked at Rose with admiration. "If we'd arrived even minutes later, you might have bled to death before we got to you. Molasses Pond isn't safe, at the moment, if you can't use a firearm." He patted the leather engulfing his ancient weapon. "We carted you away." His eyes turned to Rose. "Let's get you up," Justice said, looking back at me for anything he could be helpful with.

He hauled my weight into the air with little effort. Justice held me steady as I wobbled on my feet. "The folks in town tore down the posters Jack put up. The sketch on that wanted poster? I recognized your likeness to a pair of younger boys from years gone by. Myself and Jack. That's when I knew who you were."

I hooked my uninjured arm around his burly neck and kept the wincing to myself as we lurched toward the bench seat.

"Austin. You're a McKade."

Sahara gasped. Her hands slapped her open mouth. I would have preferred the irritating jumping, hand-clappy thing to the horror on her face.

I dumped onto the bench seat at the table.

Justice was reluctant to let go of me.

TwoFeathers sat in the chair with his leg propped. He was silent. *Overwhelmed? Or wondering if I'll turn into his enemy?*

"Os-ten." He had a crumpled poster in his fist. I reached across and coaxed it from him, smoothing it out on the table. *WANTED.*

I traced the drawing of wavy black hair falling to my shoulders from beneath a wide-brimmed, black hat. My eyes were drawn small and piggish and mean, like Lightning Jack McKade's. *That wasn't me.* My lips were thin, like a severe knife slash. *It wasn't me.* The poster gave no name, just a likeness to go by. *It wasn't me.* The charges listed were for murder and rape and horse thieving. *And all of that wasn't my doing.*

Rose ran her hand over my messy head of hair, inspecting the stitches. "I knew your ma." She slid onto the bench, next to me. Her thigh pressed against mine. Her warmth radiated up my side. Rose leaned into me as if she was a favored aunt sharing confidences. "For a short time, your ma was married in all ways but legal, to Jack McKade. She left him when she found out that I was also pregnant with his child. And further along than her." Rose paused, as if gauging my blank reaction.

"Lily is your half-sister," she said. "There could be others. I wasn't special. Not like your ma. Jack McKade was smitten with your ma."

Not smitten enough. "Sounds like he had a funny way of showing it." I clenched my jaw. It kept me from saying things I might regret.

Sahara dropped a plate of stew in front of me, from behind my bound shoulder. I couldn't tell what she was thinking, or how she was feeling. I stabbed the point of my knife at the chunks of venison and potatoes hiding in the broth.

"No doubt, your pa killed your ma that day to protect her from the cruelty of Jack McKade." Rose placed her hand around my white-knuckled fist gripping the knife. "He would have wanted to protect you too."

I growled through gritted teeth, "I didn't need his brand of protection."

"No. You didn't. But eventually, we all need someone." She got up and left me alone.

My belted six-guns banged onto the tabletop.

I shuddered at the noise.

"You're a hero," Sahara flatly said.

And I still hadn't gotten the measure of her.

"You did good," Justice added. "I couldn't be prouder of you if you were my own son."

What I did was for selfish reasons. What I did wasn't for the greater good. I was no hero. I killed Seth. I hoped I killed Jack McKade. Killing made me a killer. Not a hero.

"I'm a gunslinger."

There was silence. A log on the fire burst, sending a shower of crackling sparks into the still air.

I brushed my fingertips over the twin revolvers, brooding. *Say something, Sahara.*

On the vacant pallet, the pup paddled her legs in slumber.

TwoFeathers sucked the rim of his cup then shifted his braced leg.

Rose got up to plunk more stew plates onto the table.

Justice finally broke the deathly quiet. "This town's not ready for another gun-slinging McKade to be sure." He shook his head, lost in the moment. "This town's not ready for a lot of things. It's not ready for you, Austin."

Rose slopped more stew onto already full plates.

Justice continued. "Let's just say Jack McKade pushed you too hard. Everyone knows he's a bully. You were only defending yourself." He touched the side of his nose with his index finger. "The details will be our secret."

Sahara and Rose nodded in agreement. TwoFeathers bobbed his head.

And I didn't know which details made for *our* secret. The gun-slinging? Being a McKade?

I had so many secrets.

Peering across the table at TwoFeathers reminded me of being raised by the Navajo and siding with the Apaches against the Whites. That was a secret.

When I looked at Sahara and Rose standing as two womanly pillars, it was difficult to forget my female body. It had never matched my boy's brain. It had never matched me. That was a secret.

I had come to the Arizona Territory in search of my White pa's dream of homesteading in paradise. I had come to grow into an upstanding man. I wanted to be a good man. Then I found the lode of copper. And I knew the precious metal would nurture fevers of greed, envy, and hate around me. *Absolute wealth corrupts absolutely.* The copper strike was a secret.

I felt the weight of my secrets sucking me down. My mind churned. My stomach growled in discontent. I heedlessly played with a stabbed potato.

Sahara took my silence for indecision. "You're going to strap on those guns. And you're going to live who you are." She set her jaw forward, pursed her lips outward, and squinted.

She had tried that face on me before. I couldn't help my grin.

"I love you, Austin, late of Molasses Pond, Arizona Territory. The rest of it? We'll figure out together. All of us."

CHAPTER TWENTY

July 4, 1865, Molasses Pond, Arizona Territory

Seven months had seen a lot of changes in Molasses Pond.

We set out early from the hogan, riding toward the butte before the summer sun had any time to blister the dry landscape. The blue dog, Kadey, darted after rodents. My sorrel was a ball of restrained enthusiasm beneath me. Sahara chattered away atop a logy mare from town. The stocky mare continually pinned her ears at my high-stepping sorrel.

I grinned. Two fiery redheads. And the two that attempted to rein them in. Yup, that wasn't ever going to happen.

TwoFeathers emerged from the rocks, dragging a cayuse behind him. The animal wore a woven blanket slung with packs and pouches. Tied into its scraggly mane were beads of copper and turquoise. Feathers flapped beneath its chin from the single loop of rope through its mouth.

Across the dried flood plain, five mares, three foals, and Charlie Horse, my Appaloosa stallion, pecked at scrub among the strewn boulders near the base of the butte.

Charlie Horse raised his head. His nostrils flared, scenting the air. He snorted, pawing against the hard ground.

A periphery band of branded strays and yearlings moved farther away from the mares. A wobbly foal took too many steps in their direction. She was a fuzzy-coated bay filly with three white stockings and a wide blaze running between her large, round eyes. Charlie Horse laid his ears flat, shoving his nose toward the ground. The mare collected her foal, banding closer to the other mares.

Charlie Horse thrust his head high and bugled. He had decided we were too close. The lead mare sprang into motion, choosing a path that ascended the treacherous butte.

Charlie Horse gently nipped at a lagging dam as she carefully gathered her foal. The tiny, spotty-blanketed colt was spraddle-legged and knobbly-kneed. He floundered for balance under his dam's urging muzzle. I was content to watch them go.

In town, we met Rose and Justice on the boardwalk outside the Watering Hole.

Justice had received a letter from Lily. She wrote to say she'd be starting at a finishing school in Boston next term. She sent no words about her father, Jack McKade.

Sahara headed off to collect a slab of pork from the butcher. I could already see she had designs on raising pigs. And she wanted chickens for the eggs. I was hoping she'd raise biscuits. I liked biscuits.

It was a quiet morning. The town woke early these days. But today was a lazy holiday. Celebrations would start at noon. The new pastor was to read a sermon under the high-flying flag at the restored Spanish-Mexican fountain in the middle of town. Fiddle players were warming up for their rousing rendition of the "Star Spangled Banner." A man with a banjo led a parade of unlikely musicians with washboards and jugs and pails toward the fountain.

The Watering Hole was closed until midafternoon. Rose, it's new proprietor, took up residence in a rocker under the newly added covered porch. Justice dragged chairs out to watch the festivities.

"I heard there's going to be a horse race." I leaned against a post and contemplated the sorrel. The bowed tendon had thickened his lower leg, but he was none the worse for it.

"They're going to start off by McKade's Livery." Justice had always wanted his name over the barn doors. With his paying in good copper ore for the reconstruction of the establishment, folks got over their distaste of the name. "You thinking on running?" Justice asked. "You've got those new, blue boots on. You might want to show them off."

"I'd put my money on you," Rose said.

"I don't think it'd be fair. We all know the sorrel is the fastest horse in these parts." I polished the copper star pinned to the chest pocket of my old cotton shirt. Molasses Ponders had voted me sheriff in their fight to grow up.

"The town should be called Sorghum Pond." Sahara held up a bottle of the sweet syrup as she stepped onto the boardwalk. Her eyes sparkled and danced. Her walk jounced with enthusiasm. She wore a pale green summer shirt tucked into fine, doeskin riding breeches. Her curves had filled out in all the right places. I would never get enough of looking at her.

"Then again, there's no pond either," she said. "Sorghum Dry?"

TwoFeathers looped the rope of his cayuse to the hitch rail.

"Sounds like a promising whiskey," Rose said.

"Now that you mention it…" Sahara fluttered her free hand in the air. "Later. That can wait. I'm making us a celebration feast. I have news." She winked at TwoFeathers in a conspiratorial way.

I swear he smiled back at her.

"Er, um, Sahara?" I cleared my throat, shucked my hat, and smoothed my hair. Out of habit, I tried to pull on the silk neckerchief I no longer wore in hiding my scar.

"I don't know how to be a good husband. I'm still learning to be a good man." I dropped my hat to the board walkway and wiped my sweating palms down my holsters. I took her hands in mine. "But if you'll have me, I'd like to try to be your man. Er, your husband."

"Oh, Austin, are you proposing marriage?" she asked, exasperated.

I stood stiff like a deer that heard a crackle of twigs from the underbrush. "I hoped—"

"I think we're far too young for that. Times are changing. Folks just don't run off and get married at our age anymore." She placed the flat of her hand over my heart. "When I marry you, I want it to be for love. Not for want of a better situation." Sahara slipped her arms around my waist. "And I do love you Austin. But I need to find my own worth first."

What was she saying?

"I put a claim on the land along the Gila River next to yours. One hundred and sixty acres, to be specific. All I need to do now is stay on that claim for five consecutive years in order to gain its title. Then the sprig of land will be all ours." She puckered to kiss my cheek.

She said "ours." I turned my head quick. Our lips met.

I wrapped my arms around her and held on tight. I thought she'd pull away. But her mouth opened for our tongues to touch. We tasted of each other. And I knew if we lingered much longer our hunger would become insatiable.

"Eh-hmm," Rose interrupted.

My face heated immediately. I'm sure my cheeks were colored to crimson. Sweat trickled over my temples. I swiped my forehead with my arm and fidgeted my booted feet.

I'd wait for Sahara. I was in love with Sahara Miller. This was only the beginning of the rest of our lives.

Folks began strolling through Main Street in a pretty parade of colorful parasols and starched Sunday-go-to-meetin' shirts. TwoFeathers, with his two-colored face, sat on the walkway to watch the procession. He handed my hat back to me. Justice stuffed a pipe.

Sahara excused herself to prepare a feast. She had been cooking up many things of late.

Rose stood and hugged onto my arm. "You're a good man, Austin. Never change who you are."

She hadn't painted her face lately. I thought she was all the more lovely. Her cheeks were soft and rosy from the sun. Little wrinkles spread from the corners of her bright eyes as she smiled.

And she was quick to smile these days. She was beautiful. And fierce.

I thought perhaps my ma would have liked her had circumstances been different. I thought of my ma and pa and baby sisters. I thought of the Navajo who raised me, and the motley crew that befriended me. I was one lucky man.

Rose laid her cheek on my shoulder. "McKade won't rest until he kills you or controls you. He's out there. Somewhere. Licking his wounds. He'll be back."

About the Author

When not writing, R Kent is cowboyin'. Specifically, R Kent clinics equine behavior and language, raises horses, tends cattle, is proficient with a six-shooter, is handy with a rope, and can seriously crack a bullwhip. That's a ripe background for a mud-on-the-spurs and blood-in-the-dust Western.

Books Available from Bold Strokes Books

Femme Tales by Anne Shade. Six women find themselves in their own real-life fairy tales when true love finds them in the most unexpected ways. (978-1-63555-657-5)

Jellicle Girl by Stevie Mikayne. One dark summer night, Beth and Jackie go out to the canoe dock. Two years later, Beth is still carrying the weight of what happened to Jackie. (978-1-63555-691-9)

Le Berceau by Julius Eks. If only Ben could tear his heart in two, then he wouldn't have to choose between the love of his life and the most beautiful boy he has ever seen. (978-1-63555-688-9)

My Date with a Wendigo by Genevieve McCluer. Elizabeth Rosseau finds her long lost love and the secret community of fiends she's now a part of. (978-1-63555-679-7)

On the Run by Charlotte Greene. Even when they're cute blondes, it's stupid to pick up hitchhikers, especially when they've just broken out of prison, but doing so is about to change Gwen's life forever. (978-1-63555-682-7)

Perfect Timing by Dena Blake. The choice between love and family has never been so difficult, and Lynn's and Maggie's different visions of the future may end their romance before it's begun. (978-1-63555-466-3)

The Mail Order Bride by R Kent. When a mail order bride is thrust on Austin, he must choose between the bride he never wanted or the dream he lives for. (978-1-63555-678-0)

Through Love's Eyes by C.A. Popovich. When fate reunites Brittany Yardin and Amy Jansons, can they move beyond the pain of their past to find love? (978-1-63555-629-2)

To the Moon and Back by Melissa Brayden. Film actress Carly Daniel thinks that stage work is boring and unexciting, but when she accepts a lead role in a new play, stage manager Lauren Prescott tests both her heart and her ability to share the limelight. (978-1-63555-618-6)

Tokyo Love by Diana Jean. When Kathleen Schmitt is given the opportunity to be on the cutting edge of AI technology, she never thought a failed robotic love companion would bring her closer to her neighbor, Yuriko Velucci, and finding love in unexpected places. (978-1-63555-681-0)

Brooklyn Summer by Maggie Cummings. When opposites attract, can a summer of passion and adventure lead to a lifetime of love? (978-1-63555-578-3)

City Kitty and Country Mouse by Alyssa Linn Palmer. Pulled in two different directions, can a city kitty and country mouse fall in love and make it work? (978-1-63555-553-0)

Elimination by Jackie D. When a dangerous homegrown terrorist seeks refuge with the Russian mafia, the team will be put to the ultimate test. (978-1-63555-570-7)

In the Shadow of Darkness by Nicole Stiling. Angeline Vallencourt is a reluctant vampire who must decide what she wants more—obscurity, revenge, or the woman who makes her feel alive. (978-1-63555-624-7)

On Second Thought by C. Spencer. Madisen is falling hard for Rae. Even single life and co-parenting are beginning to click. At least, that is, until her ex-wife begins to have second thoughts. (978-1-63555-415-1)

Out of Practice by Carsen Taite. When attorney Abby Keane discovers the wedding blogger tormenting her client is the woman she had a passionate, anonymous vacation fling with, sparks and subpoenas fly. Legal Affairs: one law firm, three best friends, three chances to fall in love. (978-1-63555-359-8)

Providence by Leigh Hays. With every click of the shutter, photographer Rebekiah Kearns finds it harder and harder to keep Lindsey Blackwell in focus without getting too close. (978-1-63555-620-9)

Taking a Shot at Love by KC Richardson. When academic and athletic worlds collide, will English professor Celeste Bouchard and basketball coach Lisa Tobias ignore their attraction to achieve their professional goals? (978-1-63555-549-3)

Flight to the Horizon by Julie Tizard. Airline captain Kerri Sullivan and flight attendant Janine Case struggle to survive an emergency water landing and overcome dark secrets to give love a chance to fly. (978-1-63555-331-4)

In Helen's Hands by Nanisi Barrett D'Arnuk. As her mistress, Helen pushes Mickey to her sensual limits, delivering the pleasure only a BDSM lifestyle can provide her. (978-1-63555-639-1)

Jamis Bachman, Ghost Hunter by Jen Jensen. In Sage Creek, Utah, a poltergeist stirs to life and past secrets emerge. (978-1-63555-605-6)

Moon Shadow by Suzie Clarke. Add betrayal, season with survival, then serve revenge smokin' hot with a sharp knife. (978-1-63555-584-4)

Spellbound by Jean Copeland and Jackie D. When the supernatural worlds of good and evil face off, love might be what saves them all. (978-1-63555-564-6)

Temptation by Kris Bryant. Can experienced nanny Cassie Miller deny her growing attraction and keep her relationship with her boss professional? Or will they sidestep propriety and give in to temptation? (978-1-63555-508-0)

The Inheritance by Ali Vali. Family ties bring Tucker Delacroix and Willow Vernon together, but they could also tear them, and any chance they have at love, apart. (978-1-63555-303-1)

Thief of the Heart by MJ Williamz. Kit Hanson makes a living seducing rich women in casinos and relieving them of the expensive jewelry most won't even miss. But her streak ends when she meets beautiful FBI agent Savannah Brown. (978-1-63555-572-1)

Date Night by Raven Sky. Quinn and Riley are celebrating their one-year anniversary. Such an important milestone is bound to result in some extraordinary sexual adventures, but precisely how extraordinary is up to you, dear reader. (978-1-63555-655-1)

Face Off by PJ Trebelhorn. Hockey player Savannah Wells rarely spends more than a night with any one woman, but when photographer Madison Scott buys the house next door, she's forced to rethink what she expects out of life. (978-1-63555-480-9)

Hot Ice by Aurora Rey, Elle Spencer, Erin Zak. Can falling in love melt the hearts of the iciest ice queens? Join Aurora Rey, Elle Spencer, and Erin Zak to find out! (978-1-63555-513-4)

Line of Duty by VK Powell. Dr. Dylan Carlyle's professional and personal life is turned upside down when a tragic event at Fairview Station pits her against ambitious, handsome police officer Finley Masters. (978-1-63555-486-1)

London Undone by Nan Higgins. London Craft reinvents her life after reading a childhood letter to her future self and in doing so finds the love she truly wants. (978-1-63555-562-2)

Lunar Eclipse by Gun Brooke. Moon De Cruz lives alone on an uninhabited planet after being shipwrecked in space. Her life changes forever when Captain Beaux Lestarion's arrival threatens the planet and Moon's freedom. (978-1-63555-460-1)

One Small Step by Michelle Binfield. Iris and Cam discover the meaning of taking chances and following your heart, even if it means getting hurt. (978-1-63555-596-7)

Shadows of a Dream by Nicole Disney. Rainn has the talent to take her rock band all the way, but falling in love is a powerful distraction, and her new girlfriend's meth addiction might just take them both down. (978-1-63555-598-1)

Someone to Love by Jenny Frame. When Davina Trent is given an unexpected family, can she let nanny Wendy Darling teach her to open her heart to the children and to Wendy? (978-1-63555-468-7)

Tinsel by Kris Bryant. Did a sweet kitten show up to help Jessica Raymond and Taylor Mitchell find each other? Or is the holiday spirit to blame for their special connection? (978-1-63555-641-4)

Uncharted by Robyn Nyx. As Rayne Marcellus and Chase Stinsen track the legendary Golden Trinity, they must learn to put their differences aside and depend on one another to survive. (978-1-63555-325-3)

Where We Are by Annie McDonald. Can two women discover a way to walk on the same path together and discover the gift of staying in one spot, in time, in space, and in love? (978-1-63555-581-3)

A Moment in Time by Lisa Moreau. A longstanding family feud separates two women who unexpectedly fall in love at an antique clock shop in a small Louisiana town. (978-1-63555-419-9)

Aspen in Moonlight by Kelly Wacker. When art historian Melissa Warren meets Sula Johansen, director of a local bear conservancy, she discovers that love can come in unexpected and unusual forms. (978-1-63555-470-0)

Back to September by Melissa Brayden. Small bookshop owner Hannah Shepard and famous romance novelist Parker Bristow maneuver the landscape of their two very different worlds to find out if love can win out in the end. (978-1-63555-576-9)

Changing Course by Brey Willows. When the woman of your dreams falls from the sky, you'd better be ready to catch her. (978-1-63555-335-2)

Cost of Honor by Radclyffe. First Daughter Blair Powell and Homeland Security Director Cameron Roberts face adversity when their enemies stop at nothing to prevent President Andrew Powell's reelection. (978-1-63555-582-0)

Fearless by Tina Michele. Determined to overcome her debilitating fear through exposure therapy, Laura Carter all but fails before she's even begun until dolphin trainer Jillian Marshall dedicates herself to helping Laura defeat the nightmares of her past. (978-1-63555-495-3)

Not Dead Enough by J.M. Redmann. A woman who may or may not be dead drags Micky Knight into a messy con game. (978-1-63555-543-1)

Not Since You by Fiona Riley. When Charlotte boards her honeymoon cruise single and comes face-to-face with Lexi, the high school love she left behind, she questions every decision she has ever made. (978-1-63555-474-8)

Not Your Average Love Spell by Barbara Ann Wright. Four women struggle with who to love and who to hate while fighting to rid a kingdom of an evil invading force. (978-1-63555-327-7)

Tennessee Whiskey by Donna K. Ford. Dane Foster wants to put her life on pause and ask for a redo, a chance for something that matters. Emma Reynolds is that chance. (978-1-63555-556-1)